THE BROKEN CODE

LJ Byrne

Amazon.com

ISBN-13: 9798573009551
ISBN-10: 1477123456

Cover design by: Canva.com
Library of Congress Control Number: 2018675309
Printed in the United States of America

CONTENTS

THE BROKEN CODE

By LJ BYRNE

PROLOGUE

NeORanger21: More noise looking for an anti-antivirus toolkit.
Arch4ngel101: Info from RReagan. New botnet. DDoS.
NeORanger21: Been tracking. Sending u parts of code now.
Arch4ngel101: Received. Looks familiar. Let me run tracker tool.
NeORanger21: Hitting banks. Brits pissed.
Arch4ngel101: Tracking
NeORanger21: We gotta stop meeting like this
Arch4ngel101: In chatrooms. Lulz
NeORanger21: RReagan's lucky u work for the good guys.
Arch4ngel101: Got it. Do u see who it is? U wanna do the honors?
NeORanger21: Telling Pinocchio he's pwned.
Arch4ngel101: Tell him stop. I'll get deets to RReagan.
NeORanger21: We solved this in what 4 hrs? new record. We make gud team.
Arch4ngel101: bbl

Someone's knocking on the door. I wonder if Mom forgot her keys again. This is a common thing with Mom. I shake my head, smiling. But at the door, I realize it's not Mom. The flashing lights. The police.

"Mira Bell?"

"Yes." A chill runs up my spine. The world becomes opaque, indistinct. My knees turn to jelly as life moves in slow motion.

The police officer starts speaking. It takes me a while to

understand what they're saying. I'm sixteen years old. The police are telling me that my mother is dead. I fall to the ground screaming.

TWO MONTHS LATER

Information flow is what the internet is about. Information sharing is power. If you don't share your ideas, smart people can't do anything about them, and you'll remain anonymous and powerless.

--Vint Cerf

⊙⊙⊙⊙⊙1

When Mom died, someone handed me this brochure titled "The Five Stages of Grief." It was well-intentioned, but I haven't a clue where I'm at. I just feel lost. Here's the thing. I can't remember what Mom and I talked about that morning. I was busy online. I think I blew her off. It bothers me to no end that I dismissed her. My last words should have been "I love you" or something loving. I try not to get obsessive, but the thoughts still come. Did she feel pain? Did she think of me?

All my life, it's been Mom and me. I don't have many friends unless you count NeO, an online hacker I chat with frequently, and Kitty, who never does anything with me but brought me my homework when I was sick. She uses my name when she wants to go out with a new guy and doesn't want her mom to be suspicious.

There's a long story behind my arrival in Royalton. The short version is this. Mom was born Gwen Anderson, not Wendy Bell. And I have an aunt – my mother's twin. When Mom died, I thought I was an orphan with no family. But she left in her will –

I can't believe she had a will I didn't know about – to contact her sister. That's how I ended up in the fancy town of Royalton with my aunt, Erika De Vries.

First, Aunt Erika and her husband Robert are sweet as can be. Erika owns this small cosmetics company – think Aveda but for super-rich people – that makes goo with snake venom and snail slime. Robert owns an Internet security firm called Maven Software. I'm familiar with it. In fact, we bond talking about bots, worms, viruses. I don't tell him about my side gig as a hacker. That's still private and personal, and I guess I'm a little shy.

Second, I've gained a cool cousin. His name is Ethan, and he's eighteen months older than me. When I first met him, I thought he was a cocky pig, but he warmed up quickly when he found me crying by the pool my first night in their home. He's tried to draw me out of my shell since then with the help of his girlfriend Darcy.

I learn that living in Royalton means change. My wardrobe isn't fit for most of the homes here and appearances must be kept. I'm not comfortable buying clothes, and Aunt Erika tries to respect my wishes, but dresses and shoes show up in my closet regularly. Ethan tells me she always wanted a daughter so I must learn to live with the consequences of being her niece.

The other thing I learn is that I'll be going to a private school called Royal Bridge Academy. It's a private school with optional *boarding*, which freaks me out, and you wear uniforms! I'm told that most kids go home over the weekends – the school designs the curriculum such that weekends, in general, are relatively free, but all students get a room assigned to them. I'm not comfortable with the cost of the school. I looked it up online; it's one of the priciest schools in America.

After some debate, Aunt Erika and I come to an agreement. Because Mom disappeared before she got her inheritance when my maternal grandfather died, Aunt Erika has Mom's share, which amounts to two hundred and fifty thousand dollars. That covers about two years' worth of tuition including room and board. Since I'm not comfortable taking handouts – inheritance be damned – I tell her that I plan to pay her back. I know she thinks I'll forget about paying her back, but I won't. I already know I can since I've been doing random work on the side for the past six months.

Ethan's been trying to fill me in on how things "work" at Royal Bridge Academy. The school has two campuses: a lower school – the feeder school – and an upper school. The upper school consists of approximately a hundred and fifty students, and the kids who run the school are known as the Royals, and their groupies are called the Court. Ethan knows this because he is one of the Royals – more specifically, the King of the Royals. The King of the Royals is always a senior. Royals are selected among the seniors based on wealth, social prestige, and how many goats they've sacrificed. (I'm kidding about the goats.) By some weird process, the retiring King chooses the next King and Royals as needed. It's like they have their own social code. Currently, the senior Royals consist of Ethan, Arthur Huxley, Erin Beckett, and Elaine Blakely. The junior future Royals (no pun intended) come primarily from old money: Ryder Cabot, Cage Bennett, Ingrid Whitman, Xander Morrison, and Victoria Little. Judy Lee is the only one that hails from new money, but I've been told that she's given a pass because her family has been wealthy for over three generations. Ethan's clear I should stay away from Ryder and Ingrid, the future King and Queen of RBA.

"I know you find the concept of boarding schools daunting, but Robert and I are hardly here during the week," Aunt Erika says to me one morning. She smiles when she notices that I'm eating the oatmeal I requested. I'm just starting to get my appetite back so it must reassure her that I'm eating rather than pushing my food around. "We'll have weekends free, and you won't be alone at school. Ethan and Darcy will keep an eye on you."

Darcy Sanchez is Ethan's uber-cool girlfriend. She's in her final year at RBA, too, and Ethan's broken the unwritten Royal rules to date her. The factions at school are divided into old and new money. Darcy's parents are well-to-do, but not ridiculously wealthy, and they gained most of their wealth during the 1990s tech boom. This makes her "unworthy" of being a Royal or a Court member. (I find this ridiculous.)

With Ethan being the Royal King, he should have picked one of the other Royal girls or someone from their Court – basically, date someone established. But for Ethan, there wasn't a choice. I think it's perfectly romantic. It's thanks to Darcy that Ethan's been more supportive – she pretty much hit him in the head with her purse when he seemed insensitive about my unease about school. Darcy's arranged it so that we'll be sharing a suite. The rooms are separated into quads – basically, four bedrooms that share a common bathroom and living room – but seniors have the option of having a single place. The fact that Darcy is willing to forego this puts her in the Nice category. With pull from Aunt Erika, my other suitemates are friends of Darcy's. Ethan assures me they're nice, so I won't have to worry about mean girls.

Talking about mean girls, RBA has them too. Ethan warns me about Ingrid and her close friends, Victoria Little and Judy Lee. Ingrid is not Ethan's choice for the future Royal Queen, but she's "filthy" rich and from old money. There are rumors that Ingrid and Ryder will become the new power couple at the school, especially when Ethan's "reign" is over.

Next summer, Uncle Robert might take me to DefCon with him. He goes yearly – I won't lie, I'm excited by the idea. My aunt attends these cosmetic conferences – I never knew there were cosmetic conferences – and whenever possible, she tries to travel with Uncle Robert. That's why they're rarely home. They're still madly in love.

My aunt is a refined version of Mom. Mom looked her age. She had lines and wrinkles and her skin had lost some of its elasticity. Aunt Erika could pass for someone in her late twenties easily. What made Mom leave in the first place? It's something I think about a lot. I don't care about the money or anything like that, but it makes me sad that I don't have memories of me and Ethan as bratty kids. You don't realize how isolated you are until you find you have a bigger family out there.

NeO, who I've never met, tells me to count my blessings when I'm scared and feeling lost. It's hard to be appreciative, but I know I have many things to be grateful for. Count my blessings. I do. Everyday.

000010

NeORanger21: If we became professional cybercrime fighters, would you be Batman or Robin?
Arch4ngel101: I'd be Superman. Or Captain Marvel.
NeORanger21: You can't switch between DC and Marvel universes. That's cheating. Btw, did you see what RatGh0st posted?
Arch4ngel101: I can do anything! And yeah, saw that.
NeORanger21: FBI took down the other darknet market. Cut one head, another two rises, right?
Arch4ngel101: See? Using a Marvel reference right there. Hydra. Ur helping RReagan with the darknet stuff, aren't you?
NeORanger21: Could use your help with this pen test.
Arch4ngel101: We'll hit it this weekend. K?

First day at Royal Bridge Academy. I can do this. Ethan scarfs down his fourth croissant while I try to finish my banana and coffee. Drinking coffee. I feel grown up.

Aunt Erika eyes me after scolding Ethan about chewing with his mouth open. "I'm getting a few boxes from storage soon. When Gwennie disappeared, I really thought she'd be back, so I packed her things up and waited." My aunt's eyes shadow with sadness. "I think it's fitting for us to go through them together, don't you think? When you're ready."

I dip my chin. "That would be great, Aunt Erika. Thank you for being so kind," I whisper, tears pricking my eyelids.

Ethan puts a brotherly arm over my shoulder. My aunt covers my right hand with hers. "You're all I have left of Gwennie," my aunt says softly. "There wasn't anything I wouldn't have done for her. Maybe one day we'll understand why she left. Until then, I have her daughter. I can't replace your mother, but I can do my best to give you the next best thing."

I blink away the tears. But then Ethan checks his phone. "Crap. Come on, dear cousin, time to get going!"

We arrive at RBA in style. Ethan drives a silver Bentley Continental GT Convertible, which seems like an impractical car but who am I to judge. After helping me get checked in – and locating my dorm for me – I get to meet my dormmates.

My dormmates turn out to be just as awesome as Darcy. Of course, it helps when your cousin's girlfriend brings you in. Celeste Danvers is a junior like me. She's petite – I'm five-nine so I feel like an Amazonian to her – with ringlets of brown hair and doe-like eyes. Her mom is the famous Alisson Danvers – that's right, the only African American woman to win an Oscar twice *and* be nominated three times. Celeste is cute and I can see why Ethan thought I would like her as a friend. She's a bubblier (and shorter) version of me and we hit it off instantly. My other dormmate, Brittany Khan, is also a junior. She hails from India and her father owns this textile business. She's dressed in this beautiful sari when I meet her, and I spend over five minutes feeling the material. Her first comment to me wins me over: "Don't tell Dad, but no way am I marrying that dork back home. I want a hot Italian lover." I don't know why I find it so funny, but I do. She and Darcy have known each other since they were in diapers, but she treats me like I've known her forever.

Ethan shows up just as I straighten out the last of my uniform outfits. Blue jackets, white shirts, blue skirts. My closet is monotonous.

"Hey, babe," Darcy purrs, giving Ethan a generous kiss. Brittany rolls her eyes with good-natured affection.

"You'll get used to the lovey-doveyness on campus," she tells me, dodging Darcy's swat nimbly.

Is it wrong to want this camaraderie? It feels normal. I've never really been normal – a bit too shy and nerdy at school. I'm the girl that keeps her head lowered and hopes no one recognizes her. But here? My cousin rules this school. I think that means I'm part of something important, right? I try not to think about Mom. I know that's wrong of me, but I'm tired of crying. I force the tears back.

"Let's get something to eat," Ethan announces, and the way he says it makes it a proclamation. With his blond hair, he's positively angelic.

Celeste starts up a conversation with me while we walk. "So, first day of classes is tomorrow. There will be a first-day assembly before classes start."

"Hey, can I ask a question, Celeste? What's this old and new money thing? I don't get it." Ethan is so touchy about it that I stopped asking him.

"Well, it's a bit confusing," Celeste admits. "If your family has been rich for a handful of generations, you're old money. If you've only been wealthy for a generation, you're new money. But it is somewhat arbitrary. There are kids here whose parents are in the top five percent of wage earners, but they aren't necessarily in the top one percent."

Where does that leave me? Parentless. I mean, I don't know for sure that my biological dad is dead, but I'm pretty sure he is. Mom indicated he died unexpectedly. Right now, I'm mooching off my aunt, even though I do intend to pay her back.

"You okay, Mira?" Ethan asks in concern. Darcy flashes me a worried frown.

Startled, I try to smile. "Yeah… Just thinking."

Brittany puts a sisterly arm around my shoulder. "Darcy said this was your first boarding school. I promise it won't be so bad. We work hard during the week." She gives a saucy wink to a passing student with brown curls. "And then we *play* hard during the weekends. It really does help to pass the time. A lot of projects are done in groups. The cafeteria always has pizza – not as good as New York, but hey, it isn't bad either."

I'm guessing from their kind gestures they know my mom is dead. Duh. That's why I'm living with Aunt Erika. I'm such a moron.

"Ethan!"

A few students come jogging up to us. Ethan introduces Nate Jacobs, Connor Van Doren (who I learn is the infamous Ryder's cousin), and Erin Beckett. Erin Beckett is Ethan's female counterpart in the court of Royals. Darcy told me in confidence that Erin expected Ethan to choose her and last year was a bit of a mess when Ethan chose Darcy. Erin is old money – apparently, her family owns a lot of land that they've sold in lucrative chunks – and the thought was that the old and new money alliance would stop the infighting. But Ethan had to follow his heart. Dreamy! Erin, however, doesn't seem to be holding a grudge. She smiles at all of us, especially me.

"When I heard Ethan has a cousin, I couldn't believe it," she says in this friendly way. Her brown hair is stylishly short and there's a darling little curl that comes down her forehead. "So, do we have a future Royal here, Ethan? Pray tell."

There's a strange tenseness in Ethan's face, and I notice that Darcy's eyes faintly widen. "Hard to say, Erin. I think next year's Royals are pretty set in stone."

Nate starts talking to Ethan about soccer and Connor falls back to where I am with Celeste. It's clear that Celeste knows Connor well: I learn that he's on the swim team and soccer team. He's boyishly cute, with brown-black hair and these unusual gray eyes that have a hint of blue in them.

"I'm sure with Ethan on the team, you'll be coming to our games," Connor tells me. "Darcy's a swimmer like me, though. So, maybe I'll see you twice as much."

I dip my head in uncertainty. "I don't know. I guess. Maybe."

"You're not like Ethan at all," Connor teases, but not in a mean way. "He's all confidence and swagger, and you're actually shy."

"Stop hitting on my cousin, Connor," Ethan warns ahead

of us, frowning.

Connor pretends to zip his lips. My cheeks turn hot, but Brittany laughs out loud as we enter the cafeteria. That's when her demeanor changes and there's a strange tension as we head to a long table already occupied by four other students.

A boy with silky black hair and dark blue eyes stands as we approach. There's something vaguely familiar about him, but what astonishes me is the way the boy's jaw tenses and his eyes widen when he sees me. It lasts just for a second, but it makes me wonder if something's wrong with me. When the boy introduces himself to me as Ryder, I see the family resemblance to Connor. After the introduction, his face settles into this mask of cold indifference. Where Connor has that boyish charm about him, Ryder's looks are more chiseled, more refined. There's an arrogance about him in the way he seems to look down his nose. He's devastating. It doesn't surprise me that the pretty blond girl clinging to his arm is Ingrid Whitman. They could literally be the world's most glamorous teen couple.

I meet Judy Lee and Xander Morrison, who is distantly related to the British monarchy. Judy's family hails from China – her parents own several Chinese manufacturing firms – and her eyes sharply focus on me with disdain.

My mom never told me who my dad was, but she mentioned he was Asian. I strongly suspect Korean or Chinese. I don't really look Asian – my hair is dark brown and there's a slant to my eyes – but I'm definitely not a blond, blue-eyed creature either. I shift uncomfortably so that Ethan is in front of me.

"This is the Royals' table, Ethan," Ryder says, his voice impeccably precise. "Royals and acceptable Court are the only ones allowed."

Brittany tenses beside me and her usually cheerful face loses its brightness. Ethan's shoulders straighten. "We've been through this before, Ryder. You know that Darcy and I are together. Brittany is her best friend."

"Darcy can stay," Ingrid says like she's being the most gracious person in the world. "But not Brittany. And most certainly not your pathetic cousin."

Darcy crosses her arms. "Fuck you, Ingrid. Brittany's family is wealthy, and Mira is Ethan's cousin. They both should be considered Court."

Ingrid gives this laugh. She has this Minnie Mouse voice that is vaguely annoying. "A penniless Court member. How laughable."

A girl I later learn is Victoria Little laughs with Ingrid.

"Maybe she'll find ways to earn her way," a boy with red-blond hair says with a leer, coming next to Ingrid. The boy next to him snickers.

"Arthur, Cage, behave," Erin scolds, speaking finally. "We should allow Brittany and Mira to stay."

Judy snorts. "My understanding is that Mira has no money. She can't be Court." Her eyes take on a beady glint. "She's an orphan and charity case."

Ethan lets Darcy go and slams his hand on the table. I jump, and Connor pats my back reassuringly, causing Ryder to scowl in disapproval. "My cousin is off-limits, Judy. You take your ugliness out of here, or I will make you regret crossing me." This Ethan is harsh and mean – I don't recognize him as my fun cousin. His lips thin and his muscles tense.

Erin raises a hand. "Ethan and I agree that Brittany and Mira get to stay."

Celeste grabs my hand and gives it a friendly squeeze as Ethan gives Ryder a triumphant glare. "We've spoken."

Ingrid pushes her chest out as she leans forward, licking her lower lip. "Fine. But next year you won't be King of Royal Bridge Academy." She eyes me. "You can't protect her forever."

I'm wedged between Ethan and Celeste during the meal, but Connor sits across from me to provide a friendly person to look at. It doesn't escape my notice, or Ethan's notice, that Ryder and Xander stare at me during the entire meal. When Elaine Beckett joins us – the last of the Royals – she ignores me right away. I check her off as harmless.

Leaving RBA as soon as possible sounds more and more

appealing.

⊙⊙⊙⊙11

I close my laptop – a gift from Uncle Robert – and tuck my knees beneath my chin. I'm still getting into the flow of boarding school life. Nights are the worst because I think about Mom. I think about my life with Mom as I'm tucked into sheets I did not pick, staring at a blank ceiling with no texture, no character, no sense of individuality.

Someone taps at my open door – it's not uncommon for us to leave our doors open when we're in – and my smile is real when I see Connor. "Since we have Chem together, wanted to know if you wanted a homework buddy tonight. I was going to head to the library."

I bite my lip. *Come on, Mira, it's better than doing it alone.* "Okay. Maybe we should grab Celeste, too."

Connor nods. "Good idea. Grab your stuff and I'll let her know."

The night has a bite to it, and I regret my casual t-shirt and jeans. Connor notices my shiver and pulls off his jacket, slipping it over my shoulder. Celeste's eyes grow huge, but Connor does it so casually and naturally that I shrug it off.

Unfortunately, Ryder doesn't agree. He's in the library with Ingrid and Xander when we walk in, his eyes narrowing on the jacket of my shoulder. For some reason, I feel ashamed walking in here with a boy's jacket on my shoulders. There's a cold perusal from Ingrid as she leans over to whisper something to Ryder, causing his glare to intensify.

Ryder walks over with murder in his eyes. "Connor. What's the meaning of this?" He doesn't even address me properly, just flicking his hand my way.

I hastily remove the jacket, practically tossing it at Connor's head. Connor lifts his chin. "Chill out, Ryder. She was cold. I gave her my jacket."

"I-I'm not cold," I stammer out, shrinking in my chair.

Ryder leans over to glare at me. "Look, Orphan Annie, I'll tolerate you while Ethan's still here as long as you keep your grubby hands off my cousin. His trust fund is not your ticket out of whatever hole you crawled from. If you're smart, you'll disappear next year. When I rule this school, trash like you won't be tolerated."

My eyes fill with tears as both Connor and Celeste rise to their feet. "Do you have to be such an asshole?" Connor demands in a hushed whisper as our confrontation gains an audience.

"Boo hoo hoo." Ryder coldly mocks me. Ingrid sashays closer, her face filled with malicious glee.

"Oh, no," Ingrid derides me, "I think she's going to cry."

Don't cry, don't cry, don't cry. I clench my hands beneath the table, head lowered. Why does he have to be so mean?

"Just know you two are lowering yourselves." Ingrid straightens. "When Erin is gone, Celeste, I can remove you from the Court like *that*." She snaps her fingers to emphasize her point. "Just remember, Ryder and I will completely restore the Royals and reshape the school. Properly." She then stamps her fancy shoe on the floor for emphasis.

Ryder directs his next words to his cousin. "You're here under my supervision. I'd hate to tell your mother that you're hanging around with a commoner."

The two cousins stare each other down. I tap Connor's hand with a finger. "It's okay, Connor. Just let it go." I bite my lip when Ryder's eyes swing my way.

Celeste puts an arm around me defensively. "We're here to do homework, Ryder. Unless you'd like to join us, do you mind?" Her words are pointed but polite.

Ryder sneers, but he heads back to Ingrid and Xander without speaking again.

I pull out my chemistry assignment and hunker down. Celeste nudges me with a shoulder, brown eyes warm and kind. "It'll be okay," she whispers. "Ryder's just throwing his weight around."

Connor doesn't address the situation directly, but his eyes are mutinous when he regards his cousin. Then he looks at me with a wink and a smile.

• • •

To say that school life includes more drama than I care to deal with is an understatement, but the classes are relatively easy – at least to me. I see a lot of students stressing about the homework, but the only thing that slows me is the amount of time it takes to write everything.

I only have Connor and Celeste in Chemistry, and the only times I deal with Ryder is in math class (Calculus) and English. In general, he seems to ignore me, for which I'm grateful. To whom I'm grateful remains unknown.

There are parties on weekends, but no matter how much Ethan pesters me, I refuse to go. Ethan doesn't pressure me thanks to Darcy, but Celeste begs me constantly. I can't tell them I'm too busy online.

It takes three whole weekends, but NeORanger21 and I complete a penetration test. As usual, we get paid via bitcoins, but we're both eyeing the bounty from Escara Corporation. It occurs to me that I can pay my own way to Royal Bridge Academy – or choose to leave. It would probably mean telling Uncle Robert what I do on the side. At sixteen, I have a serious reputation online, but this might launch me into the public eye.

I do, however, agree to attend one of the swim meets after I collect my payment. When I arrive, most of the Royals and their Court are there. Other than Ethan, they aren't there for Darcy. The Royals are here for Connor – and more indirectly, for Ryder.

Ethan escorts me to where the Royals sit with their sycophants. I wish Brittany were here – I'm basically the only non-Royal, non-Court, non-whatever. When Ingrid sniffs in her posh high heels, my jeans and shirt feel lackluster.

"Got a deal at Goodwill?" Victoria jeers, eliciting a bark of humor from Judy.

It's ironic since the denim I'm wearing is designer – or that's what Aunt Erika told me.

Ethan bristles, but Erin intervenes, laying a warning hand on Victoria. "That's enough. It isn't right for the Royals and their Court to bicker publicly. Ethan's cousin is a guest."

Ryder's hard eyes linger on me as Ethan positions me between him and Celeste. Ingrid leans over to whisper something in Ryder's ear. When Ryder cocks a brow at Ingrid, Erin glances briefly at me before giving Ryder a nod. Whatever they're discussing, I feel uneasy because it seems to be about me.

When the swim competition begins, Connor's face brightens when he spots me in the crowd. Ethan elbows me in good-natured fun, explaining the different categories Connor and Darcy will be competing in. I'm on my feet with Ethan when Darcy swims her way to second place in the individual 200-meter, while Connor places first in several qualification rounds.

Celeste makes an effort to keep me engaged, talking about how Connor expects a swimming scholarship when he graduates. But I'm distracted by the times I catch Ryder looking at me. I imagine I stick out like an unfashionable sore thumb.

While it's nice having a place to sit for lunch, I remain an interloper. I don't belong with these people. I miss life when it was me and Mom. Life was predictable.

After Darcy and Connor shower and change after the meet, Connor jogs over to us. "I'm starved!" he announces to good-natured laughter.

"You're always hungry," Darcy remarks, walking up to Ethan directly. After a public kiss, she grins at me. "Let's go to the diner."

Connor's eyes twinkle at me. "If you sit next to me, I'll treat."

Ryder's head snaps up at his cousin's words. "By all means, give money to the poor," he snarks.

Any desire to eat with them disappears. I turn to Celeste. "Would you take me home? I feel unwell."

Celeste flounders as Ethan bristles. "Sure."

"Mira," Darcy begins in concern, but she stops when I shake my head.

"It's alright. I promised to call an old friend from home." The lie is bitter, but it is better than being stuck with people who don't want me.

"Um, I'll drop her off and meet you guys there," Celeste says, taking my arm kindly.

As we leave, Connor rounds on his cousin. "You're such an ass, Ryder."

000100

NeORanger21: Check your message from RReagan.
Arch4ngel101: Saw it. What you think?
NeORanger21: Don't know. Couple of hacked accounts in an area.
Arch4ngel101: Keep me posted. Ciao from No-Neck Gunther.
NeORanger21: You kill me.

Blue uniforms everywhere. And not the law enforcement kind. We're just a monotonous array of students walking to class. Mom hated uniforms. I wonder if she hated them because she grew up wearing them.

"Hey, you coming to the soccer game tomorrow?" Connor asks, jogging up to me.

I'm heading to the cafeteria, which is always a source of great anxiety. "Um, I don't know. I've been busy," I hedge. I am such a bad liar.

Connor's blue-gray eyes dim a bit, and I feel awful. As we head to the table, I notice that Ryder's in the corner having an animated discussion with Ingrid. He runs his hand over his face in exasperation, his lips flat. Ingrid says something and Ryder averts his gaze, meeting mine. He stiffens before scowling at me. They both return to the table, but Ethan barks something at them as I approach. I slide in between Ethan and Celeste.

"Where's Brittany?" I ask Celeste quietly. She points over at another table where Brittany is talking to a cute boy.

"Enrique Lopez," Celeste whispers back to me. "Basketball player."

Ingrid saunters over, draping a possessive hand on Ryder's shoulder. Her red lips are positively cruel when she says, "Now we just need to get rid of Orphan Annie."

I pale.

Cage Bennett leers at me. "I don't know, Ingrid. Lonely girls can get desperate. I like desperate girls."

I flinch, and Cage snaps his mouth shut the moment Ethan pounds the table with a fist. "Ingrid! This is the last time I will warn you." He points to Cage. "I will beat the crap out of anyone who harasses Mira! This stops now!"

I pick at my sandwich, my appetite gone. As the table settles and everyone starts talking about the weekend game and party, I doubt anyone notices that the only thing I manage to swallow is water. Over at the other table, I'm glad to see Brittany having a lively conversation with Enrique, and the possibility of sitting elsewhere cheers me up a little.

I leave for English class early, doing my best to avoid Ryder. When he arrives in class, he doesn't look at me as he passes by my desk, but he does stop for a second. He places a muffin and a bottle of orange juice in front of me. "You didn't eat," he says before moving to take his seat.

My jaw drops. Ryder ignores me for the entire period.

•••

I find the swim uniforms amusing. We're all dressed in blue one-piece swimsuits with the Royal Bridge Academy logo. Ingrid gripes about how hideous they are, but I don't mind them. This is gym class, not a fashion show.

As I head to the pool, Ingrid stops me and pushes me into the lockers hard, bruising my shoulder. "Stay away from Ryder Cabot!" she hisses in that squeaky voice of hers. "You don't belong at this school. You're nothing but a wannabe and gold-digger!" I stare at Ingrid's face twisted with hate and rage.

I open my mouth to protest, but she slaps me hard. With my head ringing, it takes me a moment to realize that Judy Lee is there, too. Judy holds me against the locker. She's so close that I can see the pores in her face. "You're nothing at this school. Ethan can't protect you all the time," she tells me in her low voice. "If you step out of line, we'll show you where you belong."

"Remember your place, Orphan Annie," Ingrid adds with a cruel smile. "If you ever need to be reminded again, I'll be happy to educate you."

Judy lets me go and the two girls walk out as if nothing's happened. By the time I leave the locker room, Celeste is looking for me. She sees my cheek, but I shake my head. I don't want to cause a fuss right now.

Celeste and I usually stick together in gym class, but the teacher assigns us to different lanes. I know she's worried about me, but since I'm not that great of a swimmer, I'm put in the slow lane with the bad swimmers. I try to tell her with a look that I'm okay. Ingrid is talking to Victoria Little in her lane and I don't see Judy anywhere.

Regardless, I work on my laps, taking breaks because I'm not used to swimming this much. I'm down to my last lap when something – no, someone – grabs me around the ankle and pulls me under. I swallow water in surprise, choking and panicking as I'm pushed under. I can't make out anything other than a few blurry arms and the feel of hands pressing me under. Everything begins to hurt, and I flail in panic. And then I blackout.

•••

My head throbs and a strange din of sounds makes the throbbing worse. Slowly, I open my eyes. And then my memory returns. I flail, sitting up.

"Mira!" Ethan is right there with Darcy. Ethan's blond hair is a mess like maybe he was pulling at it in worry. He brings me a small cup of water. "Tiny sips."

Darcy's lips are pressed into a thin line. "You passed out when they pulled you out of the water," she says. "They said you started drowning and no one noticed. Celeste was in a panic."

"They?" I croak.

Ethan and Darcy exchange glances. "Ingrid and Victoria," Ethan tells me. "Did you see anything?"

I shake my head. "I think someone pushed me under," I whisper. Just saying it makes me tremble. "Ethan…"

"I'll handle it," he tells me. "Darcy, can you help her back to her room?" My cousin stands up, his eyes distant. "I'll handle it, Mira. Don't worry." Without saying goodbye, he leaves abruptly.

• • •

Darcy and Brittany baby me, fluffing my pillows and making hot tea. Brittany takes my temperature five times before making me down a cup of chamomile tea sweetened with honey. They refuse to let me talk after I tell them several times what happened and stay with me until Celeste is done with classes. Then Celeste takes over. She tells me that someone in my lane started screaming that I was not moving in the water. Another girl pulled me out, and I spewed water immediately. In tears, she tells me that Ingrid and Victoria stood by innocently, but she thought they looked happy with my accident. Because people are in swimsuits, there aren't security cameras by the pool – this is the explanation I'm given when I ask. As such, the school decides to believe that I panicked in the pool.

Celeste and I spend a few minutes shoulder to shoulder, taking comfort that I'm okay. Finally, Celeste begins to fuss and tells me to take a nap, which I promptly do.

When I wake, I hear voices outside my room. I quickly brush my teeth and brush the tangles from my hair to see what's going on.

"No, no, no," I hear Celeste say as I leave my room.

I pause in my doorway. Ryder Cabot, Xander Morrison,

and Conner Van Doren are all talking to Celeste. From her stance and the set of her shoulders, she's clearly arguing with them.

All eyes turn when I make my presence known. Celeste covers her mouth. "You see what you did," she accuses the boys. "You woke her up!"

"I woke up on my own," I manage to say, my voice scratchy and weird sounding to my ears. I've never nearly drowned before, but I feel lousy.

Connor holds up a container. "We brought chicken soup," he says, blue-gray eyes scanning me from head to toe. "We're here—"

Ryder cuts his cousin off. "We want to know what happened during gym class."

I roll my eyes. I had to repeat the story more than once to Darcy, Brittany, and then Celeste. Why they need to hear it exactly from me is beyond my comprehension. "I was swimming. Someone grabbed me. Someone kept my head underwater." I cross my arms. "The nurse said I probably panicked when people were trying to help me and that no one tried to drown me."

Ryder and Xander exchange a look. "Someone? Just one person?"

I wander listlessly to the couch and flop down without any grace. "I didn't see. I was busy drowning." I'm normally not this sassy – in fact, I'm usually meek. But I'm not in touch with my emotions yet. It's like I'm here but not here emotionally.

Connor puts the soup down on the table. "You should have something to eat. I threw in extra saltines."

I try to smile and fail miserably. "Thank you."

Xander and I rarely speak to each other as I don't have him in any classes and only see him during mealtimes. But he walks over to sit next to me. "Did anything happen before the incident? Anyone talk to you?"

"I told Ethan that Ingrid and Judy slapped me in the locker room." Celeste stifles a gasp at my words, but Ryder's arm trembles at my words.

"It was just Judy and Ingrid?" Tension lines Ryder's jaw. He seems almost angry about it, but I can't tell if he's angry for me or angry that it was executed poorly.

"That's what she said!" Celeste emphasizes her point by stomping her foot. She's livid and snarling like a protective tiger mom.

Weary, I lean my head on the back of the sofa. "Yes."

Without saying goodbye, Ryder storms off so abruptly that even Xander stands up in surprise. "Um, I guess we should let you rest," Xander mutters awkwardly.

Celeste makes a shooing motion, but she lightly touches Connor's arm. "Thanks for stopping by."

Connor tips my chin up. "Let me know if you need anything."

I sigh as the boys leave. Celeste gives me a speculative look before saying, "Shall we have some soup?"

000101

•••

Out of perverse defiance, I go to the soccer game. I'm a glutton for punishment, but I mostly do it because Ethan begs me to. After my near-drowning, there is a shift in the Royals and their Court. I presume it has to do with Ethan giving everyone an ultimatum. Regardless, the viciousness from Cage, Arthur, and the Royal girls abate.

Just as I'm about to sit down next to Darcy, I hear my name. Connor jogs up to me, grinning. "Hey, you came." He hands me a jersey he's carrying. "It's mine," he says, looking shy. "Will you wear it? It's supposed to be lucky if a girl wears your jersey." When I frown, fingering it gingerly, he adds, "It's clean. Freshly laundered."

I notice that Darcy is wearing Ethan's jersey. "Um. Okay." I put the jersey on over my long-sleeved shirt before I think about it too much.

Connor grins before running back out to the field while I sit down. Darcy gives me a sly smile while Celeste observes the exchange quietly. I bury my head in my hand, embarrassed by the scrutiny. "I think he likes you," Darcy whispers teasingly, laughing when I turn bright red.

On the field, I see Ethan talking with Ryder and Xander.

Ethan waves at us, and Ryder follows his gaze, but Ryder's body stiffens when he sees me. He storms over to his cousin. Ryder and Connor exchange a few heated words before Nate Jacobs intervenes with placating gestures. I shrink in my seat. "Maybe I should give the jersey back," I say to no one in particular.

But Darcy just smirks. "No way. Keep it on. If it upsets Ryder, it's a good thing."

Celeste doesn't say anything.

The game turns out to be fast-paced and interesting. Connor scores twice and Ethan blocks every attempt to score. Celeste helps me understand what's happening on the field as we win easily. Erin, surrounded by a host of Court students, leads everyone in a raucous cheer when Ethan is hoisted up. Once he's set down, he bounds up the steps to us.

"You were amazing, babe," Darcy murmurs, kissing him.

Ethan notes the jersey I'm wearing with surprise, but he doesn't seem upset. Maybe wearing Conner's jersey is a bad idea. It's garnering me attention I don't want.

Connor joins us, sweaty and triumphant. "You did bring me luck, Mira. We're just going to clean up and celebrate at the house. You're coming, right?" There's a sweet earnestness to Connor that is hard to dislike.

"Absolutely," Darcy responds for me with an evil wink. "Now, both of you, get cleaned up. You guys are gross."

• • •

Darcy takes me and Celeste to Ryder's home. The place is… grotesquely huge. I mean, Aunt Erika's place is big, but this is like the American version of the Palace of Versailles. The home is made of stone and brick, giving it an almost European feel, and there's a lot of symmetry in its design. The heavy wood doors have steel grates made to look like wrought iron.

"Ryder lives here with his cousin," Darcy says. "His father hasn't been around for years. Ryder's been raised by nannies almost all his life."

I find that rather sad. Mom was always there for me: at every parent-teacher conference, at every show, at every party. "His mother?"

We step out of the car and stare at the impressive home. "Died in childbirth," Darcy says. "Ryder and Connor have always been close – more like brothers than cousins. Connor's parents don't spend a lot of time with him. They sent him here to live with Ryder and his nanny when he was twelve."

It doesn't soothe the pain of missing Mom, but I can't imagine not knowing a parent's love. Celeste chimes in quietly, "I think one of the reasons why Ryder hates Ethan so much is because his parents are so cool. And they're still in love. You can see it. They're totally into young love and all of that."

My eyes grow wide at that revelation. Perhaps under that exterior is a boy who yearns for his parents' affection. Darcy points to the other cars here to let us know we're not the first ones here. Ethan's Bentley isn't here yet, but I see Ryder's McLaren GT and several other cars that I can't identify. I only know Ryder drives a McLaren because Ethan told me.

A butler opens the door. I mean, my aunt has a cook and a household staff, but she opens her own doors. This isn't a party per se – when I look around, it's more like a bunch of kids hanging around. Arthur Huxley and Cage Bennett are talking with Erin on the couch. They both have drinks that don't appear to be sodas. In the corner, Nate chats with Victoria. He gives me a slight wave, but Victoria ignores me.

I'm still wearing Connor's jersey, and when he sees me, his face is downright smug. "There she is, my lucky charm," he says, hugging me with his hand on my lower back. I pat his back awkwardly, ignoring Darcy's muffled laughter. With friends like these... Yeah, I'm smooth that way.

Celeste furtively glances at Connor and that's when I see the shine in her eyes when he talks to her. She likes him! How did I not notice this before? When he says something that makes her laugh, her color rises. I'm no expert at romance, and Celeste isn't the type to look at someone with stars in her eyes, but I know I'm right. When he grabs my hand, the light in her eyes dim, and the smile on her face wavers. I'm the worst person ever. Celeste has been nothing but kind to me, and the guy she's crushing on is flirting with me. "Let me give you a tour. This place is monstrous," Connor says, blue-gray eyes brimming with excitement.

I'm dragged away, my mind racing a million miles a minute. This is bad. Connor likes me – is that conceited? I don't know, but when he entwines his hand with mine, I get nervous and yank my hand free, covering the suddenness with a smile when he seems surprised.

"Here's the pool," he says, trying to gauge my reaction. His eyes linger on my lips before he gestures to the enclosed pool. "The roof opens up if you want fresh air, but during the winter months, we keep it closed. Obviously."

Why are we by the pool? Far away from everyone else? Am I panicking for no reason? "Connor, I–"

I'm interrupted by Ryder showing up, and he looks pissed. "What the fuck are you two doing in here?!" he practically rages at us. His eyes fixate on the jersey I'm wearing and the muscles in his neck tighten.

"I'm showing her the place," Connor says, his lower lip jutting out belligerently.

Ryder's nose flares. "Ethan's looking for his cousin. Nate is waiting to challenge you to darts. I'll take her to Ethan."

Connor is about to argue when I intervene. I can't imagine what Celeste is thinking right now, and the sooner Connor is away from me, the better. "It's okay, Connor. I'll find you later?" I say with false brightness.

Connor bites his lip with indecision. "After you check in with Ethan, come find me in the amusement room. Maybe I'll beat Nate at darts because you're there." His eyes are warmly flirtatious.

With a sinking feeling, I agree, and he heads off with one last glare at Ryder. As soon as he's gone, Ryder rounds on me.

"Take that off," he demands coldly.

"What?"

"The jersey. Take Connor's fucking jersey off!" Ryder reaches out and yanks the jersey harshly.

I make a sound of protest and try to slap him, but he grabs me by the wrist and yanks me towards him. "You are such a jerk!" I blurt angrily.

"Take it off or I will fricking rip it off you!" My eyes widen. His words are so intense that I believe him.

Shakily, I nod, and when he releases me, I lift the jersey off and then straighten my long-sleeved shirt. Before I can say anything, Ryder grabs the jersey from me as if the sight offends him, breathing heavily. He turns away for a moment before he straightens his body and faces me again.

"I'll return this to Connor." He runs a hand through his hair and grimaces. He throws the jersey into the corner, but when he reaches for me, I flinch and step back nervously. He drops his hand to his side. "I won't hurt you. I'll take you to Ethan," he says in a calmer voice.

I turn away, trying to hide my tears. "I'll find him myself," I whisper. "Could you just leave now? I did what you wanted."

Ryder swears behind me. "If you're expecting me to apologize, you'll be waiting for a long time. I don't apologize."

"Just leave me alone, please." Weak. Pathetic. God, grow a spine, Mira!

A long pause. "Are you recovered from what happened at the pool?"

I remain silent. Did they talk about it? Ethan never told me what he discussed with the other Royals, but I know he thought Ingrid was responsible.

"I'd never hurt you." Silence. He shifts. Then very gently, "I'll tell Ethan you're here."

I don't move. I don't move until Ethan and Darcy find me, and even then, I don't say anything. I let Ethan take me home. I let Aunt Erika coddle me. I don't leave my room until it's time to return to school.

000110

NeORanger21: You've been busy.
Arch4ngel101: I found an exploit. Sent to company with recommended patch.
NeORanger21: gg. Lucky you work for the gud guys. See RReagan's message?
Arch4ngel101: Yes. Want to take first shot?
NeORanger21: He must be desperate to trust us with this.
Arch4ngel101: Or he knows who we are.
NeORanger21: Unlikely.
Arch4ngel101: Sending you code screenshots now. Look familiar?
NeORanger21: Real familiar.
Arch4ngel101: what is he up to now?

I close my laptop and look at the dresses on my bed. Aunt Erika went shopping and she wants me to wear one of these tonight because she invited two special "guests" to dinner. Even Ethan doesn't know who's coming, although we know Darcy will be eating with us tonight.

Mom and I cooked and baked a lot together. Feeling adventurous, I convince Aunt Erika to let me do this baked apple dish for dessert. It's apples wrapped in pastry, baked in this gorgeous syrup. We came across the dish at an apple festival in Wisconsin one summer and spent the rest of the summer trying to deconstruct the recipe.

I narrow the choices between a pink sheath dress or a

soft-knit mini dress with a V neckline and empire waist. I go with the minidress. It's a bit shorter than I'm used to, but the three-fourths length sleeves are modest. Besides, the pink one is too girly for me. The mini dress is in deep green and seems more elegant.

I skip down the stairs feeling better than I have been in a while. When Darcy sees me, she grins. "Girl, those legs go for miles!" she squeals, giving me a hug. She's in a pretty wrap dress with a dark floral print, and she's left her chestnut hair loose and shiny. "It's probably some old friends of your uncle coming. You'll get used to being dragged to these dinners – we're basically there to prevent your aunt from dying of boredom."

I giggle a little, but I step back when Ethan arrives, looking handsome and older than his eighteen years in a dark blue suit. I sigh inwardly, wishing he'd picked anything other than blue.

Aunt Erika smiles at me fondly, complimenting how I look. "Ethan will tell you that I've been dying to shop for another female," she says with a roll of her eyes. There's a strange nervous energy in her voice. "I hope you don't mind, but I heard Darcy telling Ethan that she thought Connor Van Doren was interested in you."

I feel the blood drain from my face.

Ethan and Darcy exchange a horrified look as the doorbell rings. Aunt Erika continues blithely, "Those boys live a mile away and they lack parental supervision. I invited them over for dinner. To my surprise, they accepted."

"Oh, my God," Ethan mutters, closing his hazel eyes. Darcy clutches his arm like she's afraid she's going to fall.

"Mrs. De Vries, thank you for having us over," I hear Ryder say, entering the room arrogantly with Connor in his wake.

Ryder is holding flowers and he hands them to my aunt before handing me a single red rose. "I wasn't aware Darcy was going to be here, but this is for you." His fingers brush mine when I take the flower from him. He notices the pallor and the slight flinch. The jerk seems faintly amused. Unlike Ethan,

Ryder's wearing a charcoal gray suit without a tie. He's gorgeous, which is totally unfair because he's not very nice. His cousin's outfit is similar, but with fine pinstripe detailing.

"I'll just go and put this in some water. Ethan, why don't you take them to the solarium until dinner is ready. We're still waiting on Robert," Aunt Erika says, shaking her head in mock despair.

Both Ryder and Connor fall behind me as Ethan, his face tense, walks briskly ahead of us. I pause with Darcy right before the solarium, letting Connor and Ryder enter first. Connor flashes me a tight grin as he passes me. Darcy whispers in my ear, "I swear those two were checking out your ass."

Two? "Darcy!" I nearly strangle her as I turn beet red.

My cousin's evil girlfriend laughs as she drags me in. Ethan closes the door firmly, grabbing the rose from my hand and throwing it in the trash. Ryder's face darkens at the action.

"What the hell are you doing here, Ryder?" Ethan doesn't beat around the bush.

Faking innocence, Ryder says, "Your mom invited us."

"After the things you and Ingrid have done to Mira, you are not welcome here!" Ethan gets right into Ryder's face. The younger boy doesn't flinch. "Sorry, Connor, but your cousin is a Grade A asshole!"

"No arguments here," Connor says glibly, ignoring Ryder's scowl. Connor walks over to me. "You look beautiful." He stares at my legs but then does a slow perusal of me that causes me to blush.

Immediately, I think of Celeste. This is not good, but before I can respond, Ethan points at Ryder and says, "You and Ingrid have undermined my reign at RBA every single day. It stops now, or God help me, I will throw you out of this house."

Ryder grows cold. "Get your hand out of my face."

"Make me!"

Darcy grabs Ethan's arm and Connor holds Ryder back. "Stop this! You're acting like little kids!" Darcy snaps, and her sharp tone makes both guys pause.

I sit down, shaking my head. I miss my quiet dinners with Mom. This is way too much drama. Life with Mom was fun. And uneventful.

Darcy swears, releasing Ethan and coming over to me. "It's okay. Just ignore these big babies. They're too busy trying to figure out who's a bigger ass."

"A truce," Ryder says suddenly. "At least, for now." Connor frowns at his cousin in surprise.

Ethan tries to relax but not before he gives Ryder a final glare. "Fine. Mira, sorry. I just hate assholes." He smooths his suit. "Dad's probably home by now."

In the dining room, I'm seated in between Ryder and Connor. Darcy and Ethan are across from me, both trying to be supportive while feeling my pain. At least Connor is easy to talk to, but I'm nervous about seeming too friendly. I don't want to lead him on.

"Any thoughts about college yet?" Uncle Robert asks Ryder while the dinner dishes are cleared.

"Robert!" Aunt Erika admonishes.

But Ryder merely smiles. "I've given some thought to it, sir. What about you, Ethan? What are you doing?" There's a coldness to the question like he's relishing the moment Ethan leaves RBA.

Before Ethan can respond, Aunt Erika says, "Mira, you hardly touched dinner."

I glance guiltily at my plate. I'd moved the veggies around, but I could barely taste the food. Ryder pipes up. "We'll do our best to make sure she eats at school. She's incredibly studious and sometimes forgets." Connor flashes his cousin another frown.

Uncle Robert simply agrees. "She's got a good head on her, our Mira. She might even have a knack for programming. She's asked me some great questions."

I start coughing to cover my nervous laughter and Connor thumps my back as my eyes water. "You okay?" he asks in concern and I wave him off, not trusting myself to speak. Ryder's hands clench under the table as Connor rubs my back. Awkward.

Desserts are plated and I nervously wait as everyone takes their first bite. I even manage to spoon a bit into my mouth.

"Oh, God," Darcy moans, closing her eyes. "This is so good, Mira. Seriously, I would make this every day if I knew how."

Ethan chuckles. "With that kind of reaction, I hope Mira does make it every day for you, Darcy."

I expect Darcy to be mortified, but she just laughs and both Aunt Erika and Uncle Robert laugh along. Maybe I'm too uptight, but Darcy clearly has won Aunt Erika over, and my aunt seems unfazed by the clear intimacy between her and Ethan.

"You *made* this?" Ryder asks to my left, astonishment evident in his blue eyes.

"Mom and I used to cook and bake a lot," I whisper, staring at my plate.

"Gwennie was like that," Aunt Erika adds fondly. "Wherever we went, she was deconstructing dishes left and right."

"Sounds like you and your mom were pretty close," Connor says, and I hear the slight envy. I wonder what it's like to be forgotten by your parents and sent away.

I take a sip of water. "We were. We did a lot together. We were best friends. She was – everything to me." My voice hitches a little. I clear my throat nervously. "She came to every event, every art show, every parent-teacher conference." I see Aunt Erika wipe a tear.

There's a brief silence at the table. I'm afraid that everyone's looking at me with my depressing comments. Ryder asks far too kindly, "What is your favorite memory of her?"

This is, by far, the nicest words Ryder's said to me, and when Connor tenses to my right, I wonder where the curiosity stems from. I think for a moment. "Right before Christmas last year, Mom won these basketball tickets at a raffle." My eyes close as I remember. "I'd never been to a basketball game before, and Mom thought it'd be a great way to celebrate my birthday.

We got hot dogs and drank way too much soda. And then, during halftime, the camera focused on me and my name flashed on the screen. The crowd sang to me, and I just remember Mom being ecstatic about it." I bite my lip, looking at everyone.

Aunt Erika has a misty smile on her face. Both Ethan and Darcy listen with respectful affection. Uncle Robert is gently sympathetic, while Connor squeezes my hand before releasing it. But it's Ryder's expression that I find strange. He's incredibly still, his eyes distant and unfocused. When he realizes I'm looking at him, he starts a little.

"Halloween is next week," Aunt Erika changes the subject. "I presume RBA is having its usual party."

Don't think about what you used to do with Mom, I tell myself. Of course, RBA doesn't do anything normally. Their on-campus party is a mask ball. While some of the guys do dress up in costumes, the party is really an excuse to wear fancy dresses and outfits.

Darcy and Ethan engage with Aunt Erika about Halloween, and I filter their voices out while I try to stop the tears that want to flow. Even though I'm not paying attention to him, I have this strange feeling that Ryder is acutely aware of me. The thought makes me uneasy.

Uncle Robert's phone buzzes and he checks his messages with a frown. Sighing, he stands up. "Well, I hate to be the party pooper. Ethan, I leave you in charge of hosting abilities." He gives me a weary smile. "We're dealing with a bit of an issue. Some new threat hitting banks."

My eyes widen when my phone buzzes with a Discord notification. I stand up to check Discord and see that NeO has been trying to reach me.

My uncle is halfway out of the dining room when he mumbles, "Bot causing DDoS."

Denial of service. I want to see the code. "Um, Kitty from my old school needs me to call her." I need to see the code. I don't care if I look crazy when I flee the room. I open my laptop and connect with NeORanger21. He already knows about it

– several major institutions have been hit hard. (I wonder what this guy does for a living – I swear he's online all the time.) He sends me samples of the code to confirm my suspicions.

I tell Ne0 that it looks like a modified version of a program called Kallisto. Some hackers post their code just to show off. Some hackers take that code and weaponize it. In my mind, I see the code come apart into functioning parts. I know how to cripple it.

In certain circles, we compete against each other. Arch4ngel101 has a reputation. Ne0Ranger21 has one too. We form teams and go after each other: Red versus Blue Teams. It's like role-playing games but with code instead of characters. Although we run them for fun and to show off, the competitions give us insight into the hacker behind the name. The way this code is mashed together, it reeks of RatGh0st.

When I send the fix to Ne0, he promises to disseminate it for me. This is what I do. I play behind the scenes whenever possible. Programmers know I exist, but the only one truly close to me is Ne0Ranger21.

Here's the thing. When I run the code in my protected simulation, and then launch the fix, a script runs. This message flashes back: *Don't chase the rabbit down the hole. It's nice to be noticed.*

I exhale sharply. Whoever launched this knew we'd find a fix. Ne0Ranger21 sees the same thing. He pings me, insisting we should talk later. I agree before closing my laptop. It sounds almost like a warning, and I have this nagging suspicion that it may be aimed at me. RatGh0st knows me and Ne0 by reputation. We've been in the same chat rooms. Is he trying to communicate something to us?

I rejoin Ethan and the others in the living room. It doesn't surprise me that Ryder and Connor are still here, but I am surprised that no one is fighting. Darcy's stern expression makes me think she lectured them into submission.

"That was one hell of a break," Darcy mutters. No one else comments about my odd exit from the dining room.

"Sorry, you know, issues," I lie, wincing as I wait for lightning to strike. Ryder and Ethan are in deep conversation, but they're not arguing so that's progress. I wish I could hear what they're talking about especially since Ryder and Ethan look my way a few times.

Connor waits until Darcy steps away to talk to me. "Mira, it isn't unusual for students to show up at the Halloween party with a date," he begins.

Could this night get any worse? My mind is still scattered. From where my cousin stands, I see Ryder's eyes widen briefly. He looks worried.

"Would you go with me?" Connor asks quickly, his blue-gray eyes on my face and his breathing rapid. He's nervous.

I try to hide my feeling of horror. Crap. Crap. Celeste romantically likes him. I like Connor, too, but as a friend. No matter how lonely I feel, it would be wrong to try and find comfort with Connor when I don't feel that way about him. "Like as your date?" When he nods, I close my eyes briefly. "Connor, we're friends, right?"

The flash of pain tells me that Connor expected a different reaction. "You like me, but you don't *like* like me," he states heavily.

"I'm sorry," I whisper. "You're super kind and super sweet." Ugh. I think I made it worse. I just friend-zoned him. I twist my hands. "Please don't be mad."

Connor averts his gaze for a minute. "I'm not. Disappointed? Yes. Maybe a whole host of other emotions."

"I could still use a really good friend," I say back to him. Yeah, I'm making this worse.

He smiles at me sadly, but the awkwardness opens a chasm I don't want between us. "For you? Always."

This will go down as one of the most uncomfortable nights of my life; at least I stopped some malware thingy. It's only a matter of time before authorities track down who sent it, and if it is RatGh0st, then it will be one less bad guy out there.

Connor awkwardly leaves to join Ethan and Ryder. Darcy

wanders over with a knowing look. "I'm guessing from Connor's sad face and your freaked-out expression that he asked you out and you said no," Darcy says very quietly, linking her arm through mine and walking me towards the veranda. We don't head outside, but it gives us some semblance of privacy. "He's a nice kid. If it'd been Ryder, Ethan would have tossed him out before he had a chance to ask." We both look at the three boys now talking. When Ryder meets my eyes, I quickly avert my gaze.

I make a derisive sound in my throat. "Ryder wouldn't touch me with a pole," I scoff, "and I don't think he's ever asked for anything in his life."

Darcy makes a face. "Fair enough. Besides, Ingrid's all over him. She truly is revolting. Did I ever tell you that she tried to hit on Ethan last year?" We shudder. "Ethan literally threw her off him when she sat on his lap. Then Erin chewed Ingrid out." Darcy pushes her chestnut hair back. "Erin hounded Ethan, too. She was furious when Ethan asked me out."

I'm surprised by that. Erin has always been nice to me.

"Don't be fooled by her," Darcy warns, reading me correctly. "Erin is old school – she truly expected Ethan to start something with her when they both became Royals. I had no idea that Ethan even noticed me when we were sophomores. But the head Royal at the time was a supreme asshole. Ethan knew I'd be targeted if he made a move, so he waited until he had the clout. It was gutsy. Erin and Ethan had a huge argument."

"But she accepted you and Ethan after a while?"

Darcy twists her lips. "Sort of. Nate and Xander supported Ethan last year. They have sway as Court members. You never met her, but Sarah was a fellow Royal who graduated last year. She never liked Erin and she sided with Ethan. It's all weird and crazy, but Ethan had enough support to make it difficult for Erin. Eventually, Erin realized it wasn't worth the fight. I mean, would you want to 'date' a guy who wasn't into you?" Darcy makes quote signs around the word *date*. "Erin is generally okay to deal with, but she only pretends to accept things as they are. She's as bad as Ingrid. If she senses an opening, she'll come down hard. Be careful with her."

"We've probably over-extended our stay, Ryder," Connor says, and guilt gnaws at me. Darcy squeezes Ethan's arm as if to say *I'll explain later*, and I wonder if I'm supposed to follow everyone out or if it's polite to run to my room and hide.

The decision is taken out of my hands. "We'll see you all at school on Monday," Darcy says, communicating to Ethan with a look.

Ryder's eyes narrow as if he's contemplating whether or not to accept this brush off, but Connor doesn't bother to wait. Ethan walks the two boys out, and Darcy turns to me. "You and I are going to the kitchen to eat more of that apple dessert. And I'm going to make you eat every bite while we talk."

It's a shame Erin is technically the Royals' Queen. Darcy would be so much better at it.

⊙⊙⊙111

When I forayed into the world of hackers and darknets and networks, I attracted the attention of a certain individual – likely because I was fourteen at the time and doing things major companies couldn't. Ne0Ranger21 and I know him as RReagan, and, as a sign of his creativity, his actual name is Ron Reagan. He works for the FBI's Cyber Division. Let's just say one online conversation led to another. We've helped him with some tiny jobs.

The Monday after the disastrous dinner, I receive a message from RReagan. He wants to *talk*, which means he'll probably be using a burner phone. Or maybe I'll be the one using a burner phone. Regardless, it sounds so secretive that I feel like I should buy shades and ride in a black Range Rover. I puzzle over his request all day until Ryder corners me right before English class.

"Are you going to the Halloween party?" he asks without much explanation.

The short answer is maybe. The long answer is that I'm undecided, but I have a feeling I'll be strong-armed by Celeste, Brittany, and Darcy. Since Darcy and Ethan will be showing up dressed as a king and queen, Brittany wants us to dress up as princesses. Celeste is worried that will make Erin, Judy, and Elaine angry. Anyway, I give Ryder the short answer. "Maybe."

For some reason, that makes him frown. "Connor asked you, didn't he? The other night." Ryder doesn't wait for me to answer. "But you turned him down. Why? He's rich. Wealthy enough to make your life pretty luxurious."

My brows rise. "What are you talking about?"

"Connor. He'll inherit quite a bit of money. Why wouldn't you agree to date him? He wants you."

The way Ryder speaks makes me think he believes this is a normal conversation. "Why would I want to know if he'll inherit anything?"

For a moment, the strange tension in his face disappears, replaced by an earnestness that seems foreign on Ryder. "You're not interested in Connor? Not even for his money?"

My mouth opens in horror. "That's a really awful thing to say," I finally whisper. "Not everyone is so obsessed with money."

Ryder laughs harshly. "Everyone is obsessed with money. Anyone can be bought. Even you."

I blink. This is probably the longest conversation I've had with Ryder, but it isn't one I'm anxious to extend. "That's a sad way to think about the world," I say very quietly. "I intend to make my way into the world, not live off some trust fund or inheritance. You know, I'd give anything to see my mom again. Money will never take that pain away."

We stare at each other in silence. I'm about to leave when Ryder says, "Are you sure about that?" He reaches out and grabs my right hand that is curled into a fist. Like an idiot, I watch him coax my hand to relax and find myself blushing at the contact. "I hope you come to the party, Mira." Our eyes meet again as he smiles faintly. He releases my hand and leaves.

I'm starting to think that some of the students at RBA suffer from personality disorders.

• • •

Whatever Ethan does to force the Court and the Royals to settle makes a difference. Or at least, I think it does. Arthur and Cage still leer at me, but they do it at a distance. Erin remains benign. Judy and Elaine ignore me. Ingrid and Victoria continue to give me withering looks, but they are silent. I take a moment to consider Ingrid. She hates me and I find the concept odd and unsettling. Is it just because of the whole Old vs. New money issue? When she attacked me in the locker room, I can't forget how angry she was.

I don't have a degree in psychology, but that kind of anger doesn't seem normal to me. I ponder this in the library as I start the research process for my English paper. We're writing a paper on *Heart of Darkness* by Joseph Conrad, which isn't that difficult of a process. Just thirty years ago, it was considered an important literary work to analyze due to its dark imagery and themes. But the book itself is controversial. Its depiction of the horrors of colonization is often lost by overanalyzing the psychological meaning of the novel. It's characterizations of the people of Africa – making them savage and uncivilized – leaves a bad taste in my mouth. I get the stirrings of my paper as I sit and think about the hate Ingrid blasts my way, and the way Conrad depicts the oppressed populations in Africa as his book's protagonist searches for the wayward Mr. Kurtz. Both are formed by prejudicial beliefs.

"So serious," a voice teases unpleasantly. Cage Bennett stands between the stacks of books. "No big cousin around. Just you and me in the library."

That's not true. I could scream and alert the librarian, but something tells me that Cage is the kind of guy that likes girls to be afraid of him. I start backing up slowly. I'm not afraid of him doing anything too terrible, but I don't want to give him the pleasure of terrifying me either.

"There you are. I've been looking for you."

I can't tell if I'm in greater trouble now that Xander Morrison has joined us. His hair is gently tousled like he just woke up from a nap, but his blue-green eyes are surprisingly serious. Even though Cage is older than Xander, the two boys are evenly matched, and there's a set to Xander's shoulders – he's not there to help Cage bully me.

"Cage." There's a finality to Xander's tone. "Need to borrow Mira." He doesn't wait for Cage to respond, grabbing me by the hand and yanking me out of the library.

The moment we're outside, he spins me around. "Are you completely stupid or just oblivious?" he demands in a harsh whisper. "After what happened to you at the pool, why in the world would you wander around campus alone?"

I'm stricken mute as I stare at him foolishly. A part of me wants to tell him that I shouldn't have to worry about walking around the school on my own. Another part just wants to go to my room and cry. *Like a baby*, I mock myself.

Xander swears under his breath. "Come on. Let me walk you back to your dorm." He scowls as I follow him meekly.

I'm in my uniform, but this is the East Coast and I'm not used to the chillier nights. I presume winter is going to be a deal-breaker for me. After seeing me shiver – and scowling about it, too – he removes his jacket and drapes it around me.

"Your cousin needs to keep a better eye on you," he grumbles, sounding less angry. "He should know better."

"Why does he need to keep an eye on me?" I bristle at his criticism of Ethan.

Xander exhales sharply, his eyes dark as he regards me. "Because the Royal girls don't like you, that's why." He stops at my dorm. "Go inside. And for God's sake, Mira, don't wander around on your own at school again." He removes his jacket from my shoulders. Without saying goodbye, he turns and walks off into the dark, leaving me puzzled.

001000

Despite my intention not to go to the Halloween party, Aunt Erika has other plans. Darcy and Brittany do a terrible job hiding their smiles when I return to the dorm with Celeste and find a dress waiting for me.

The sky-blue ball gown is possibly the fanciest outfit I've ever worn. Celeste tells me it's a fairy gown. The off-the-shoulder dress has a rather low back – I'm shy about how much of my back shows – but Darcy tuts at me when I cringe. I admire the flower appliques on the tulle skirt. Because it is a mask ball, there is a half-mask made of silvery lace. It doesn't do much to conceal my face, but it frames my eyes and makes them seem exotic.

It doesn't surprise me that Darcy's gown is threaded with metallic gold. It's very regal and her mask is a cross between a circlet and a half-mask. Nope, the symbolism is not subtle. I try not to get teary when Darcy and Brittany help me with my makeup while Celeste pulls my hair back in a half-ponytail.

"Missing Mom?" Celeste whispers empathetically. Mom promised to help me with my makeup one day, but now that day won't come. When I nod, the girls hug me collectively. "She's here with you. Always."

I help the others with their dresses and hair – not with the makeup since I'm hopeless when it comes to that. When we're done, I look like a fairy, Darcy is a queen, Brittany is a Greek goddess, and Celeste is a princess.

Ethan whistles as he enters our suite, handsome in a black tux. His eyes fill with pride when he beholds Darcy in her queenly attire. Brittany, Celeste, and I giggle on the side while the two share a moment.

We take a bunch of pictures so that Aunt Erika won't throw a hissy fit about a lack of photos, and then Ethan offers me and Darcy an elbow and escorts us to the ball, Celeste and Brittany flanking us to either side.

The school was once part of an estate, and only the mansion remains. Used only for special occasions, the mansion was built in a southern plantation shape, with brick walls and long columns in the front. Many of the rooms were consolidated during various renovations to provide a large area for dancing. The upper rooms were converted into bathrooms and sitting rooms. During the summer months, the school rents the mansion out for weddings and receptions.

Ethan takes us through the tunnels so that we don't have to walk through the chilly evening air. Walking into the building, I'm swept away by how surreal everything is. The interior of the mansion practically glows with fancy lighting and students in elegant attire.

"Ethan, you look amazing," Erin says. She's in a black evening dress, and her smile falters when she sees Darcy's outfit. With the memory of Darcy's words, this time I note the brief flash of fury Erin hides. "You look lovely, Darcy."

"Thank you. So do you."

Erin glances at the rest of us, her dark eyes lingering briefly on me. "A sweet fairy," she comments. "How fitting."

Nate Jacobs whistles as he joins us. He twirls Brittany around and then spins Celeste in a quick dance. When he approaches me, Ethan scowls. Nate discreetly backs off. "How is it that the most beautiful girls are around you, Ethan?" he complains with a good-natured sigh.

"It's good to be the king," Ethan deadpans.

"Excuse me. I need to find Arthur," Erin says stiffly, moving off into the crowd of students.

I'm not exactly sure if Erin and Arthur are an actual couple, but he's become her pseudo-escort. I feel bad for her because Arthur gives me the creeps. I'm not sure any girl finds it easy to be around him.

"You showed up," Ryder breathes into my ear, causing me to jump. There should be a law against that. He smirks when I spin around in alarm.

Ryder, Xander, and Connor greet Ethan with varying degrees of enthusiasm, but the long look Connor sends my way has me fidgeting. I impulsively grab Celeste and say, "I'm really thirsty."

Ethan pauses mid-conversation with Darcy and Nate to glance towards me. I wave him off. I have Celeste with me, and, as we move, Connor and Ryder follow.

When we get to the drink station, I'm dismayed by the amount of alcohol. Hello? These kids are underage! And I'm further dismayed when Ryder, Connor, and Celeste grab champagne flutes. I reach for a bottle of mineral water. I'm not sure I'll ever be able to touch alcohol. A drunk driver killed Mom.

"Looks like our king is starting the dance," Ryder tells us with narrowed eyes.

Connor hasn't taken his eyes off me. Just as he opens his mouth, I suddenly grab Ryder's arm, nearly causing him to spew his drink. "I think Ethan's looking for me," I blurt in a panicked tone. "He wanted me to be one of the people on the floor with him."

Ryder's blue eyes meet mine, and something like pleasure rolls off him. "Let's not disappoint him," he murmurs. "Dance with me, Mira."

I remind myself I don't like Ryder and the only reason why I agree is to push Connor and Celeste together.

Connor's face falls in disappointment, but he immediately turns to Celeste and escorts her out to the floor. I sigh in relief at her delighted expression. Erin and Arthur move next to Darcy and Ethan. Ryder positions himself to the left of Ethan, making sure my displeased cousin notices us. Brittany and Nate pair up, and down the row, I see Xander with Elaine, while Ingrid is with Cage. Victoria pairs with Daniel Jameson, a Court member who I rarely interact with, and Judy seem to be sitting the dance out.

We move in a coordinated waltz, joining with our partners in the middle as we dance. I match Ryder step for step, his eyes never leaving my face. "Why are you staring at me like that?" I ask him at one point.

"Perhaps I like what I see," he replies, the hand holding mine moving in a caress.

Startled, I stumble a bit. Ethan catches my eye with a concerned look. He's not happy that I'm dancing with Ryder. Meanwhile, Connor and Celeste smile and laugh with each other – Celeste is glowing. I flash her a quick smile.

Ryder shifts to hold me closer. "I'm guessing Connor will kill me before the night is over."

"This is really close," I say stupidly. I'm practically against his chest.

"So it is," he says, his eyes lidded.

My heart does a weird, fluttery thing as we dance: it feels natural dancing with him. When his leg brushes mine, I blush.

"Why will Connor kill you?" I finally manage to ask, my color high.

"Because I want to kiss you," Ryder confesses, bringing his lips close to mine as the song ends.

His lips barely touch mine before he's pulled away by a furious Connor. Ethan intervenes immediately. "Not here!" he snaps. "And not in front of Mira. You two take it outside!"

The devastation on Celeste's face cuts me as Ryder and Connor belligerently push each other while they make their way outside. Xander holds Ryder back while Ethan keeps Connor from slamming his fist into his cousin's face. The other students, hungry for gossip and drama, circle like sharks as Ryder and Connor continue to rage at each other. Ingrid, standing with Cage and Victoria, pushes her way forward, her eyes sharp and bitter.

The two boys face off in the courtyard, their breath frosting as they try to reach each other. Ethan and Xander do their best to calm the cousins down. Erin finally appears, and Cage and Arthur move to flank her as she watches. Celeste takes my hand. I want so badly to turn to her, to apologize, but I don't know what to say. Instead, I squeeze her hand back.

"I don't understand," I say stupidly, glancing at Darcy and Brittany.

"You *knew*!" Connor bellows at his cousin, Ethan still holding him. "You knew. You got in the way, and now you're going after her! What the fuck, Ryder?!"

The other boy holds his head arrogantly, shaking Xander's hold off. "You're coming to the wrong conclusion, Connor. You're acting like a fool. She doesn't belong to you."

My brain works too slowly. "They can't be fighting about me. He hates me," I whisper. "Ryder hates me."

"Does he?" Celeste wonders aloud.

The fight goes out of Connor suddenly. Ethan staggers a bit, letting Connor go. "That's enough, both of you," Ethan orders in a hard voice, gesturing to them. "She didn't come here with you, Connor. She's free to do what she wants."

I cringe. This is my fault. I shouldn't have let Ryder almost kiss me. Now Celeste is hurt, and Connor is angry.

Connor hangs his head, but then his body tenses as he launches at his cousin. The two exchange blows before they're dragged apart.

"You think you can have any girl you want, don't you?!" Connor seethes, his blue-gray eyes dark and stormy. "The great Ryder Cabot, Whore of Royal Bridge Academy! It wasn't enough for you to come between us, was it? You just couldn't stand the thought that maybe a girl would pick me over you!"

"Is that true, Ryder?" Ingrid asks in a ringing voice. "Are you lusting after our Orphan Annie?"

Ryder sneers at Ingrid, the corner of his mouth bloody. "You only wish I'd lust after you!"

Everyone's so focused on the confrontation between

Ryder and Connor that they don't notice me release Celeste's hand. Celeste meets my eyes, and I shake my head. I head back in, pushing past students. Erin stops me inside with a frown. "You should leave, Mira," she says. "You'll only get hurt staying here. Boys like Ryder play mean games. You're not one of us, and you don't know how to play the games we play. I'd hate for you to get hurt."

I take two steps back, staring at her in confusion. And then I flee, disappearing into the underground tunnel as fast as I can.

⊙⊙1⊙⊙1

The tension between Ryder and Connor continues into November. Ryder and I ignore each other in class, and I do my best to mend my relationship with Connor. He's hurt, but he's not angry with me. I can't imagine how awkward things are at home.

Slowly, though, I see something close to normalcy between me and Connor. The resentment with Ryder remains. As Connor tells me in a moment of honesty, "I'm upset that he did it so soon after I told him I was interested in you."

I avoid the parties after the soccer games, watching the first snowfall from my window instead. I don't want or need a social life. I withdraw from the physical world and spend my weekends doing available bounties. After playing Mission Impossible with RReagan, he says that his division is tracking "activity". That's his obtuse way of saying he may need a favor soon.

Right before the Thanksgiving break, Aunt Erika asks if she should invite Ryder and Connor to join us. I'm not sure she realizes that Ethan and Ryder aren't best friends, but I think about those two spending Thanksgiving alone. I don't know how to feel about Ryder, but I can't let that stand in the way of simple kindness.

"God, Mira, you're too soft," Ethan groans as I drag him to Connor's suite that he shares with Nate, Ryder, and Xander during the school week.

"Thanksgiving is about sharing and caring," I say, my hand around his arm.

"That's Christmas, Mira. And for crying out loud, Ryder and Connor are not talking. Do we really want them fighting in our home?"

Xander opens the door to their suite in surprise. Like a boss, Ethan sweeps right in as if he's the one dragging me and not the other way around. Connor glances up from the book he's reading, getting hastily to his feet. Both Xander and Connor are still in their uniforms.

"Where the hell did you put my shaving cream?" Ryder gripes, coming out of his room in nothing but a towel slung around his waist. Correction, the towel is slung *low* around his waist.

Ethan covers my eyes and spins me around so that I face the door. "Goddammit! Put some clothes on, Ryder!" Once I'm primly turned, he uses his hands to keep me in place. "Why are you walking around naked?"

"What the fuck are you doing here? And I'm not naked, you ass."

Since I'm now staring at the door, Connor walks over to me. "Mira?" He's torn between mirth and puzzlement.

"Hey," I say. Ugh, I sound all breathy and flustered. I am definitely *not* going to think about how low that towel was. Definitely not going to think about Ryder's Orion's belt. And how the hell do I know what an Orion's belt is?

"Aunt Erika wants to invite you both," I use my thumb to point at Ryder over my shoulder, "to Thanksgiving. I know you don't do Thanksgiving in England, but you made it sound like your uncle isn't around much. And that seems lonely to me. You should be with family. I mean, we're not family. But you should at least be with friends. I know we're not all really friends either but we're nice. Or usually nice." Now I'm babbling.

"You came to invite us to Thanksgiving?" Ryder asks slowly behind me.

"I didn't," Ethan grumbles under his breath.

I'm about to turn but Ethan prevents me from doing so. "Ethan, I've seen boys' chests before," I protest, ignoring Xander's huff of laughter, the low chuckle from Ryder, and Connor pressing his lips together.

"Answer her, Cabot, so I can get her out of here," Ethan snarls, not letting up on his grip. "I don't want my cousin seeing you like that."

"If you are spending Thanksgiving alone, you should both come," I pipe up.

Connor glances over my shoulder at Ryder with a strange look on his face. "We'd love to."

I ignore Ethan's groan, but that doesn't stop him from dragging me out, ensuring I'm not exposed to anything improper by covering my eyes.

• • •

Thanksgiving was just me and Mom. Sometimes we cooked. Sometimes we went out. With Aunt Erika, I think she's excited to have a full house. Her chef prepped everything for us beforehand with detailed instructions. After seeing Aunt Erika in the kitchen, I take over the timing of the dishes.

Since Darcy is with her family, Ethan does a video chat while I put the pie in the oven. "Look at her, babe. She's a pro in the kitchen at sixteen," he says proudly. "There isn't anything Mira can't do."

"Aww, she looks cute in an apron," Darcy says, leaning towards the camera. In the background, I hear a cacophony of voices. "Ma, I'm coming!" She blows us a kiss. "Babe, got to go. The annual volleyball competition is about to begin." She rolls her eyes. "Call me later and tell me what Thanksgiving is like with those two." She gives me a funny wink.

We say our goodbyes as Aunt Erika escorts Ryder and Connor in. "I can have Martha keep an eye on the food if you want to be with your friends."

Ethan snorts derisively, but I take my apron off and nod.

"You're cooking?" Ryder asks with a surprised look while I wash my hands.

I shrug. "Sort of. Just putting things in the oven. But I have made dinner before."

"You're not even flustered. I thought cooking Thanksgiving dinner is supposed to be stressful," Connor comments as we follow Ethan out of the kitchen.

"I know how to follow a recipe, Connor. It's not neurosurgery," I say drily. Why make a fuss over a simple thing?

Connor raises his hands defensively. "Alright, don't bite my head off."

Ethan takes us to the amusement room, tossing a cue stick to Ryder with a challenge shining in his eyes. "Come on, Cabot. A game. And a wager."

Ryder spins the stick smoothly, tilting his chin up as he answers. "Fine." His deep blue eyes glance my way. "I win and I ask Mira to the Winter Ball."

My jaw drops. I glance at Connor surreptitiously, but Connor only narrows his eyes. They don't seem to be fighting anymore. Ethan, however, tenses. Scowling, Ethan steps closer to Ryder in challenge. "Fine. You lose and you stay away from my cousin. Permanently."

They're making a bet about me?

Ryder doesn't blink and gives my cousin a cocky smile. "Deal."

I take a seat, eyes wide. I guess no one plans to ask me what I think. I tuck my legs under me while Connor takes a spot across the room. Both Ethan and Ryder are solid players, calling out their shots calmly and confidently. Towards the end of the match, when Ethan has only two balls left on the table, Ryder misses and Ethan takes over. The current king and the future king stare each other down as Ethan examines his shot. A slow smile tells me Ethan's sure he'll win. After a second, Ryder leans down and whispers something into Ethan's ear.

My cousin's eyes widen, jaw tensing as he glares at Ryder. Shaking himself, Ethan makes a visible effort to relax. He takes the shot and swears when his ball nears the socket but stops at the edge. He misjudged the power he needed. Ryder smirks, keeping his eye on Ethan as he lines up his shot. He sinks his last ball and then goes after the 8-ball.

Ethan throws the cue stick on the floor hard enough to make me flinch before storming off. Ryder slowly pivots to face me, but I'm not smiling. "You can ask but I don't have to say yes," I snap, crossing my arms. Childish, I know.

Connor chuckles. As I move to leave, Ryder grabs my arm. "Connor, I'd like a moment with Mira," he requests quietly.

"Let me go," I hiss. I am *not* going to be weak.

"Hear me out," Ryder says, and it sounds like a plea.

Connor cocks his head at me, and I sigh. "If he gets obnoxious, shout and I'll come in and punch him," he promises right before he steps out of the room. Why is Connor being so agreeable? Why am I being abandoned with the mean boy?

Ryder lets me go. "Mira."

Stop being a baby, I chide myself. I face him. "Ryder."

"Will you attend the Winter Ball with me?"

Why is he asking me? "The last time I went to an event, you and Connor ruined it. Besides, you're supposed to go with Ingrid, right? Aren't you two dating or promised to each other or something?

Ryder doesn't smile. "I'm not with Ingrid. I'm asking you." When he takes a step towards me, I step back. A flash of hurt confusion crosses his face. "Don't be afraid of me. I'd never hurt you." His voice drops to a near whisper. "I'm asking you to be my date, Mira."

"You don't even like me," I blurt, backing up into the pool table.

Ryder leans until his hands are resting on either side of me. "Is that what you think? Because I thought I was being pretty obvious about my interest. I think everyone knows. Even Ethan." He brings his face close to mine. "There are things you're not ready to hear from me yet. But you should know that I do like you. Connor was right. I didn't want to see you with him because I want you to be with me. You don't flaunt yourself, but there isn't a guy on campus you couldn't have. You think no one sees you, but we do."

"We?"

"The guys." His eyes are amused. "You don't notice it, do you? Prettiest girl on campus. Protected by the great Ethan De Vries. Untouchable. That makes you so much more interesting." His hands run up my arms to clasp my elbows. "Mira, you almost let me kiss you that night. I haven't been able to stop thinking about it since."

Okay, he makes me sound like forbidden fruit or something. I should want him to see me for me, right? "Why are you being nice now?" Mom warned me about teenage hormones. Actually, she warned me about hormones in general. She said they make you impulsive and stupid. Ryder makes me feel very stupid. Worse, he smells good, too. My brain is malfunctioning.

Ryder's lids lower. "I know my behavior hasn't been stellar."

"Is it true you've dated a lot of girls?" I ask suddenly, trying to clear my head.

"I've never dated anyone," Ryder murmurs. "I've never asked anyone either. I'm asking you. And after the ball, I intend to keep on asking you." When my eyes widen, he adds in a lower voice, "There won't be anyone else. I don't want anyone else, Mira."

Wait, what is he saying? It's gotten very warm in this room. I'm overwhelmed. More than overwhelmed. I avert my head and close my eyes when Ryder brings his lips to my ear.

"I'll beg if you want me to," he whispers into my ear.

"Yes." What am I doing? What am I saying?

"Yes, you want me to beg, or yes, you'll be my date to the Winter Ball?" I hear a hint of laughter in his voice.

"The latter."

Ryder straightens, his knuckles brushing my cheek gently. "Thank you."

My eyes snap open. "A favor?"

"Anything."

"Do you think you could get Connor to ask Celeste?"

Ryder's smile is genuine. "I think I can try."

● ● ●

"You did what?!"

It's after dinner. Ryder and Connor have gone home, so I stop by Ethan's room to tell him I agreed to go with Ryder to the ball. Darcy's face, peering at me from Ethan's laptop, is full of snarky glee.

"I told you he liked her, Ethan," she practically crows.

Ethan scowls at his girlfriend. "Dammit, Darcy, I don't trust him. You *know* he and Ingrid have been pissed since last year."

"I can't wait to see Ingrid's bitchy face." Darcy winks at me.

Ethan exhales heavily. "Mira, just don't rush things, okay? Ryder doesn't have the best reputation."

"He basically sleeps with a girl once and then ignores her," Darcy agrees, then continues thoughtfully, "but he's never asked a girl out before."

That's consistent with what Ryder said, but the mention of his prior behavior makes me scrunch my face. "I don't intend to have sex anytime soon."

Ethan groans. "Okay, I don't even want to hear the three-letter word from your mouth, Mira. Gross. You're like a sister and I am going to kill Ryder if he even tries anything like that. You shouldn't be dating until you're twenty-one or something! God, why aren't there nunneries to send cousins and sisters to anymore?" Darcy breaks into laughter in the background.

"I'm just going to a dance with him." I lift my hands in a futile gesture.

Ethan's shoulders slump with resignation. "Just be care-ful. Don't let him into your heart, cuz. The Royals don't play nicely." Ethan ruffles my hair.

"I'll be careful," I promise.

OO1O1O

I nibble at my lower lip before I close my laptop. Rat-Gh0st's never escalated before. Why now? He's a dull hacker – no ingenuity. This makes me think that someone – or something – is motivating him. But what? He attacked banks first through a DDoS. Then he tried to blackmail a city by locking their systems up.

I shake my head. The truth is that I could do this all day. Hacking, coding, investigating. I love the chase, I love the strike and counterstrike aspects, the challenge of breaking barriers and finding mistakes. It's easy to get caught up in it and forget the outside world. But right now, I'm putting my cyber world aside for the real world.

It's strange shopping with other girls for clothes. We go from store to store trying on gowns. Darcy picks an A-line gown in deep purple. Brittany gets a form-fitting sheath dress in emerald green. And Celeste chooses a metallic blue gown that graces her curves perfectly. None of the girls blink at the cost of their dresses, but I do. I refuse to buy any of the gowns I try on.

Mom and I never had a lot of money. To spend four to five figures on a gown I might wear only once seems like a crime. When I tell Aunt Erika this, we compromise. She has me look at the gowns in her closet and then we work with a seamstress to alter the gown to my taste.

Much to Ethan's irritation, I agree to let Ryder grab a stretch limo for us to share. Darcy and I get ready together, and when we descend the stairs, I fight the flutter of nerves in my stomach.

My redesigned dress is in deep red silk. It is softly checkered in shades of dark red, making the fabric seem textured and vibrant. Without the long sleeves, the now sleeveless gown has a younger, more elegant feel with the deep sweetheart neckline. The moment I see Ryder's eyes on me, I know I look as good as I feel. In the background, my aunt and uncle look on with sentimental pride.

Ryder's voice is faintly husky when he says to me, "You look and smell divine." He takes a velvet jewelry case out and opens it. Inside is a white-gold necklace with a ruby pendant. "I want you to have this."

I step away, my brow furrowing. "I can't accept that." When Ryder frowns, I glance at him anxiously. "Ryder, that's too much. It's far too expensive."

Ethan and Darcy look at us as I keep shaking my head. The distress on my face causes my uncle to step forward. "Ryder, I must agree with Mira. It's inappropriate to give her something so lavish. As her uncle and guardian, I must insist that you only let her borrow it for the night," Uncle Robert says. When he sees me hesitate, my uncle adds, "I think it would be okay for you to borrow it."

The shadow in Ryder's eyes tells me he's either angry with me or disappointed or hurt. I honestly can't tell, but some of the tension leaves him as he drapes the necklace around my neck. His eyes linger on the way the ruby lies against my skin, above the curve of my dress.

In the limo, Ethan is torn between keeping an eye on Ryder and drooling over Darcy. This is their last Winter Ball at RBA. I haven't paid that much attention to what their plans are after high school. They've applied to the same schools, but there's been talk of taking a gap year and traveling.

Ryder trails a finger down my right hand. "You're quiet and thoughtful looking. You're turning seventeen in a few days."

How in the world does Ryder know that? Ethan and Darcy, in deep conversation, pause when they hear Ryder's comment.

"Are we having a party? You'll be seventeen! How did I not know this?" Darcy's reproach to Ethan is evident.

Ethan sighs. "She doesn't want a big party. She doesn't want a party at all."

It's both pathetic and not pathetic that my birthdays were often quiet affairs. Mom and I would go to the local diner, and I would eat a whole stack of pancakes drenched in syrup and butter. We'd pick a movie, order a pizza, and wear pajamas. Our gifts were small and personal.

Darcy makes a sound of disappointment. "But, Mira, we should have a party!"

"What did you do with Aunt Gwen?" Ethan asks much to my dismay and embarrassment.

I avoid everyone's eyes when I recite what my birthdays were like. I know it sounds lame. I was never popular and struggled to make friends. In elementary, I was awkward, the one last picked on teams. In middle school, I kept to myself.

Darcy snaps her fingers. "Let's do a slumber party!"

"What?" I blink at her a few times.

"It's perfect. We'll invite a few friends, hot tub, pizza, cake. Get dressed in pajamas." Darcy claps her hands in excitement.

"Girls only?" I squeak.

Ethan protests. "I want to be there, too. This is my first year as a cousin!"

"Co-ed," Darcy laughs with a wink at me, ignoring my red face. "I'll plan it. Please let me plan it!"

I hide my face in my hands, but Ryder gently lowers them. "Exactly what kind of pajamas are we talking about?" His question is suggestive.

Ethan reaches over and swats Ryder. "Normal pajamas. Flannel. Get your mind out of the gutter!"

Ryder just smiles and shrugs.

"Alright, anything on your wish list?" Darcy asks, and I see her mind working out the details.

"No presents!" The thought of meaningless presents is painful. I don't want empty gifts to make up for what I lost.

Darcy huffs. "Mira, we're bringing gifts. I saw this sweet Coach purse you should have."

"Nothing over twenty dollars, then." I ignore Ethan's horrified look. "I mean it. I'll reject anything more than twenty bucks! My birthdays were never about getting things." Mom always said I was her gift.

When everyone starts to protest, I lay my foot down. "I'd rather just have a card with a personal note than anything else."

While Darcy continues to plan, I meet Ryder's slightly confused look with a shrug of my own.

•••

It's somewhat apropos that the current king and future king arrive together. Erin graciously comments on it, and if her smile falters when she says Darcy's name, no one mentions it. Elaine, in her jaded way, just yawns and ignores everything, while her date, Cage, wanders off to flirt with several girls at another table. Nate and Victoria would be cute as a couple except he looks deathly bored.

But I feel a wave of happiness when I see Celeste and Connor together. Ryder's hand lingers possessively on my waist as Connor moves our way, but nothing in Connor's demeanor suggests he's displeased with his partner or displeased that Ryder is with me.

"You look amazing," Connor comments easily, Celeste's hand secured through his arm. The words he and Ryder exchange are without tension or rancor, and Celeste's eyes are bright with joy.

Ryder and Conner track Ethan and Darcy, and that's when I see Ingrid. If looks could kill, I would be dead with a slit throat, my body riddled with bullets, and a dozen knives sticking out of my chest. She's here with Daniel Jameson, since Xander's on his own, and the evil glare she sends Xander's way when he stops to talk to Ethan is a clear sign of her displeasure.

Ingrid struts towards us, dragging Daniel with a long-nailed hand. "Well, Ryder." Her red lips turn down with distaste. "I guess you do have a thing for little orphans." She whispers something in Ryder's ear, and he tenses slightly next to me. Then she addresses me. "Clever girl. Ryder's worth a lot of money. Hopefully, you can hold on to him long enough to enjoy it. He's not known to be… faithful."

Ryder's eyes burn, but his tone is viciously cold. "Careful, Ingrid. Your petty ways are unattractive. And no amount of plastic surgery can fix that. We're attending the Winter Ball together, not plotting marriage. If you'll excuse us, Ethan wants us on the floor. We can't disappoint the King."

Ryder's cruelty is back in full force. I bite my tongue as Ethan indicates we should position ourselves next to him. Erin and Arthur move to Ethan's right, and Erin's face is curiously impassive as Ingrid and Daniel join us on the floor. I wave as Brittany joins us with Enrique, our basketball star. Her saucy wink speaks volumes – Enrique is not Court status yet, but it's believed that he'll take us to state next year. If Ethan has him starting the dance with all of us, that's a statement in itself. Celeste and Connor take the last spot on the floor.

The moment the music starts, Ryder's focus is all on me. The hardness on his face eases slightly, but with Ingrid watching us two couples away, I'm wary at the way his thumb strokes my hand. He isn't looking at me directly. He seems focused on my lips, dropping his gaze suggestively at times to my exposed skin and the necklace around my neck. When he spins me, he yanks me back into his arms, letting me feel the long length of his body through my dress. I'm confused and bothered by his actions, and when the song ends, I step away when he reaches for me, my brows knitted in a frown. I ignore the sharp way he calls my name as I make my escape to the restrooms.

I've always wondered why many of the women's restrooms have a weird little sitting area. Now I know why as I sit down to take a calming breath, closing my eyes.

"Are you okay?"

Erin walks over to me, her face filled with concern.

"I'm fine. Just a little headache."

She hesitates. "You're being played. If you're curious about the game, you should talk to Daniel Jameson."

When I stare at her in confusion, she averts her eyes.

"There are things I know in my position. Things I'm not allowed to tell you, but you seem like a nice person. I'd hate for you to get hurt." She steps closer to me. "Ryder plays games. He plays to win. There are things Daniel knows that might be helpful to you." A shadow crosses her face. "I've already said too much."

I wait a few minutes after she leaves before walking out. Ryder snares my arm. "You were in there for over ten minutes. You left me on the floor." He sounds hurt.

I try to push him away, but he forces me further down the hallway and away from others, pinning me to the wall and forcing my head up. I go limp, averting my head. Even with the music in the background, I hear our combined heavy breathing.

"Tell me what's going through your mind right now," Ryder says in a tight voice.

"You're acting like a jerk," I say finally. "I've never gone on a date, much less gone dancing. I only know how to waltz because my mom taught me. Whatever you're trying to prove out there," I wave to the main hall, "I don't understand any of it. I don't—" I break off. "I don't put out or whatever you call it, so don't treat me like I'm going to give you whatever you want."

Ryder goes still. "I didn't—"

"You did. Or at least, that's how you made me feel."

He bends his head until his forehead presses against my temple. "I'm sorry."

Ryder once told me he never apologized. Clearly, this is no longer the case.

"Mira, I'm sorry," he repeats. "I—I'm a bit confused right now." His body leans against me, loose and soothing. "We grow up hard and fast in my world. And you're—" He stops, holding me to his chest. My ear hears the loud thud of his heartbeat, his harsh breaths. "I know I have a reputation, but that's not me. Not to you. That's not who I want to be for you."

Ryder has an amazing ability to say epic, swoon-worthy stuff. He's too beautiful for his own good, too, and I don't understand why he's focused on me.

"What the hell are you doing to Mira?!" Ethan roars from down the hallway, storming towards us with murder on his face.

Ryder slowly moves away, his face cool and impassive. "We were talking, Ethan."

Ethan's skepticism is obvious. "Cabot, you don't touch her. For God's sake, don't do to her what you do to other girls."

Ryder goes rigid. "Just be blunt, De Vries. You want to know if my intentions to Mira are *honorable*." He says the last word derisively.

Darcy lays a hand on Ethan's arm. "Ethan, let it go. This isn't the place. Don't ruin the night by making assumptions here."

Darcy's gentle reasoning wins Ethan over and he makes a visible effort to relax. "Alright, alright." Ethan gives me a stiff hug and then nudges me over to Ryder with a stern look at the other boy.

"Okay, can we put the egos aside for a second and just enjoy the dance?" Darcy demands with a hint of exasperation.

Ryder leads me back to the dance floor. "I've done a poor

job so far on our first date," he says to me. He glowers briefly at a furious Ingrid. "You should know that I think I'm prone to jealousy."

"You think?" I query archly.

His faint smile doesn't quite reach his eyes. "I think." His hand drifts to my waist.

"Well, the good thing about starting poorly is that you can't get much worse," I quip.

His warm laugh vibrates against my head. "I guess so."

001011

My birthday begins with me and Aunt Erika over a plate of pancakes. It's just the two of us and she regales me with stories of Mom. Then she hands me a file box that is worn and tattered on the edges. Inside are my mother's journals.

"She wrote in them faithfully from age fourteen and on." My aunt grows thoughtful. "She was certainly better about journaling than I was. She stopped not long after high school, I think. After Robert and I married, it put a damper on how often we were together. I didn't expect to fall in love so suddenly." Her voice lowers conspiratorially. "Did you know that our father wanted Gwennie to marry Ernest Whitman? He threw them together all the time. She went on a few dates, but Ernest was an unpleasant young man. He remains unpleasant to this day. I always felt bad for Sally being married to such a snide man."

"Ernest Whitman? Ingrid's father?" I make a face.

"I know, right?" Aunt Erika sighs. "No, Gwen had more sense than that."

"It didn't bother me when I was little – not knowing who my dad was, I mean. But now I wish I did know something about him," I admit.

Aunt Erika takes my hand sympathetically. "I've wracked my brains about this." With her other hand, she lifts my chin. "You've definitely got some Asian blood in you, but I can't think of anyone who Gwen knew at the time that would be a potential father for you. We weren't very diverse back then, but it must have been someone that Gwen didn't want anyone to know about." Her lips turn down. "To be honest, I wasn't a great sister. I was obsessed with getting pregnant. Robert and I wanted to have a lot of kids." Her eyes cloud. "It wasn't in the cards for us, though. I must've done something to make Gwen think she couldn't trust me. Or she must've been afraid of Father finding out."

"Maybe some things aren't meant to be known," I say finally. "I asked her once about her parents. She never said she was an only child. In fact, all she told me was that she had to strike out on her own because it was necessary." I pause, recollecting something. "I remember a neighbor complaining about her sister, and Mom got very emotional. She said to never take a sister for granted because your sister is your other half. Not better, not worse, but still a part of you."

Aunt Erika closes her eyes briefly. "Thank you...for that memory." Her blue eyes shimmer when she opens them. "And thank you, Gwennie, for giving me your daughter."

•••

How Darcy manages to get Ethan to agree to this party is beyond me. At precisely two in the afternoon, Darcy, Celeste, and Brittany show up. We go up to my room with sleeping bags and blankets. At three, Ryder, Connor, Nate, and Xander show up, ignoring Ethan's faint frown as they barge into my room. Somehow, Ethan gets a pillow to his face, which results in a massive pillow war. I'm not sure if the guys pick sides, but somehow it ends with the girls declaring victory.

Ethan snags Darcy and swings her over his shoulder. "I'm kidnapping your ringleader. We'll meet you in the hot tub." He disappears with her.

I cover my mouth with a hand when Xander waggles his brows suggestively. Nate leans his head against Brittany and asks, "Hmm, feel like being kidnapped?" Brittany pushes him away with a huff.

We shoo the boys out so we can change into swimsuits,

and the boys beat us to the hot tub.

"Honestly, if you weren't Ethan's cousin, I'd be in here naked," Xander announces. Nate reaches over to smack the back of his head. "Hey! As if you guys wouldn't do the same!"

"You don't need to announce it to them," Connor grumbles.

I'm conscious of Ryder's eyes following my every move. The hot tub is blissfully warm, and I give a little sigh as I sink into the bubbly water, but I start feeling shy when Ryder sits next to me, his lids slightly lowered.

Ryder rests his arms outside the tub. "You okay with this?" he asks me quietly. When I nod, he doesn't bother to hide his pleased smile. He presses a kiss to my temple. "Happy birthday, Mira." I hope no one notices that I'm blushing.

"We should think about pizza," Nate announces. "I'm hungry."

"You're always hungry," Ryder scoffs.

Xander leans forward to tap my nose with his finger. "What does the birthday girl want on her pizza?"

Ryder stands abruptly, grabbing Xander by the throat. "Back off, Xander!" he snaps furiously, ignoring my wide eyes.

Xander just laughs. "Easy, man. I get it."

Ryder lets go, stretching his neck. His eyes darken as he looks at me somewhat apologetically. He reaches for my hand in the water. We went to the ball together, but we're suddenly on hand-holding terms?

"Pineapple? A sin or not a sin, that's the real question," Connor says.

"I like pineapple on my pizza," I say timidly.

Nate groans in despair, but Ryder flashes him a dark look. Nate lifts his hands in surrender. "You get whatever you want, Mira."

By the time Ethan joins us with a flustered Darcy, the guys unanimously decide that while we're waiting for pizzas, I should open presents. I reiterate my threat to reject anything that looks egregiously expensive.

Ethan goes first. "It's a gift from Mom, Dad, and me," he explains, as I open the box.

Inside is a collection of photos set up as a collage within a frame. In the first row are pictures of Mom and Aunt Erika as babies and then as teens. The second row contains pictures of Ethan throughout the years. And the final row has pictures of me. I give Ethan a huge hug.

"Oh, you were such a cute baby," Brittany coos. "Look at all that hair!"

"Ethan was a grumpy baby," Connor teases, pointing at Ethan's crabby face in a picture.

"Wow, I never realized your moms were identical twins," Celeste comments. "I can't tell them apart in the pictures." I look at my mother's young face and grow misty.

Nate hands me an envelope. "This is from me, Connor, and Xander. Your twenty-dollar limit was difficult to work around. But we used Groupon and got a membership discount."

Inside are four tickets to a play in February. "I thought you and the girls could go together," Connor explains with a glance at Celeste. "The play is called *Proof*. I think you'll like it."

"Thank you," I say shyly.

Brittany, Darcy, and Celeste hand me their box. Inside is a collection of items. There are four silver bracelets. Each of the girls put one on and hand me the fourth. I notice that the inside is etched with our names, the year, and the words *Best Roommates Ever*. There's a USB drive containing a variety of K-pop songs that I told Celeste that I like. And the final thing is a small, framed photo of all four of us dressed up for Halloween.

Celeste says softly, "I know you came to us full of sadness and loss. But you've also gained a few friends this year."

I blink back a few tears and we do a group hug while Ethan rolls his eyes.

Ryder goes last and I take his gift suspiciously. The box is rather large, but not very heavy. I'm not prepared to find a sketch of myself inside the box. In the drawing, I'm sitting in my school uniform, leaning over my laptop with a slight smile on my face. My hair is pulled into a messy bun, but a lock has escaped and drapes over my cheek. My fingers are drawn in fine detail. I have one hand on the keyboard and the other is tucked beneath my chin.

"Did you draw this?" I ask as everyone goes quiet. Ryder dips his head once, watching me intently.

Beneath the sketch is a plain leather keychain. I lift it out and glance at Ryder quizzically.

"I'm going to teach you how to drive this coming summer," Ryder announces. His lips quirk upward. "That's for the car keys when you finally get your driver's license."

I'm speechless. Darcy covers Ethan's eyes. "If you're going to kiss her, Ryder, you need to do that while Ethan's not looking."

Ethan makes a rumbly sound, but he doesn't fuss. With a smirk, Ryder leans over, planting a tiny kiss at the edge of my mouth before kissing me gently on the lips. The kiss is both sensuous and chaste. When he backs up, Celeste whispers in my ear, "I could be wrong, but I think Ryder Cabot likes you."

001100

RReagan: The DDoS attack used several hijacked computers. Do you recognize this address?
Arch4ngel101: Do you?
RReagan: I know it's your school. If I didn't know you better, I would have suspected you. But all of this is linked. There are no coincidences. RatGh0st is helping someone. This isn't his usual MO.
Arch4ngel101: You're going to ask me for a favor, aren't you?
RReagan: If I send you dates, are you able to send me a list of users who were online at the time?
Arch4ngel101: Are you asking me to illegally break into the school's system?
RReagan: National security overrides school security. Look, if this is what I think it is... I could use your help.
Arch4ngel101: Send me dates, I'll get you the info.

You'd think that after Christmas, my relationship with Ryder would escalate. It doesn't – at least, it doesn't escalate in a big way. It's quieter. We work on homework assignments together. Are we dating? Are we a couple? I haven't a clue because I never ask. We don't hold hands publicly, but we walk side-by-side. He stares at me a lot, and during lunch, he finds reasons for our hands to meet or our shoulders to touch. Maybe Ethan makes him nervous. It doesn't help that Ethan glowers at Ryder whenever possible.

One afternoon during gym, Ingrid corners me in the

locker room. "It won't last," she hisses at me as Judy and Victoria circle me. "Don't get comfortable. Ryder can have whatever toys he wants, but when it's all said and done, Ryder and I will be King and Queen next year and you'll be nothing." One thing I'll say about Ingrid is that she has lightning-fast reflexes, which she uses to pull at my hair. "Ryder will never jeopardize his chance to become king, and I could turn the tables on him just like that." She snaps her fingers. "Ethan had political clout and money. Ryder only has me."

I stare at her mutely, not trusting myself to speak. Besides, I don't understand what she's talking about.

"Remember what we told you, Mira," Judy intones in her resonant voice. "If you need a reminder of what you are and your place at RBA, we would be happy to re-educate you."

"You're just like your mother," Ingrid spits out. I stare at her in confusion.

Victoria mutters an epithet at me. "You're pathetic. Throwing yourself at guys left and right." She tosses her hair back over her shoulder.

The three girls move to leave, but Ingrid changes her mind at the last minute, delivering a stinging slap that makes my head snap. "I warned you to keep your greedy hands to yourself. Maybe I should show the world exactly what kind of mother you had."

My head rings as the mark on my cheek blooms, leaving a bright splotch. By the time Celeste gets suspicious enough to look for me, the three girls are long gone.

• • •

Darcy hands me an ice pack for my cheek. "Ingrid is out of control," she fumes, her eyes dark. "Erin's supposed to control the girls, but she does absolutely nothing!"

Celeste snorts. "Erin won't lift a finger to control Ingrid. You know that!"

"What did Ingrid mean about the political clout and

Ryder becoming king?" I ask. We're in our shared living room. Celeste is next to me while Darcy paces. Brittany sits across from me, cross-legged, with a worried frown.

Brittany, surprisingly, is the one that answers. "The hierarchy is based on wealth, connections, and influence over others. When Ethan and Darcy got together, Ethan was supported by several Royals. Erin's old money and rich, but she's not the type to make a major fuss. Ethan, on the other hand, is well-liked. He's always been popular, especially among students who are neither Court nor Royal. Ryder is a bonafide asshole. The girls want him, the boys hate him. In fact, the only time Ryder isn't an asshole is… when he's with you."

I consider Brittany's words. Ryder was a jerk when we first met, no doubt. But now? He runs hot and cold.

My cousin shows up a few minutes later, swiftly examining my cheek. I wave him off. "It's fine," I tell him. "I just bruise easily."

That doesn't placate him. Ethan pulls out his phone and calls Erin. The moment she picks up, he starts yelling. "You're a lousy Queen, Erin! Ingrid hit Mira! I told you to deal with this!" He's silent as she says something to him, but his mottled face tells me all I need to know. "You know that the school sides with me! Out of respect, I didn't replace you, but if you can't control Ingrid, your reign ends and Darcy's begins! She lays another finger on Mira and I won't hesitate!" Whatever Erin says doesn't make Ethan happy, but it's clear she's pleading with him. The rest of his words are terse. Once he's done, we stare at each other wordlessly for a long time.

•••

"Why didn't you tell me? Why didn't you call?" Ryder demands. He heard through the grapevine – actually, he heard Erin chewing Ingrid out – and tried to reach me several times. Eventually, he made his way to my dorm where Celeste ran interference until I finally relented.

"I didn't want you to get upset. Ethan's already mad."

Ryder paces in front of me, his black silky hair falling across his forehead as he keeps frowning down at me. "Mira, I'll keep you safe. Ingrid won't touch you again."

I wonder if he understands what he's saying. Unless he plans on being with me every minute, I'm vulnerable. And even then, there are more of Ingrid's posse to contend with.

"You used to be on Ingrid's side, remember?" I've never brought this up with him before. "She's mad because she thinks she has a claim to you – a claim you reinforced when we first met."

Ryder freezes, his eyes wide. "I know." His voice is a near whisper. He sits down on the bed next to me, reaching out with long fingers to tuck my hair back. "I know my behavior, in the beginning, was terrible. It's not who I am. It's not who I want to be."

Could Ryder Cabot be any more confusing? My consternation must show because he leans his forehead against mine for a moment. "I'm sorry, Mira." When I'm silent, he changes topics. "Have you finished the math assignment yet?" I shake my head. "Come over to my room and we can work on it together."

Remembering that I promised RReagan a file, I hesitate. "I'll meet you. I need to talk to Celeste first. I'll be over in twenty."

His smile is slow and sure. "Alright. Don't take too long or I'll get lonely." His kiss to my cheek is chaste and sweet.

I laugh when he winks before leaving. Once he's gone, I close my door and open my laptop.

When I ran through the list of logins on the dates RReagan asked for, I found that someone sent out a rather large, encrypted file under a mock account that isn't registered to an actual student at the school. I have a simple program that runs common passwords and was able to access the account. When I open the file in a protected environment – just in case it's a virus or something – I freeze.

I head to Discord and message NeORanger21. He responds

within a few minutes and I invite him to a voice chat.

"This is a surprise," he says as soon as we're connected.

"I'm sending you something. Someone sent this out a few weeks ago. Do you see what it says? Like, this isn't a hacking scheme."

There's silence and then, "Shit. Fuel-air explosives. These are various mix ratios – and their results."

"Duh. I know." I rub my hands nervously. "I'm sending this over to RReagan, but I'm freaked out. People who are interested in things like this…"

"It would be bad people, Angel. Are you in danger?" He sounds concerned.

"Um. No, I don't think so. I mean, no one knows that I do stuff like this. But the email it came from doesn't belong to anyone here. Someone entered as an admin and created this email account." I exhale sharply. "It's not difficult to do, and the person did a shoddy job hiding his or her steps." I think quietly. "You know, the person logged in using the room with the super-computers. You have to badge in."

"You might need to pull that information, too. What can I do to help?"

I blink in surprise. "I guess not much. Is RReagan having you work on something, too?"

"Yeah. He wanted me to look at the attacks – on the surface, the usual stuff. But the viruses and worms and bots… RatGh0st is a script kiddie. The cut-and-paste of various codes. I also found some wire transfers."

"Excuse me?"

He laughs. "Yeah, don't ask. So, you know how banks keep an eye on transactions that exceed a certain amount?"

"Yes."

"Well, they also keep an eye on mini-transactions that add up. Up until the first wave of attacks, the banks that were attacked were investigating some of these mini-transactions."

I frown. "You sound like you're more involved with this than helping with a few files."

"I am. Angel, if what you found is connected, this might be a really big deal. I need you to be careful. Don't leave any footprints. Do you want me to contact RReagan for you and get this over to him?"

I sigh. "Yes, please. I'll upload it now. And don't forget who you're talking to. I know how to be invisible."

After we end the chat, I start infiltrating the school system. Yes, this is on the shadier side of things, but I know the school's security system is integrated with their network. I'm so caught up in my work that by the time I'm set up, hours have passed, and I've totally forgotten my plan to meet up with Ryder. I fall asleep near my laptop.

001101

In the morning, I see a host of messages from Ryder. My phone was in silent mode. He likely thought I blew him off. The first few texts are teasing and curious, but the messages become irritable. I feel like a texted apology isn't enough. I will apologize profusely when I see him.

Celeste, Connor, and I spot Ryder on our way to chem class. He's clustered in a corner with Xander and Ingrid, but Ryder's stony expression tells me the conversation is unpleasant. His lips barely move when he speaks to her, and he hardly looks her way. Xander has his hands on his hips, lips pressed thin, as Ingrid gestures to them, her face sharp and intent. Ryder shakes his head once, hands clenched, at something Ingrid says to him, while Xander runs his hand down his face in exasperation. Then something Ingrid says causes Ryder to glare at her. Every line of his body tenses with anger and irritation. He moves as if to push her but stops when Xander barks a warning. Ryder stiffens, turning to look at me. I'm taken aback by the hostility rolling off him in waves. He snaps a response to Ingrid before walking towards me, Xander on his heels. Ingrid doesn't follow.

"Where were you last night?" Ryder demands irritably. "I texted and called you."

Oops. Right. I mean to apologize for that. "Sorry, I fell asleep," I tell him. Wow. That might go down in history as one of the worst apologies ever.

"I waited for you." There's a bitter tone to his voice. He sounds hurt and angry at the same time.

"Want to walk with us to class?" I ask, flinching a little under his scrutiny.

"No, I don't." Without a goodbye, Ryder storms off. Xander hesitates before following his friend.

I shouldn't be hurt. I'm guilty of not being a good – girlfriend? Friend? What am I?

"What bit his ass this morning?" Celeste grumbles to Connor.

"That's just Ryder. He was born a prick. He'll die a prick," his cousin says without much rancor. "What are your plans for spring break?"

Celeste makes a little moue with her lips. "Mom's dragging me to Europe. France really."

"I'll be heading to England. Mother and Father have asked me to attend some event." Connor's shoulders slump a bit. He's been in the States so much that his accent is an odd mix of British English and East Coast twang. "If you get bored in France, let me know."

I suppose telling them that I intend to be doing a hackathon with NeORanger21 is not a good idea, although the chances that they're into fuel-air explosives aren't good. Still, I'm not comfortable talking about my online skills.

Ethan and Darcy are heading to Florida, and then, as the King of the Royals, Ethan is hosting a major party at the school's lake house. I've been invited to Florida, but I seriously doubt they want me to tag along as a third wheel.

"We should do a joint trip together next year," Celeste suggests as we slip into class. "Maybe I won't even be a Court member with Ingrid running things."

Connor smiles at her. "Would that be such a bad thing? We could escape Ingrid's annoying presence together."

Their friendly banter keeps my mind off Ryder. We tease each other until class begins.

• • •

"I'll be glad when we don't have gym anymore," Celeste tells me.

We tense when Ingrid saunters by with Victoria. "Hello, Orphan Annie," Ingrid says cheerfully. "Did you know my father knew your mother?" Before I can respond, she continues, "He told me wild tales about her. Let's just say your mom got around."

Celeste comes to my defense. "You have no idea what you're talking about!" she snaps.

Ingrid pretends to examine her nails. "Maybe. Or maybe the apple doesn't fall far from the tree. Gwen the Wench. That was her nickname. She tried to ensnare a few rich men. You just have to wonder what loser fucked her to create you."

Ingrid's crudeness is appalling. "You're pathetic," I tell her, but Ingrid just laughs with Victoria. It's like they know something I don't.

"Well, maybe now that Ryder knows, he'll have second thoughts about getting involved with a gold digger's daughter." Ingrid flips her silky hair. "Have a nice day."

Celeste huffs in disbelief. "Can you believe that girl? There is not one nice bone in her body."

I agree with her, but the encounter leaves me troubled. Why bring up Mom now? I remember Aunt Erika's comment about Ernest Whitman, Ingrid's father. Is he the one giving Ingrid information? Whatever is being said, it can't be true. Mom was a decent, good person. She explained how hormones shouldn't blur the lines when it comes to respect and decency.

Remember, Mira. Love yourself as much as I love you. If the guy you fall for isn't Mr. Right, then love yourself enough to leave. Don't get trapped. The right man makes all the difference. You'll know because he'll become a better person because of you. You can't fix someone who's broken. The right man will fix himself because he wants to.

The memory of her voice is fresh. It envelops me and brings tears. The memory of her is still brutal. Celeste thinks I'm hurt about Ingrid's words. I'm not. But I could really use my mother's arms right now.

001110

Ethan pulls me aside for heart-to-heart cousin talk. (To be honest, I don't know if that's even a thing, but it's the only description I could come up with.)

Sitting on the edge of my bed, my handsome cousin looks troubled. "Mira, I know you and Ryder are sort of a thing."

That's an understatement. Ryder can't seem to decide how serious we are. Rather than complicate the matter, I nod slowly.

"Do you like him?" Ethan asks, eyes lowered.

If I were feeling snappy, I'd point out that the answer is an obvious yes. "I think so," I say instead. Of all the conversations I want to have with Ethan, this is not high on my list. "I've never been in a relationship with a guy before."

"Darcy says I can't protect you from everything." Sighing, Ethan pats me awkwardly on the back. "I'm going to try and ease up on being overly protective. This is all I ask. When we're on campus, I don't want you in Ryder's room after nine. And he doesn't need to walk you back to your room or anything. That just leads to him wanting to linger. This is new to you, so don't rush into the relationship."

"Um, that's easing up? I'm seventeen, Ethan, not ten."

Ethan evades my glare. "I know, I know. Just for the time being, can you do that? Can you not rush into full-blown boyfriend-girlfriend mode with Ryder?"

Ethan's concern is touching and weird. To be honest, how

am I supposed to react? Then again, Ryder and I are moving at glacial speed. Agreeing to Ethan's requests is harmless. Maybe it will make him less anxious. "Okay. I mean, I will take it slow. When we're at school, I will be in my room, safe and sound, by nine whenever possible. Safe and sound and alone," I amend.

Reassured, Ethan relaxes. "I'll try and explain my worries to you later. Just, for now, believe me when I say that I'm trying to protect you the best I can."

• • •

After my odd conversation with Ethan, I take the time to go through some of my mother's journals back at the house. It's something I've been doing gradually. Not unexpectedly, there is the usual gossip.

Today Cassidy told everyone that I have a crush on P. It's not true. I can't stand him. I'm just irritated because he pulls my pigtails all the time. Erika acts like she's ten years older rather than ten minutes older. Her hair is not in braids because she's too mature.

I notice that Mom only uses the names of family and friends. All guys are referred to with a single letter.

Erika has met the man she's going to marry. She told me this today. She's sixteen. R is very nice and he's good looking to boot. But love at 16? Can you fall in love so quickly and easily? I'm sure it is just a phase. I find myself ambivalent at 16. All the things Erika loves — the parties, the dresses, the shoes — mean little to me. I am a doll for my parents' pleasure. They parade us around: the pretty Anderson twins. We're well-to-do. Not grossly wealthy like some of our neighbors. That's why we're dressed up like pretty offerings to rich boys around town.

Am I wrong to dislike these things? I always go like I'm supposed to. Erika would be sad if I didn't. I think she knows that my mind and heart are not in it. Dad would very much like it if I were willing to date E. I don't like him. There is something about his hands that bothers me. When we were little, I remember he found an injured bird. He killed it just to make me cry. E likes me a little too much. When we sat down at dinner the other night, he put his hand on my leg under the table! I thought I would be sick.

E? Ernest Whitman? I want to ask Aunt Erika, but I'm not sure if I want to know yet.

I bounce over when someone knocks at my door. I'm guessing it's Ethan freshly returned from Darcy's swim meet. I'm a terrible friend. I know I should be there for Darcy and Connor, but Arthur Huxley is also on the swim team. That means Ingrid is likely to be present. So, I told Darcy the partial truth: I wanted to read my mom's journals. I also spent the morning doing a pen test with NeORanger21.

When I open the door, I gape like an idiot. Ryder Cabot stands in my doorway, and he doesn't look particularly happy. It's been weeks since we've talked even though we see each other during mealtimes and classes. The avoidance hasn't just been on his side either – it's also been on mine. I want to tell him about my alter ego as a hacker. If we're to progress, I need to share that part of myself with him.

"Hi," I say somewhat awkwardly. Should I invite him into my bedroom? Do I need Ethan's permission? Is it sleazy to let a boy walk into my room?

Apparently, sleazy doesn't bother Ryder because he saunters right in, our shoulders brushing as he walks past me. He sucks in his breath before continuing.

He paces, running his hand through his hair so that it's gently tousled. He's all in gray today: gray wool coat, gray slacks, a pale gray shirt that stretches over his chest. A literal walking teen model. "We should take a break," he states suddenly, his blue eyes averted.

Okay, does this mean we were together and he wants a break? I mean, we hung out. We kissed. We went to a dance. But we never went out on dates. Is this normal? My first relationship ends before it begins with me getting dumped. Pain? Disappointment? I'm not sure. "Alright." My voice is curiously faint. "I guess we never really made anything official."

Ryder latches on that. "Right. Exactly. You seem occupied with school."

I rub my temple with my right hand. "I've been busy." It's strange. I know I'm speaking. I know Ryder is speaking, but everything sounds far away.

Ryder steps towards me, reconsiders, then turns away. "Yeah, I've noticed." The way he speaks cuts a little. I know I'm to blame. "Mira, this is just—a temporary break."

Now I'm utterly confused again as I stare at his back. He looks at me over his shoulder and whatever he sees causes him to face me. I can't decipher the range of emotions on his face. Abruptly, he hugs me. "This doesn't mean we're over." Before I can reply, he kisses me with an odd, almost desperate, intensity. He stares at me, eyes burning, before he releases me, leaving me gasping for breath.

And just like that, he storms out of my room.

⊙⊙1111

In order to stave off curious relatives and friends, I loop Kitty, my "friend" from home, in. She agrees to be my cover for spring break. I manage to convince Aunt Erika that Kitty's mom is getting me a free ride on an airline she works for. As such, I pack my bags, buy my ticket with my money (squeal!), and arrive in Washington ready to hack my way to first place. It's exciting when you have your own money – the sleepless nights were worth every bitcoin in my electronic wallet – and can do your own thing.

When I converge at the arena, I'm vibrating with energy. My phone is off. Everything on my laptop is disabled. You'd be stupid to go into this with anything hackable. After I check in, I find a specific coffee shop and order an iced mocha, wearing a cap with the movie "The Matrix" emblazoned on it so Ne0Ranger21 can find me.

"You know, my favorite movie is *The Matrix*," a guy to my right says to me.

I try to hide my smile. "Who's your favorite character?"

"Neo, of course."

I turn my head. He's taller than I expected – not as tall as Ryder but close. His shoulder-length blond hair falls loose. He's lithe but not overly thin. His green eyes twinkle at me. "Do I pass inspection?"

I don't bother to hide my smile this time. "Sort of." I stick my hand out. "Arch4ngel101 at your service. But you can call me Mira."

"NeORanger21." He flashes a teasing smile. "You can call me Liam."

I've known this person online for a while, but this is the first time we've exchanged real names. It's both strange and refreshing.

"You're taller than I thought you'd be," I say.

"You're prettier than I thought you'd be," he responds. "Especially since I expected Mr. No Neck Gunther."

I burst into laughter. "Want to grab some food?"

"There's a place around the corner that's good."

I squint at him. "You live around here, don't you?"

"Yes, ma'am. And don't worry, we meet and work in open areas. I won't be following you to your hotel room either." He cocks his head at me. "I am going to ask how old you are, though."

I shrug. "Seventeen."

"I'll be nineteen this summer. So, I'm like super experienced and a lot more mature than you," he says with a wink, chuckling when I roll my eyes.

Over lunch, we talk a bit about RReagan. Since I've started tracking the account, the mysterious user hasn't logged back in at school. In fact, it's been unusually quiet. Liam's seeing the same thing in the cyberworld. We talk in hushed tones like nervous Nellies.

"You think RatGh0st is tied up with what I found, don't you?" I ask. "I mean, that's why we're both involved. It's why we were both brought in."

Liam thinks carefully, chewing on a chip. "Don't get mad," he begins, wincing when I narrow my eyes at him, "but I have security clearance."

"What?"

"NSA. FBI. That kind."

Well, that makes sense. "You work for the government? You work with RReagan?" I whisper.

"Sort of. More like a consultant right now." He presses

a finger to his lips. "And maybe someday we'll be coworkers, Angel." He notes me picking at my sandwich. "Are you mad at me?"

I shake my head. "No. But I think I stepped into something a teenager really shouldn't be involved in."

Liam grimaces as he pulls his hair back into a loose ponytail at the nape. He's got that surfer boy appeal. "Honestly, I didn't think you were this young. We certainly didn't expect it to evolve into something bigger."

"Geez, it's not like you're forty. We're barely a year or two apart in age. And you look like you could be my age. I can handle the technicalities. I just don't want to think about the ramifications."

"That's because you're still a kid."

My eyes widen incredulously. Is he trying to pick a fight? "You can't drink alcohol."

His eyes crinkle in mirth. "I surrender. The field is yours." Taking a long drink of his soda, he changes the subject with a sly smile. "So… this boyfriend or ex-boyfriend of yours still giving you problems?"

Sigh. Liam knows the gist of everything through our online chats. "Sort of. It's complicated. I mean, I'm seventeen. I'm too young to have romantic notions, right?"

My partner-in-cyber shakes the ice in his cup. "It depends. There's a lot of shows out there where it sounds like teens find their epic lovemate early. *Buffy the Vampire Slayer. The Vampire Diaries.*" He shrugs. "I heard something like this in *The Vampire Diaries* – no laughing! I have two older sisters and they loved that show. But I think it's true for you. You want a love that consumes you. A guy who will endure anything to be with you, a guy who will give up everything for a chance with you. When you find the guy who does that for you, you'll know. And it won't matter if you're seventeen or seventy."

"That's why I like being behind the scenes. There's a purity, an elegance to programming. You see the pieces and move them. No emotions to deal with. Just satisfaction."

He leans forward on the table. "Angel, you're out for blood, aren't you?"

I know he's talking about the competition. "Yes, I am. I'm here to win."

· · ·

Liam and I make a powerful team. While guzzling Red Bull – which is a terrible habit, by the way – and eating pizza, we tackle the hackathon. Most teams consist of more than two people, but the synergy between me and Liam more than compensate for our lack of manpower.

There are two challenge events. The first is to develop a filtering program to wipe negative associations about you in your social media feed. I nickname it the "happy status" filter. The second challenge is to find a solution to negative reviews on products and services.

The first challenge is easy. Liam and I use existing code to flag potentially negative associations. Think of it as a virus, except instead of infecting a computer, it infects certain words. The second one is more difficult. We decide to create a program that alerts a company when certain negative words are used during the review process. A chat box opens that connects the reviewer to a representative, thereby bypassing the negative review before it happens. Liam works on the user interface while I work on the main body. Programming is a lot like putting a puzzle together – at least to me. I start with the edges – the framework, you might say – and then fill in the middle. It's hard to explain how the code comes to me. It just appears.

Hackathons are won through sheer determination, fast programming, and a viable solution. We have all three and snag the top prize. It's fun, exhilarating, and, five days later, I'm still on a high.

Here's the thing, though. I need to come clean with Aunt Erika and Uncle Robert soon. I mean, my name is on a check, the event was public, and Uncle Robert works for an Internet security company. It's possible that being CEO means he only gets tidbits of what happens at hackathons, and there are a lot of them around the world. I'll have to wait and see for now. Right now, I'll keep Arch4ngel101 under wraps.

010000

"I'm so glad you decided to come," Darcy says to me at the lake house. She's dressed in a hot pink strappy mini dress that Ethan can barely take his eyes off. "I know Ingrid is a PITA, but it means a lot to Ethan that you're at this party since he's hosting."

My cousin is at the bar grabbing drinks for us: wine for Darcy, club soda for me, and a rum thingy for himself.

"What's going on with you and Ryder?" she tries to ask me nonchalantly.

"We're on a break." It sounds weird even to my ears. "I don't know. Maybe I'm not ready for a relationship."

Ethan hands us our drinks. Brittany won't be here for two reasons: Royals and Court only, and she's still overseas. I'm not officially Court, but Ethan is my cousin so I'm pseudo-Court. I know it rankles Ethan that he can't invite who he wants. He's a king with limited powers. Across the room, Erin salutes him – or we think she does. We return fake smiles her way.

That's when Ryder shows up with Ingrid. There's a twinge of resentment when I spy them. Are they here together? No one expects me to come to parties, so maybe Ryder thought it was safe to come with Ingrid. Xander, Connor, and Nate enter right after them, but it's Xander who realizes I'm here first. He looks alarmed next to Connor.

Ingrid grabs Ryder's arm and says something at the same time as his eyes meet mine. If they are together, it shouldn't surprise me. Ethan may have broken tradition, but Ryder isn't Ethan.

"Oh, boy," Celeste says, arriving at my elbow.

Ryder frees himself from Ingrid's grasp, but he doesn't move away. He's dressed far more casually than normal – button-down shirt with slacks – and I hate that he looks so good in clothes. It's just not fair.

Connor joins us while his cousin continues to stand and stare. "Hey, Celeste," he says, and I note the way he rests a hand on her back in a familiar way. I raise a brow at Connor.

"Is there something I should know about you two?" I tease gently.

Celeste blushes. "Maybe." Her brown eyes are filled with affection.

Connor returns Celeste's look. "Sorry my cousin is being a dick," Connor says. "I have no idea what's wrong with him. Why he wants to take a break is beyond me."

Ingrid, wearing a near see-through dress, walks over to Ethan on wobbly heels. I'm tempted to push her. Her sly eyes flicker over me before she tells Ethan, "When I'm ruling the school, we'll have to fix all the things you broke during your reign."

"Ingrid, go fuck yourself," Darcy says sweetly.

Ethan pushes Ingrid's shoulder with a finger, eliciting a shrieky gasp. "Ingrid. You aren't Queen yet. Get out of my face."

Ingrid's face mottles with rage, turning downright unpleasant. "You've sullied the Royals with your lowlife girlfriend! Erin didn't have the guts to tell you off, but I do! We'll be glad when you're gone."

Darcy puts her drink down and slams her hands into Ingrid's chest. "What's the code again? Girls deal with girls, right?" In one smooth move, she grabs her wine and throws her drink into Ingrid's face. "You're nothing but a needy bitch!"

There's a satisfying silence as the wine stains Ingrid's dress and makes it even more transparent.

"Ingrid!" Erin's voice shatters the silence. "That's

enough." Her heels tap loudly on the floor. "You need to leave. Now." Erin is furious, her words are full of warning. The two girls stare at each other. Then Ingrid bursts into tears, fleeing the room. Erin's face turns stony as she addresses Darcy. "You may be Ethan's girlfriend, but I'm the Royal Queen here, not you. Remember that."

Ethan snaps, "Watch yourself, Erin!"

The two key Royals glare at each other, but Erin breaks eye contact first, and the Court members whisper among themselves as Erin walks back to Arthur Huxley. The music starts up, and Celeste and Connor dance on the floor together. I head to the bar to get another club soda.

"You look nice."

I don't have to turn. "Did you have a nice spring break, Ryder?" I'm all politeness.

"Not really. What about you?"

With my fresh club soda, I face him, lifting my chin. "I did have a good break."

A flash of pain before the walls go up again. "I'm glad. If you'll excuse me."

I spend most of the party with Celeste or with Darcy, but eventually, all the club soda gets to my bladder. But when I leave the toilet, I'm cornered by Daniel.

As a Court member, Daniel's loyalties lie with Ingrid. He lurks and does whatever Erin and Ingrid ask of him. Frankly, he seems shady. He's taller than me but not by much. His slightly hooked nose gives him a haughty appearance.

"Mira. Been wanting to talk to you," he says, glancing around to be sure we don't have an audience. We're down a hallway away from the main room.

"Um, okay." Talking is harmless.

"Be careful with Ryder Cabot," he blurts, leaning towards me. "You probably don't know this, but the old money guys here run bets. The guys are laughing about you behind your back. You're part of the game."

"I have no idea what you're talking about." I start to

leave, but he grabs both arms and pins me to the wall.

"Listen, Ryder has a bet that he can ruin you to get back at Ethan," Daniel says urgently, his eyes running up and down my body. "Everything's a game to him."

I struggle to free myself. "Let go of me!"

"I'll help you if you want. You only have to ask." Daniel's eyes are bright with lust as he pushes himself against me. "If you help me win the bet, it'll ruin Ryder."

Trying to buy time, I ask, "How am I supposed to help you win a bet?"

"I think you know, babe. All I need is to take the top prize."

What is he talking about? I try to push him away, but it makes him more determined to hold me. His slimy lips come closer. Gross! Is he going to kiss me? Just as I'm about to scream, Daniel's mouth opens in pain as he's yanked away. Ryder, his face cold with anger, hauls Daniel back by his hair and flings him against a wall. Xander helpfully holds Daniel upright for his friend.

"Do not touch her!" Ryder snarls as his fist slams into Daniel's face. When Xander lets go of Daniel, Ryder grabs the boy by the shirt and hits him again.

Daniel slumps, blood streaming from his nose as he struggles to stand. When he manages to hold himself upright, Xander punches him in the stomach. "He didn't tell you to stand. Stay down if you want to live," Xander sneers.

Ryder turns to me, his eyes wild as he scans me head to toe. He runs his hands gently over my face and my arms. "Are you okay? Did he hurt you?" His words are at odds with the anger rolling off his body.

"I think you broke my nose," Daniel whines.

Xander grabs Daniel by the collar. "I'll throw the trash out," he says to us, dragging Daniel away.

"I'm okay, Ryder." I bite my lip. "You hit him rather hard." I glance at the hand that's beginning to swell.

Ryder brushes my hair back from my face, cradling my

cheek briefly. "He touched you," he bites out, rage in his eyes. "I'll kill him if he touches you again." Despite his harsh words, he closes his eyes and presses his forehead to mine, steadying himself. "No one touches you."

I try to move away, but Ryder refuses to let me budge. "Ryder, I'm fine. I should head back."

"No, wait. Don't go, Mira. Not yet." Very slowly, he wraps his arms around me. "I need to hold you for a minute." He tucks my head under his chin like I'm precious.

"You're giving me emotional whiplash, Ryder," I whisper. I hate that Daniel's words linger in my mind, poisoning this moment. A bet? Get back at Ethan?

Ryder holds me tighter and makes a muffled sound. "There's so much I want to say right now, but I don't know where to begin. I should leave you alone. I should let you go. But I can't do it."

I press my ear to his chest, hearing his thundering heartbeat. Beneath my fingers, his body burns at my touch. "Ryder, what is it you want?"

"You. I want you." When I squirm in his arms, he whispers, "Don't. Don't push me away. I need you, Mira. I know I keep messing up, but I don't want to stay away anymore. Be with me."

This is the part where I should give myself a pep talk about being strong. But I don't. "You want to – date? Be together?"

"Yes. Yes to all of it."

"What about Ingrid? I mean, you came here with her and…" Ugh, I sound like a jealous twit.

"Ingrid can go to hell. I didn't come with her. I came with Connor." He cradles my face with his hands. "Mira, please, give me a second chance."

I bite my lips, trying to blink back tears. Ryder kisses the corners of my eyes, his murmured apologies fanning my skin.

"I'm sorry. I'm such a screwup." He caresses my cheek with a hand, his breath hitching faintly. "I want to kiss you."

I consider his words for a bit, and then my cheeks grow

hot. "What's stopping you?"

Startled, he looks at me with wonder before grinning. When he kisses me, I decide I'm glad I came to the party after all.

• • •

"Is it just me or did you and Ryder go from zero to sixty last night?" Celeste asks with a coy smile.

I throw popcorn at her as she laughs at my embarrassed expression. "Sort of. He's mercurial. Take a break. Don't take a break. Make up your mind." I roll my eyes with exasperation.

"But you like him?" Celeste presses me with a raised brow.

I sigh. "I do. A lot. It's weird. I blame hormones, but I can't think clearly when he's with me. He was an ass to me and then he suddenly stopped."

Celeste hums. "Everyone could tell he was jealous when he saw you in Connor's jersey." She reaches out to grab my hand. "You didn't have to push Connor away, you know. He liked you."

"He liked the thought of me because I was new," I correct her, and for some reason, I know this with confidence. I was an unknown, a mystery.

She considers my words. "You did that for me, didn't you?"

"Yes and no. Connor landed in the friend bucket pretty much after we met. It isn't right to lead someone on if you have no romantic intentions." I pause to look her straight in the eye. "I think he just needed time to see what was in front of him."

The flush deepens her beautiful skin. "I won't lie that I'm a bit giddy with how things are going with Connor. But Ryder... The way he looks at you, Mira... He looks at you like you're his world." She chews on some popcorn thoughtfully. "Maybe he wanted a break because he felt vulnerable?"

"I don't know. I just hope Ryder is careful. I'm not sure I could handle a broken heart right now."

Celeste squeezes my hand. "You're stronger than you

think, Mira. A lot stronger."

010001

Ryder rests his head in my lap, morosely reading Emily Brontë's *Wuthering Heights* while the weather outside rages. He's clearly not enjoying the book, but we need to finish it since we're working on the project together.

"Just because it's a classic doesn't mean you have to love the book," I say, brushing his black hair back. He captures my hand briefly to kiss it, and I want to giggle like an idiot.

Ryder's gestures of affection make me tingle and feel warm. He doesn't hide our relationship anymore. Much to Ethan's chagrin, Ryder holds my hand in public and kisses me whenever possible. This new and improved Ryder is sweet, intense, and thoughtful. Ingrid constantly looks like she's eating lemons.

"I don't like the characters in the book," he corrects me. "Heathcliff is a lousy antihero. He doesn't even do the right thing. He isn't a Byronic hero either. He's capable of great affection only in the beginning. All he does is become consumed with bitterness and rage, hurting everyone along the way. He's a total monster to his wife."

I tilt my head at him. "I feel sorry for him. Think of all the pain he might have avoided had he bothered to talk to the girl he loved rather than storming off in a hissy fit."

Veiled blue eyes hide Ryder's thoughts. "Do you put the blame solely on Heathcliff, then?"

"No. Catherine herself is partially to blame. He had pride

and she had her vanity. She shouldn't have thrown away a chance at true love for money and security." I bite my lip, thinking about my words.

Ryder sits up suddenly and the look he gives me is earnest, almost eager. "Do you believe that?"

"Money can't buy love." I frown, recalling a time when Ryder thought money could buy anything. "Or it shouldn't." I check the time on my phone. "Ugh. I better return to my room before Ethan gets upset with me." I can hear the hard patter of freezing rain as it alternates between sleet, hail, and whatever else Mother Nature is whipping in her frenzy. "Will we lose power?"

Ryder shakes his head. "We've got backup generators," he says before lowering his voice with a smile. "Let me walk you back to your room."

"I'll be fine, and you know how Ethan gets if he hears I've returned to my room late with you in tow."

Ryder huffs, but after a short debate, Ryder gives in. "I'd rather you invite me back to your room since I don't care about keeping Ethan happy. But since you want to keep him happy, I'll just suck it up. Text me, though, so I know you're still thinking about me," he murmurs, snaking an arm around my middle. For a few minutes, we kiss, and I can feel his body yearning for *more*, but he never presses the issue. Okay, I yearn for more too. I know he's *done things* – I don't even want to think about that too much – but he lets me control the pace. I know I'm nowhere near ready to have sex. Call me old-fashioned, but sex is a big deal. It shouldn't be done casually.

He groans a little when I pull away, but then he gives me a rueful smile before gently pressing his heated forehead against mine.

I take one of the tunnels towards my dorm – convenient that the school had these built – while checking my phone for messages. Just as I'm about to reach the elevators, I bump into Ingrid, my phone falling from my hands and landing on the floor with a sharp crack. Crap.

Ingrid's pale eyes gleam as she smiles at me with her red lips. "Hello, *Mira.*"

A wad of cloth is shoved into my mouth before my head is rudely covered with a pillowcase. I don't get a chance to scream. Someone grabs me from behind, and I get a whiff of cologne. Whoever it is, he's stronger and taller than me. I've watched a lot of self-defense videos, but I can't remember a single move or manage a cohesive thought as I panic and thrash uselessly.

I don't have a sense of how many people are helping Ingrid as I'm pushed, hands on my legs and ankles, and hauled. I hear the elevator open and close, and then a feeling of going up. I try to scream past the gag in my mouth.

I continue to struggle, twisting and jerking my body around. I don't want to make it easy for them. My terror fuels me, but I can't focus it to free myself. I'm being dragged somewhere; the main person holding me drops me slightly and I feel the sharp edge of a step dig into my side. I scream futilely in pain as I'm yanked up steps.

We stop, and I hear the clanking of something metallic. What sounds like a knob turning is drowned out by a burst of freezing air and icy water. I'm pushed, not carried, and drenched instantly as the hands holding me let go. I yank the hood off my head in time to see a door slam shut and to realize I'm outside in the storm, sleet pelting my body hard.

Pulling the rag out of my mouth, it takes me longer than I'd like to see that I'm on the roof. I run to the door, my fingers already numb, and find the door locked. I pummel the door with my hands, screaming. I run to the ledge. I'm six stories up, and there isn't anyone walking around outside. Still, I scream for someone to help me. The wind rips away my words.

My clothes, now heavy with rain, saps my body's heat. The wind pushes the cold in further. I run back to the door, hitting it repeatedly, sobbing. I'm not stupid. I could die from hypothermia.

When Mom died, there was a moment I wanted to die

too. I wanted to be left alone. I wanted the world to disappear. With sudden clarity, I now know I don't want to die – not like this. I should be allowed to finish my school year. I want to go to see what I can do in the real world.

I hop, shout, and pound at the door, trying to stay warm with little success. Eventually, I tire. My movements slow. I don't feel as cold anymore, just tired. Sleepy. I remember drinking hot cocoa while watching movies with Mom.

The sun will be up soon. I imagine the sun's warmth and it feels real. I'll tell Ryder how good the sun feels when I wake up.

• • •

I'm dreaming. I smell cinnamon, sunshine, strawberries. I walk through a field of daisies, startling butterflies that fly into the bright sunlight. Too bright. I shield my eyes. Someone's calling my name.

The field is too pretty to leave. But someone calls my name again. Insistently. Pulling. Going towards the person hurts. My skin is on fire. I don't want that.

"Stay with me, Mira! Mira, look at me! Mira!"

I turn away.

010010

My mind flits in and out of awareness. Voices come and go.

"Start the IV. Get the machine hooked up now!"

Darkness. Quiet. Cold. Sharp pain. Sleep.

I move. There's a mask on my face. The air I breathe is warm against my nose and lips. My fingers twitch. It takes more energy to move my hand.

"Shh. Be still. I'll get the nurse."

The voice is soft and sweet. It sounds like Mom. I start crying. I want to tell her to stay and not go away. Hot tears leak from my eyes.

Gentle, warm hands grab me.

"Mira? Mira? Can you open your eyes for me?"

The mask is removed, and the gasp of air into my lungs is sharp and painful. It takes so much energy to open my eyes, but finally, I manage it.

The world is a bleary, bright mess that moves discordantly. "What?"

A man with owlish eyes peers at me. A doctor. "Can you tell me your name?"

Didn't someone just say it? "Mira. Bell." It sounds like I said *wonderful.*

"That's right. You're in a hospital. You're being treated for moderate hypothermia. Your guardians are here and you're safe." He speaks slowly, enunciating every syllable. The doctor looks over his shoulder.

At first, I almost scream *Mom.* But then I see the lines of the face – the brighter features, the smoother skin. Aunt Erika.

"Mira, God, we've been so worried and scared," my aunt cries, trying to hug me.

Uncle Robert blinks back tears, trying to stay out of the way of the nurse. "We've been waiting for you to wake up, kiddo."

"Careful," the nurse cautions. "Her body is still recovering." She smiles gently at me as the doctor leaves

I realize I'm attached to an IV and enveloped in a balloon-like contraption circulating warm air. I'm puffy. I blink. The nurse fiddles with a few monitors. "I'll give you some time to talk to your family."

Ethan comes into view, his face drawn and tight. My brows knit in confusion as his eyes tell me more than words would.

"Do you remember what happened?" he asks.

"How did you find me?" I return with a question of my own in a weak voice. Aunt Erika strokes my head.

"We couldn't find you at first." Ethan's jaw clenches. "Celeste found your phone in the lobby with the screen badly cracked. Ryder got worried when you didn't text him back."

"That's when Ingrid grabbed me," I say.

Aunt Erika starts, her eyes darting to Ethan. "Ingrid?"

"We thought she was involved," Ethan says, "but she was at a small party with her crew. There's a video."

Cold runs up my spine. "That's not possible. Ethan, I saw her."

Aunt Erika very kindly tells me, "The school reviewed videos around the time you must have left Ryder's room. It shows you walking alone, throwing your phone, and then taking the elevator up. It was lucky that Ethan searched for you."

My throat hurts as Uncle Robert continues, "Honey, depression is common in teens. We got your suicide note…"

"I didn't write a suicide note." Okay, I've woken in an alternate reality. I know I saw Ingrid. The videos make no sense. What the hell is going on?

Ethan unlocks his phone, showing me a picture of a wet, printed note: I MISS MOM SO MUCH. I CAN'T TAKE THE ROYALS AND THEIR CODE. ONCE ETHAN IS GONE, MY LIFE WILL BE OVER. PLEASE TELL ETHAN I'M SORRY. LOVE, MIRA.

So, first, that is the worst note ever. I would never write a note like that. It doesn't even sound like me. Second, anyone could have written it! It's typed, for God's sake.

"I talked to the school," Aunt Erika says. "They're being wonderful. You have straights As across the board. They've agreed to let you rest at home, take your finals from home. You'll be excused from homework until then. The condition is you have to agree to counseling."

Finals. Which is in one week. Counseling. This is insane.

"I was dumped on the roof." I look at my arms, pushing down the puffy contraption, and pull my hospital gown a bit to show my upper arms which are bruised. "Look! This is where I was grabbed!"

Aunt Erika doesn't believe me. It's obvious with the way she's nodding. Uncle Robert says, "I'll get the nurse."

I start crying. "I swear. I didn't try to kill myself! You have to believe me!"

"Darcy, Brittany, and Celeste were here, but I sent them home. Mom and Dad just wanted family around you." Ethan hesitates. "Ryder refused to leave. He's outside, but we told him to stay away. Has he said anything to you? Done anything to you?"

I'm still weeping. "No. No. We were hanging out."

"I'm going to let him come in for a bit until the nurse gets back," Aunt Erika decides, giving Ethan a warning look. She heads out with Uncle Robert. About a minute later, Ryder enters, pale, livid, shaken.

"Mira." He reaches for my hand. "Shit, I should have walked you back. Why didn't you let me walk you back?" He kisses the back of it.

"You know why," Ethan practically growls.

"I didn't try to kill myself," I try to say calmly, but I'm still crying. "Ingrid grabbed me with her friends."

Ryder's eyes darken. "Who was there?"

"I d-don't know," I stammer, realizing how bad that sounds, "because they covered my head with a pillowcase or something. I only saw Ingrid."

Ryder is silent. "Ingrid was with friends. There's video – school video and they posted a picture on social media. The videos show you walking alone."

"That isn't possible!" I want to see these videos. "I need to see the videos."

"The doctor said that you withdrawing, not attending parties or being social… It makes sense." Ethan lowers his eyes.

What the hell?! I turn to Ryder, and there is doubt in his eyes. My heart squeezes. Why would I lie?

"Get out," I say in a flat voice. Ryder starts. "Ryder, get out. You don't believe me. Neither of you believe me. That means you think I'm lying."

They continue to stare at me in disbelief. "Mira, let me—" Ryder tries to grab my hand again and I swat him away.

"Get out!" I start screaming hoarsely at the top of my lungs, ripping off the heated circulator. "Why won't you believe me, you asshole?! Get out! You did this with Ingrid, didn't you?"

Nurses come in to grab me as I shout and scream at Ryder and Ethan. My eyes burn with rage and betrayal as I start ripping the IV out of my arm, reveling in the sharp pain telling me I'm real. Then I feel a prick in my arm. Things get fuzzy. A strange calm overwhelms me. And then there is nothing but a dreamless sleep.

010011

I agree to counseling. It's a farce, to be honest, but it means not being forced into long-term treatment. I get my things delivered from school and hole up in my room. I'm watched and checked all the time, going to a half-day outpatient program at a nearby clinic before I'm smothered by attention by Aunt Erika.

I haven't seen Darcy, Celeste, or Brittany, although they send me warm messages. My aunt and uncle are wary of letting me see my friends since I blew up at Ethan and Ryder. Ryder doesn't contact me, and it stings. It stings that he doesn't believe me. I remain silent, too.

At home, I hack into the school system and find the video files in question. In the first clip, you don't see my face, just the back of my head in my school uniform. I throw the phone down on the ground. In the second clip, I'm still alone. This time, you can see my face as I walk to the elevator and get in. That's all there is. I'm alone in both clips.

I chew my lower lip, watching the second video again. And then I pause, rewind, and watch again. In the first clip, my phone lands close to the elevator. In the second clip, I don't see anything on the floor. Okay, you don't see my face in the first video. It could be someone with long hair – maybe even a wig – dressed in a school uniform. I mean, people look the same from behind.

I watch the first video again. I've never seen myself walk

so I can't tell if the person walks like me. But when the hand throws the phone to the ground, I freeze the frame. The wrist is visible. There's no bracelet.

These videos have been manipulated. It wouldn't be hard to hack the video feed and upload an old file of me going to the elevator. The timestamp can be altered by bypassing the feed with the faked video. The first video may not even be me. It could be someone in a wig. I start compiling my evidence. It doesn't take a talented person to create and doctor photos and videos, but school security systems are relatively robust for casual hackers.

I start working on a little remote access tool and rootkit that I want to put on Ingrid's devices. Even cellphones are more like computers these days. Anything open to a network can be made vulnerable. Talking about cellphones, Aunt Erika got me a brand new one right away since my old one was unsalvageable. I make sure my old phone was properly destroyed just in case.

When the weekend rolls around, I'm released from my half-day outpatient therapy with a doctor's signature verifying that I'm on my way to recovery. It wasn't all bad. I got to talk about my mom. I got to talk about being a wallflower. I let Ingrid hit me. I let Ryder dump me and then I took him back. I'm sick of being a victim.

Celeste is the first person to get permission to visit me. My loving but incredibly stupid cousin has forbidden any contact with me until today. The moment it's lifted, Celeste texts me and visits me with Brittany and Darcy in tow.

As soon as I see them, Celeste bursts into tears, and I blurt, "I didn't try to kill myself."

What surprises me is that all three of them nod. "We believe you," Celeste says, and then I start crying, too.

It is a relief to be believed. Next thing you know, we're all blubbering messes. After we get our cry fest out of the way, Celeste speaks up. "We were suspicious right away. Ingrid and Cage said the same thing – Ingrid hosted a gathering and invited certain Court members over. It was too specific."

"Not just them, but Judy, Erin, and Victoria," Darcy adds, blotting at her eyes. "It was the same thing. *Oh, we were all at a party with Ingrid. See, here's a picture of us on social media.*" Darcy mimics Victoria's pretentious voice. "I told Ethan my suspicions, but he thought the videos made it obvious."

"There are time stamps on the videos and stuff, but can't those be faked?" Brittany asks.

I'm grim when I reply, "Yes. Many things can be altered." I decide to reveal a few things. "The video with me breaking my phone? I don't think that's me." I point to our friendship bracelet. "I'm not wearing this. It's someone wearing a wig with the time stamp altered."

"Shit." Darcy's whisper echoes all our sentiments. "Well, we have the proof, right? Let's get this cleared up."

"Not so simple," Celeste says thoughtfully. "Ingrid has the alibi of half the Royals *and* some Court members. Plus, they could simply say the bracelet didn't show because it was hidden by the sleeve of our jackets. They could argue the angle is all wrong." She demonstrates this by lifting her arms and sliding her bracelet so that the sleeve bars it from view.

At this point, I don't give them what else I've gleaned. I don't want them to get entangled in this until I'm done collecting evidence. It will reveal too much about me – and create questions I'm not ready to answer.

"I've been so angry with Ethan," I admit, "that I haven't spoken to him since I was released. He's staying out of my way."

Darcy sighs, reaching to hug me. "Ethan is being illogical because he's struggling with guilt. He thinks it's because of him that you felt this pressure to fit in. In both situations, he thinks he's failed you in some way. He also doesn't think women are that vindictive."

Brittany snorts. "Yeah, we are. We hold grudges. Or I do."

I manage to laugh as Celeste adds, "I think Connor doubts Ingrid too. He doesn't know what happened, but he doesn't think you tried to freeze yourself on the roof of our dorm. The Royal girls believe in the code about sticking together, even if it means lying."

No one asks about Ryder. For that I'm glad. I'm still upset with him. Okay, we didn't profess undying love, but I thought… I thought he would believe me.

"We'll keep digging, and I'll talk to Ethan," Darcy promises, but I'm not sure what she can do with regards to Ingrid. Ethan and Darcy are a week away from graduating. Next year, it will just be me, Brittany, and Celeste. It's a sobering thought.

"At least Monday is mostly for those who need extra time to finish projects," Brittany says.

That's true. It's mostly set aside for cleaning out lockers, dorm rooms, and returning borrowed materials. Since I did my finals remotely, Aunt Erika has already had my room cleared out. There is an evening party Tuesday night for the departing seniors, and then the seniors have their graduation ceremony the following weekend.

After the girls leave, I send my little rootkit out to Ingrid's email address and hope for a bite. My phone buzzes and I see Ryder's name. It's with trepidation that I accept his call.

"I wasn't sure if you'd answer," Ryder says, his voice smooth but solemn. "Mira, I need to talk to you, but I can't get away right now. My father is in town." There's a hesitancy in his words. "I'm hosting a party Monday night. It's tradition for the outgoing king to recognize the new king." His laugh is harsh. "Would you come early so we can talk?"

"Do you believe me? About Ingrid?" I wait, holding my breath.

"I do. Mira, I believe you."

I want to cry. Or maybe hug him. "That… means a lot."

"Mira, I'm sorry for not being there. But I'll tell you everything, I swear." He sounds rushed and anxious. "If you'll have me, next year it won't be Ingrid. You'll be my queen. I'm tired of the games. I want to tell you everything, even if it means I lose everything." He takes a deep breath. "The party starts at eight. Are you able to have someone drop you off around seven?"

"Yeah, I think so." I suck in my breath. I want him to prove this isn't a game. My heart wants it to be real, but my mind has doubts.

"Great." He's quiet. "You're the only thing that matters, Mira." I hear some background noise and Ryder grows hushed. "I need to go. I'll see you soon."

He disconnects and I stare at my shiny new phone for a long time.

010100

Monday, Ingrid bites. I spoofed the principal's email address so that Ingrid gets a message asking her to return her books. Normally, I would cringe at doing this, but Ingrid could have killed me.

While rummaging through her laptop, I come across something curious: Ingrid has a Discord account. It's curious because Discord is popular among gamers – and folks like me. Ingrid just isn't the Discord type.

Once I'm in Discord as Ingrid, though, I feel like my world falls apart. There is only one server Ingrid is subscribed to: Old Royal Bluebloods. When I click on the server, I check to see who's subscribed to the server. It's almost all the old money Royals and some of the Court members: Erin, Elaine, Judy, Victoria, Ingrid, Cage, Arthur, Ryder, Xander, Nate, Daniel, a few others. Ethan, Connor, and Celeste are missing. I do a quick scan of the available categories. There are the usual voice channels, but the category I click on first is labeled THE BETS.

There I find channels identified only by names. There are a few names I don't recognize, but I recognize these: Celeste D, Darcy S, Brittany K, Mira B. I click Celeste D first and cover my mouth in horror.

Arthur writes about Celeste's body in lewd detail. There are bets placed on getting kisses or getting pictures. I'm dismayed when Daniel wins money for getting nude pictures of Celeste. The post is recent. Cage suggests Daniel ask for sexual favors if she wants the pictures deleted. Daniel thinks it's a great idea, but he doesn't know how to get past Connor.

I next go to Darcy S. Most of the posts here are older: Darcy would have been a sophomore and it's clear that Erin was aware Ethan was attracted to her. Erin rants about Darcy, calling her several names. She tries to get Cage to seduce Darcy. He fails. Erin is horrifically vicious, asking Cage to give Darcy a date-rape drug so pictures can be taken. Xander objects and Erin claims it's a joke. Recent posts are mainly from Erin complaining about Ethan overstepping his role and disregarding the honor of the Royals. I nearly choke at the hypocrisy.

I click on Brittany K. There are pictures of her. Erin goads the boys into making bets on who can get pictures of her in certain positions. I stop reading after Cage posts lurid thoughts on her.

When I click on my name, I start at the beginning. A month before my arrival at RBA, Erin announces my existence. She doesn't know my name yet. Ingrid says I'm the perfect tool to hurt the King of RBA. Erin demands that I'm ruined so she can rub it in Ethan's face. Arthur, Cage, Ryder, and Xander agree that they'll help. There's back and forth between everyone about what would be the best thing. Nate disagrees with everyone.

Erin writes: *I think we leave it to our future king. Make her love you and then dump her. Are you game, Ryder?*

Ingrid says that I'll be ugly, but Erin claims that would be even better. Ingrid suggests maybe I'll jump off a bridge. Xander finds the thought disgusting, but he says that there's a rumor that I'm pretty. Ryder responds: *You'll secure my position? If I take her, screw her, and dump her?*

My stomach curls when Erin agrees. Their crude words make me cringe.

Ingrid writes: *I'm all for it if I see tears on her face when you're done with her.*

Xander asks if it is open season on me and whether he can take a shot. After a short debate, it's agreed that Ryder will try first.

Erin decrees that if Ryder can break my heart and ruin me, she'll ensure he is the next King – she alludes to Ethan threatening Ryder's position. The next set of posts occur on the first day of school. Erin has seen me from afar and writes that she thinks I'll be sweet enough for Ryder's taste. Through my tears, I see Arthur declaring that he wants me after Ryder is done with me. Cage says he doesn't want to wait. Daniel wants to drug me and have his way. Ingrid mocks Ethan's protectiveness and says I must be a virgin. There's a gross description from Cage about sex with virgins.

Ryder writes: *She's mine. No one else gets to touch her until I'm done with her.*

Ingrid responds: *You can have her any way you want, but don't forget I'm your future queen.*

Ryder replies: *How could I forget?*

Concern erupts from Erin when Connor shows interest in me, and Erin demands Ryder put an end to it. Ryder agrees and promises Connor won't ruin Erin's fun. There are a few more posts, mainly from Ingrid and Erin, both demanding that Ryder humiliate me when he throws his party for Ethan. It's decided by Erin that she'll only be satisfied if Ryder seduces me. Ingrid demands pictures.

I close my laptop, crying violently for a bit. Eventually, my sobs subside. When Ethan comes knocking on my door, I don't respond. My door is locked, and, after a while, he gives up. I can't face Ethan. I can't show him all of this. It would devastate him if he knew I was targeted because of him.

It was a game. I should have known. Ryder reeled me in by running hot and cold. He threw epic nonsense my way and I believed it. Now his request to see me before his party makes sense. He would've seduced me and then thrown me in front of everyone. I want to believe I would've held back, but I don't know. Maybe he would've forced me. Just the thought makes me shudder.

I continue to sit in the darkness as seven o'clock rolls around. Not long after, Ryder begins to text me, asking me if

I'm on my way. My phone buzzes and I see his name flash on my phone. His messages get increasingly worried. I get incoming calls from Darcy, Brittany, Celeste, and Ethan.

Ryder messages me again. *Please tell me you're okay. I'll wait for you. Ethan's here and he doesn't know if you're at home.*

I ignore Ryder. I text Ethan that I'm ill and will talk to him tomorrow. I grab a backpack and stuff it with my laptop before I fall asleep fitfully.

010101

I ask the driver to wait for me as I arrive at Ryder's in the morning. I promise him extra money if he stays. I see Ryder's car and another one that I don't recognize, so I know he's here. The butler lets me in without question, indicating that Ryder is upstairs.

I wander up to Ryder's room, pausing when I hear voices. Like a creep, I press my ear to the door and listen.

"…why now?" Ryder asks. I hear him pacing.

"It's simple." Ingrid. Her voice grates on my nerves. "There is no way I'm not going to be Queen. And now, you'll be King."

"My position was never threatened!" Ryder snaps. "There is no one who comes close."

Ingrid's laughter sounds cruel. "Only if Daddy doesn't take it all away." When Ryder swears at her, she adds, "It doesn't matter. I'm here. Let's do this. Or is it Mira?"

"You know where I stand with Mira," Ryder snarls, coming to a sudden stop.

Ingrid laughs again. "You love adding notches to your belt. You should've added her. Or couldn't you do it because she's so sweet and innocent? Tell me, Ryder, what made you hold back?"

I clutch my stomach. Oh, God. His promise to Erin and Ingrid to ruin me. Since he failed to ruin me, is this some other sick thing to stay in Erin's good graces?

"Shut up! Don't mention her name."

"Touchy, touchy."

Silence. "You know why…"

"I promise," Ingrid coos, "Ryder, you can end this. You'll have everything. King. The girl. Money. You just have to keep your end of the bargain. I imagine certain people will be grateful."

More silence. Finally, Ryder speaks hoarsely, "I want you to stay away from Mira. Leave her alone. She doesn't deserve any of this."

"Agreed."

Another long pause. "This is… I just… You swear?"

Ingrid makes a weird sound in her throat. "Yes, I'll give you everything."

More silence. "Come here."

I try not to gag as I hear light footsteps and then the sounds of kissing. The unmistakable sounds of clothes being removed and heavy breathing keep me frozen in horror. I feel like a pervert.

"Come on, baby, I'll make it better," Ingrid says as I hear a zipper followed by the thump of pants falling to the floor. "I can make you feel good. I can make this good."

Tears stream down my face as my heart hammers painfully. This is what it feels like to be humiliated. This is what it feels like to have your heart stomped on. Something inside me shatters.

"You know what I want, Ingrid," Ryder whispers. "Keep your promise."

The sound of two bodies shuffling on the bed spurs me to action. I push the door open gently but with enough sound so that Ryder hears me. He jerks upright in bed next to Ingrid, who is borderline naked. His blue eyes widen in horror.

"I admit, you got me, Ryder," I say bitterly, my tears clear on my face. But I'm no longer crying. "You almost made me believe you were sincere." I choke on my breath, but when I speak again, my voice becomes harder, stronger. "You can have him, Ingrid. You're perfect together. A match made in heaven."

"Mira, no!" Ryder jumps out of bed. Well, who knew? He's a boxer boy. When he reaches for me, I slap him hard, shocking him. The red mark on his cheek fuels my tirade.

"Why? What did I ever do to either of you? All this work just to humiliate me and hurt Ethan!" I don't care how loud I get or who hears me. "I read all about the *deal* you made with Ingrid and Erin! Ingrid sure knows how to pick her targets. I can't believe you went after Celeste, Darcy, and Brittany too. You're not Royals. You're monsters! You play with people because you're not human!"

"I can explain, Mira," Ryder says, his hands out in supplication. Are those tears? What a joke!

I shake my head, my eyes catching Ingrid's smirk. She doesn't bother to hide her body. "You don't have to. I saw everything on Discord." I give him a scathing look. "Why is Connor being left out of the fun and games? Didn't think he was worthy? Or didn't think he'd play? What made Daniel worthy but not Connor?"

Ryder tries to reach for me again. "Mira, please. Listen to me," he pleads.

I knock his hand away. "You have no idea what I'm capable of," I hiss, stepping back, and I know that every ounce of my hate is in my face. "You disgust me. Both of you. You deserve each other."

A tear slips from his eyes. "No, don't," he chokes out. "No, let me—"

I walk back slowly. "You two better get back to business. Don't keep your queen waiting. Don't call me, Ryder. You don't exist in my world anymore. You're pathetic. I hope you both burn in hell."

I hold his eyes until I reach his bedroom door, and then I run to the car waiting for me. If he manages to put his pants on to chase me, I never find out.

•••

I don't return home. I send my compiled video files and my suspicions to Uncle Robert via email. I tell him that I'll be in touch, but I need to leave Royalton right now. I tell Ethan I'm sorry I'll miss his graduation and to give my love to Darcy, Brittany, and Celeste.

Then I turn off my phone. I purchase a burner phone and a one-way ticket to Washington. I don't look back.

THREE MONTHS LATER

The Internet gave us access to everything; but it also gave everything access to us.

--James Veitch

There are no secrets on the internet.

--Paul Babicki

⊙10110⊙

During the summer, I contact Aunt Erika and Uncle Robert periodically. My cowardice isn't the stuff heroines are made of: I ran to escape my problems. I break. I cry. I come to terms that everything with Ryder was based on a bet, a lie. I hide to lick my wounds. To the rest of Royal Bridge Academy, I can't be found. No matter how much Ethan begs his mom, she gives me privacy and peace. Ethan knows the gist of it. I sent him screenshots of the Discord channel for him to read.

It takes me nearly all of three months to decide what to do. I know Aunt Erika enrolled me back at RBA, but I wasn't sure if I wanted to go back. In fact, I planned on not coming back at all.

I return a few days before school begins. I'm pale and weary, but Aunt Erika doesn't judge me or get angry. I think she doesn't want me to run away again. We hug for a whole minute, relief flowing from her to me.

"If you don't want to go to RBA, I understand," Uncle Robert says with a heavy sigh. Even though I have evidence that the videos were doctored, it's still my word against Ingrid's. And Ingrid has people lying for her. There's no evidence that Ingrid did anything to me.

I've returned because I promised RReagan and Liam that I would. You see, I spent the summer in Liam's guest bedroom. During that time, I got dragged into Liam's work on the strange fuel-air explosives file I found and the strange money transfers.

Liam Jacobi is now the newest student transfer at RBA. He's essentially pulling off a *21 Jump Street*: he's pretending to be a student but really working for the government. So why am I, a high school student, helping the government with suspicious activities? Desperate times call for desperate measures. (Jokes aside, I think the government's not as efficient as RReagan would like. And there really isn't anyone that can compare to the way Liam and I operate.)

Ethan rushes home the moment he hears I'm back. Both he and Darcy are at the U. As freshmen, they're living on campus, but the U is only an hour away. As soon as I see him, I burst into tears. I forgive myself for crying. Ethan's been hurting too.

"I'm so sorry, so sorry," he says as soon as we hug. His eyes are suspiciously moist. "Those assholes did that to you because of me. They took it out on you instead of me." Ethan is full of guilt and pain.

"It's okay. I'm okay. They are responsible for their actions alone." I pull back to look at him. "I'm sorry I missed your graduation. I had to get away."

"You scared the living daylights out of me disappearing like that," my cousin growls, but his mock anger is ruined by the sad smile. "You're seventeen, Mira. I worried about your safety and well-being, but Mom insisted you needed space. You had to deal with everything alone. Mom *said* you were okay, but she wouldn't tell me anything!"

After I left, Ethan confronted Erin, Arthur, and Cage, showing the posts to their parents. Ethan and Cage came to blows. Ethan won. Erin disappeared like the coward she's always been. And Arthur's parents moved him away from the neighborhood.

When Ethan talks about the new Royals, I tell him I don't want to hear about Ryder. Instead, Ethan tells me that Ingrid denied the posts, said they were fake, and claimed someone was trying to frame her. Beyond that, not much has changed. Ryder is King. Ingrid is Queen. The Court exists. That's fine. It's more than fine. I plan to topple a monarchy.

• • •

Ethan spends the weekend with me. I know Darcy wants to be here too, but I'm not ready to face her. Although she feels guilty, I make sure Ethan is aware that I don't blame her. No. This is all on Ryder and Ingrid and Erin.

Lounging by the pool and soaking up the last of the summer heat, Ethan gives me a quick update. Brittany, after seeing what was written about her on Discord, is overseas. The school has her doing a study abroad program, but the plan is that she'll be back for the spring term. Ethan says she's currently in France drinking too much coffee and eating too much chocolate. Celeste has been quiet. Nate and Xander took some heat and have been laying low.

I regret hiding from Celeste, Brittany, and Darcy. From what Ethan says, it sounds like they understood the reasons why I disappeared. It was a necessary evil. "It took me a while to piece myself together," I tell Ethan. "I'm not afraid of them anymore."

Ethan, dripping from a quick dip in the pool, drapes himself on a lounger under the cabana. "I know you don't want to talk about *him*. You should know, if he had completed the bet, I would've killed him." His hands clench into fits. "I would've strangled them."

I shudder. "I don't need you to protect me," I say softly. I'm going to fight with my weapon of choice and on my terms – and I know I'm going to win.

A commotion silences Ethan as he glances away from me with a frown. I hear shouts, and then Uncle Robert yelling, "I will call the police!"

Ryder bursts into the pool area, his eyes frantically searching for me. "Mira." He says my name almost painfully.

How the hell did he know I was back?

Ethan stands. If I were into dramas, I'd be eating popcorn because it's old King versus new King. "Ryder! Get the hell out of here!"

Ryder ignores Ethan. Uncle Robert grabs Ryder from behind, and Ethan moves in to help. Ryder struggles between them, his anger rising, his eyes intent on me. "Mira, please, talk to me! Let me explain. Just hear my side of the story!"

I worried that I wouldn't be able to face Ryder, but now that he's here, I let the emotions in. There is the inevitable pain. But there's more now. Anger. Frustration. Looking at Ryder, I almost believe he cares. And maybe he began to care for me, but it wasn't enough to stop him from his games.

"Go inside the house, Mira," Ethan says. "I'll deal with this." Ethan flexes like he's Tarzan.

Noppity-nope. I was meek and fragile last year. I am not that girl anymore. I walk right up to Ryder in my swimsuit. "Alright, I'm talking to you," I say as my uncle and cousin glance at me in surprise.

A spark of hope flickers in Ryder's eyes. "Mira—"

I cut him off. "But I'm not listening to you. Nothing you could say would make a difference. I'm a person, not a bet, not a tool for revenge." My voice is cold and steady. "My *mother* died last year. She was my best friend and losing her gutted me. That alone should've earned me a measure of your pity. But pity would have required a heart. A *soul.*" Ryder inhales sharply. "I may not have earned your pity, but you've earned mine. I pity you, Ryder, because you're a lonely, horrible person, and you're unlovable. I don't think you even have a soul."

Ryder blinks. My words are deliberately cruel, but I have three months of bottled anger inside me. "Give me another chance," he finally chokes out.

Seriously? He must love verbal abuse. How many chances does he think he deserves?

"You're pathetic." It's Ethan's disdain that snaps Ryder's attention away from me. "You're a lemming, Ryder. A follower, not a leader. I fought for what I believed in when it came to Darcy. You just went with the status quo. Look at you now. I can't believe I made you King. Nate would've been a better choice."

Ethan's words hit a nerve. Tugging his clothes back in place, Ryder's mouth tightens as he straightens. Dark blue eyes return to me painfully. "I'm sorry I wasted your time, Mira." He nods at Uncle Robert. "I will see myself out."

"Are you okay?" Ethan asks me as I watch Ryder retreat.

"More than okay," I say. "I feel strong."

010111

Liam picks me up for the first day of school. In the school uniform, he looks the part of a high school student. We exchange snarky grins as he parks the car – a Range Rover, I kid you not, in jet black – and we step on campus together.

"Mira!" Celeste runs towards me, nearly toppling me in her haste.

Liam's eyebrows rise with amusement as she rattles off a list of questions. "I'll tell you everything later," I promise, grabbing her hands so I can look at her.

It's only then that Celeste sees Liam. He sticks his hand out. "Liam Jacobi. RBA's newest senior."

Celeste blushes – which means she thinks he's cute – and introduces herself. Her eyes dwell on how close Liam stands by me.

Liam, ever the showman, drapes his arm over my shoulder. "Mira and I got together over the summer." Liam's overdoing the boyfriend bit. I try not to sigh. "She's my girl."

Her surprise is quickly replaced by a smile. "Wow, that's…"

I know she wants to say "sudden" or "fast," but for some reason, she falters.

"Okay, let's go to the first-day assembly," I say, on the verge of hysterical laughter.

Liam meticulously entwines his hand with mine, giving me the kind of smile you might give to a dog. He ignores my semi-sardonic glare. We enter the gym, and I deliberately choose one of the front rows. Celeste, my loyal and sweet friend, sits with us. There are murmurs as other students enter and see me. Obviously, most have heard about the whole Discord fiasco because there are speculative whispers and a few chuckles. But it isn't until Connor enters that I tense. Will he side with me or his cousin? He came alone, not with the Court. That is telling. Blue-gray eyes grow huge, but he doesn't hesitate in joining us and takes the spot next to Celeste.

My defiant group waits for the Royals. When they file in, it's like *Village of the Damned*, which is this old horror movie I watched with Mom. In the movie, the women of a village are impregnated by some alien species, and the result are these pale children with white-blond hair and overly blue eyes that have freaky mind powers. When the kids get old enough, they walk in mated pairs wherever they go. Anyhow, that's how the Royals enter. Ryder is in front with Ingrid Whitman at his right. After them is Xander Morrison paired with Judy Lee. Then Nate Jacobs walks in with Victoria Little, whose newly red hair does not look natural. Behind them, the Court follows. I see Daniel Jameson and shudder.

At first, only Ingrid sees me as they climb up to sit in their exclusive cluster in the back. I expect any moment for Ingrid's eyes to glow red when I meet her glare. Then Ryder stumbles when he realizes who Ingrid is looking at. He hesitates, and for a moment I fear he's going to walk over. But he doesn't. His thoughts and emotions hide behind a wall of arrogant entitlement.

Our principal gives a rousing speech on a new year, and a chance to right the wrongs and become a better person. She's clearly referencing the Discord situation, glowering at the Royals in the back a few times. When my hands clench, Liam puts his arm around me in a very boyfriend-like move. I try not to giggle. My only thought is that Ingrid won't know what hits her next.

I'm not content to let bygones be bygones, and I'm done avoiding people. As seniors, we get the option of living in a quad or having a single. I'm in a single because I need privacy this year if I'm going to destroy the Royals. Correction. When I destroy the Royals.

• • •

Liam arranged his classes to be in line with mine, but he's only enrolled in three classes instead of six because he's not really a student. His enrollment here causes all sorts of questions to run through my mind. Will he do his homework? Does the administration know he's not a real student? If not, is this really a good use of our taxpayer dollars?

I curse my luck at having Ryder in three of my classes: math, science, and English. Ugh, and so is Judy. Fortunately, these are the same classes Liam's taking, and our "relationship" takes center stage.

Liam hovers and flirts, but he's careful about getting handsy. I may have privately threatened him a few times. Even without looking, I know Ryder watches us. Judy watches us too with her beady eyes, and I have no doubt she's reporting to the leader of her coven about what she sees.

When lunch rolls around, I hide my smile when Connor and Celeste follow me and Liam outside to one of the open tables. It'll be cold and dreary soon enough – enjoying the sun is a luxury we can't afford to waste. I take a moment to feel happy about Connor and Celeste. At least one good thing evolved from my terrible last year.

"You look well despite everything," Connor says with a shamefaced look. "I just… I'm sorry."

I shake my head. "You weren't part of it."

Celeste covers his hand sympathetically when he says, "In a way, I am. I'm an entitled prick, too, you know." He hesitates. "Ryder's barely spoken to me all summer."

I turn away when Celeste hisses at Connor. I guess Ryder is the person who shall not be named.

While Connor feeds Celeste some fries, Liam whispers in my ear, "I need to connect the names to faces. I have a list we need to vet thoroughly." Anyone who's watching will think we're being affectionate rather than giving each other information. "We can clear the low hanging fruit first."

A shadow falls across the table; Ryder looms like a grim reaper. "Mira. I need to speak to you."

Not this again. I take my first real look at Ryder Cabot. If anything, he's handsomer. He's grown a little more, his shoulders are broader, and the lines of his face are more mature. But his dark blue eyes are the same: cold, hard to read.

Liam stands, rolling his shoulders. Maybe he saw that move in a movie because I've never seen him do that before. I remind myself to tell him that movie boyfriends aren't always the best ones to mimic. "Exactly why do you need to speak to my girlfriend?"

Ryder's eyes dart from me to Liam. His jaw tightens, and I'm surprised I don't hear teeth cracking. "Girlfriend." Ryder snaps the word like he can't believe it. "I wasn't aware I needed permission to talk to Mira."

Liam has the body of a surfer, and he's not your stereotypical hacker with bad hygiene. His blond hair is longer than most boys, but it adds to his charm. He may not be as gorgeous as Ryder, but he's sexy in a lithe sort of way. (I do a mental check – am I analyzing these two guys based on looks? Boy, am I shallow or what?)

Celeste listens to the drama with huge eyes. She's avoided the Royals and the Court the past few months except for Connor. While we haven't had a chance to talk about the events right before summer, her resentment against the Royals is clear. A glance at Connor tells me that he's torn between his feelings for Celeste, his residual anger at Ryder, and the fact that his cousin is his best friend.

"It only applies to you," Liam says, resting a hand on my shoulder.

I half expect Liam to pat me on the head.

Ryder's nose flares slightly. "Worried she'll be tempted? She was mine last year."

Okay, I've had enough. "I was never yours, Ryder. We dated. If you can even call it that." A flash of hurt flickers in Ryder's eyes, and I hesitate. I'm turning into a major bitch, aren't I? "Don't worry, Liam, my time with him wasn't very memorable." Now that's a complete lie. And yes, that was super bitchy and immature.

Liam has no qualms about twisting the metaphorical knife. "I'm not worried about temptation." He gets in Ryder's face. "I know how to treat a woman right."

The insinuations from that statement! And apparently, I'm a woman now. Does that make me cooler? I don't know.

A muscle moves in Ryder's jaw as he stares at me. And then, with a visible swallow, he says, "I'll be here when you're willing to talk, Mira."

Liam sneers, "You'll never get close to her again."

Ryder fists his hands, and I wonder if a fight's about to erupt. But then his shoulders slump, and he nods at Connor, not meeting my eyes, before he… walks away.

Connor breaks the silence. "Ryder… struggled this summer."

Before I can respond, Celeste slams her hand on the table. "You know what he did to Mira! How can you defend him?"

Connor lifts his hands pleadingly, his blue-gray eyes sincere. "I'm not. It's just – there are things that you don't know."

I huff. "Stop. I'm a big girl. You can defend or villainize Ryder all you want." I shrug listlessly. "It's irrelevant to me now."

Only Liam knows the truth, and his green eyes observe the twitch of my fingers and the set of my mouth. He squeezes my hand before returning to semi-boyfriend mode. By the end of the day, Liam has dropped a whole series of hints about our relationship. With his West Coast looks, the girls at school ogle him wherever we go.

"You should know that you've snagged the girl everyone

wanted to hook up with last year," a boy named Emmett, a new Court member, tells Liam during dinner. I try not to wince.

Liam takes it all in stride. "It doesn't surprise me. She's the hottest girl here. She's an angel."

I wince internally. Even though I'm tempted to puke, I manage a cross between a smile and a grimace. This is going to be a long year.

011000

While Liam taps into the school's systems, I focus on homework. When needed, I help him narrow the list of "suspects" – I start to feel like Nancy Drew in a computer sort of way. First, I eliminate Connor and Celeste. I know they're clean, but it's nice to check the boxes anyway. I bite the bullet and screen the Royal boys, clearing Ryder, Nate, and Xander. Liam takes over the Royal girls, promising to keep me posted. Since he's so secretive about some of his conversations with RReagan, I don't press him. My participation is supposed to be peripheral, and I want to keep it that way.

To the school, Liam and I are perfectly lovey-dovey with him hanging out in my room or vice-versa. In private, our relationship is strictly platonic. We talk; we don't touch or kiss. I give him some advice on how not to sound too cheesy in public. He runs programs and ignores me. I explain that *Fifty Shades of Gray* isn't a good example of a healthy relationship.

The atmosphere at RBA has changed. Thanks to Ethan, some details of the Discord site were leaked: the bets, the ringleaders, the victims. Needless to say, fewer students hold the Royals in awe. Although the Royals are trying to maintain a sense of unity, the tension is palpable, and last year's antics are fresh in the mind of the Court as well – some of whom were excluded from the "bets".

Ryder doesn't approach me again, but Liam catches him staring more often than not. "That guy still wants you," Liam observes, tapping on his laptop with his pen thoughtfully.

I make a face. "Don't. Ryder Cabot is never getting close to me. I'm still taking them all down." My chest feels tight every time Ryder enters a room. If I'm over him, why does he still bother me?

Ingrid flaunts her status as Queen whenever possible, clinging to Ryder's arm when they're together. I don't know if they're officially dating, but it sure looks like it. It rankles me that he simply moved on.

Liam cocks his head, and a lock of blond hair falls across his cheek. "I know he hurt you. But I also know you."

He's not wrong. Once I got past my weepy stage, Liam and I talked a lot. He probably knows more about me than Celeste. "I was naïve last year."

"You're still you. Inside, you want something real, something full of passion." Liam picks at his nails. "The only guy worthy of you is one who will walk through fire for you. I think you thought it would be Ryder. Maybe you still do."

That won't be Ryder. He may be sorry, but I can't forget the cruelty in which he agreed to the bet. Maybe he wants me back because of his damaged pride, but I won't forgive someone just because he looks good in a uniform. My phone buzzes with an incoming text from Celeste.

"Ingrid is hosting a party this weekend. Celeste says we're specifically invited." I roll my eyes.

But Liam stops me from declining. "You know Ernest Whitman? We've flagged him."

I thought the girls had been cleared. Apparently, I'm wrong.

"We're pretty sure he has a shell company that's laundering money for him, too." Liam leans back on his bed, hands behind his head. "I say we go."

I narrow my eyes. "What do you have planned?"

"Oh, no. Not trading secrets with you." His green eyes turn wicked. "I do have a dress for you to wear, though."

• • •

I grit my teeth. "I think half the dress is missing."

The silvery dress Liam gives me skims my body and leaves little to the imagination. The halter top leaves my back bare all the way to my waist, making it rather obvious that I'm not wearing a bra. Because the skirt is short, I'm afraid to bend over. Maybe I should offer to wear a bikini instead.

Liam gives me a thumbs up when I scowl. "It's supposed to be distracting. I want people looking at you and not me." With an apologetic look, he adds, "Yes, it's sexist. Make the girl look hot to distract everyone, but it works. And you look hot. I mean that in a non-pervy way, of course."

"I will kill you one day." My smile is deliberately unpleasant. "Fine. What do you need me to do?"

Straightening his suit, he does a mental checklist. "Just look amazing and act like you can't keep your hands off my hotness." When I roll my eyes, he laughs. "I need to do a few things," he says obtusely. "And I need to clone Ingrid Whitman's phone. If her father's involved, she might be as well."

"My rootkit is probably still on her computers," I recall. "I can hand the access over to you."

Liam brightens. "Perfect. At the party, I may need a distraction, but we'll have to play it by ear."

I remember that Daniel Jameson indicated he had pictures of certain girls. If so, Ingrid may also have access to those files. I regret that I never bothered to hack her phone.

When we arrive at Ingrid's mansion, I'm appalled by the deliberate opulence. While not as huge as Ryder's, it's like they took designing tips from Donald Trump and dipped everything in gold.

"I wonder why she invited us," I muse out loud.

Liam snorts. "You're adorable when you're clueless. She wants to see what happens between you and Ryder. If she's digging her claws into him, she'll want proof that you're not a threat. Have you ever looked at them when they're together? Ingrid's into the whole thing, but Ryder is ready to walk the plank. Ingrid wants to confirm either a lack of interest from you or loyalty from Ryder." He pauses right before we enter the place. "Look, I might get a little touchy tonight. I'm not saying this because I want a reason to grope you. It would be all sorts of wrong to, you know, cross a line."

I roll my eyes. "Whatever." Liam's such a dork. It's not like I'm fourteen.

"Just don't hit me."

Wait, what? We step inside, and for a few seconds, I can only stand there and blink. The only word that comes to mind is shiny. Everything is very shiny.

"Mira Bell?"

Nate Jacobs is not looking at my face. I turn red with embarrassment as Nate, who was the politest on that Discord site, stares at me. Or my legs. Or my cleavage. "Wow. I mean, sorry." He blushes under his dark skin. "I've never seen you like this before."

"Wipe the drool, man," Liam says with good-natured heat. He places his hand on the small of my back as we walk past.

"If you grab my ass, I'm going to castrate you," I hum to him quietly. "No, I'll just destroy your cyber life. Ruin your credit score. Create evidence that you're wanted in five countries..."

Liam laughs, but the glance he sends me is apologetic. "It's disturbing how violent you've become. Where's my angel?"

Sometimes I cringe at how stupid I was last year. I don't smile when I reply, "She got wiser." Liam sobers in memory. He witnessed the fallout: my tears, my cold rage. When I wasn't mourning, I was programming. On that level, Liam and I fully understand each other.

Celeste and Connor are dancing when they spot us. Connor's eyes grow huge, and when he glances over his shoulder, I learn where Ryder is. Of course, Ingrid presses herself to Ryder's side as if to say *mine*. Celeste gives me an approving thumbs-up, mouthing *hot*.

Ingrid wears a red dress as tiny as mine, but hers is so tight that you can see the outline of certain parts of her anatomy that shouldn't be outlined. It's very Kim Kardashian. Ingrid grabs Ryder's arm possessively, her mouth tightening when Ryder stiffens at her touch. His face, even when he notices me, is carefully blank. The light hits my dress. I sparkle, and as Liam expected, people look our way when Liam takes me out to dance. The cousin to the former King with the mysterious new boy.

"Let's make them ogle a bit," he murmurs in my ear, using his blond hair to hide that we're talking. He's careful about the way his hand caresses my back, but I'm glad he warned me about being handsy because I nearly jump at the touch.

With deliberate movements, we do a slow kizomba dance. It's something Liam taught me over the summer, although this is the first time Liam holds me like we're lovers. As we move, it causes my dress to flutter around my thighs, and it isn't long before we have more than one set of eyes on us. When Liam guides me with a sensuously moving hand, I note that Ryder looks downright pissed. In fact, he's seething with jealousy. Standing with Ingrid, he's so tense that I'm surprised he doesn't pull a muscle. Xander comes to stand by Ryder, his mouth open.

"Right now, every guy wishes he were me," Liam says with a faint laugh. "Ryder Cabot is about to pop a blood vessel. Just as I predicted. I'm going to dip you and then kiss you. If I'm right, your boy is going to storm over and hit me. And by the way, sorry about this."

Even though he warns me, and I manage to get dipped without looking like an idiot, the moment he kisses me is still shocking. Without the warning, I would have misread his action because he wraps my hair in his right hand possessively before pressing his lips to mine. This could seriously be in a movie. All in all, it's not bad. Liam doesn't stir the same reaction I had with Ryder, but the heat is slow and tempting as he parts my lips. I remember that it's a show, but honestly, the PDA is rather extreme because his tongue is in my mouth. I feel trashy because

I'm letting a guy I've never kissed before do this in public. To everyone, we seem ready to make out on the floor. Then I feel Liam's hand on my bottom.

I don't get a chance to punch Liam. He's yanked back roughly, and the next thing I see is Ryder slamming his fist into Liam's face. "Holy shit!" I gasp, my lip gloss smeared.

"Don't touch her!" Ryder yells as he looms over Liam on the floor.

Liam's mouth bleeds, but rather than getting angry, he chuckles, touching his lip with the back of his hand. He stands and the two guys face off. "Have a problem with me kissing my girlfriend, Cabot?"

I stand idiotically, not rushing to Liam as a concerned girlfriend should. Oops. Maybe I should go over and say something. I try to stamp concern into my features. "Are you okay?" I'm about to bend over when I remember the damn short dress. Not bending over in this thing!

Ingrid sneers, grabbing Ryder's arm, but he rips her hands off and pushes her away. "Get away from me!" he shouts into her astonished face, and then he lunges at Liam again. This time Xander and Nate grab him before he reaches Liam, but they struggle to hold him back.

Xander says something quietly into Ryder's ear, and the crazed fury clears a bit as Ryder's eyes find me. What surprises me is the devastation and pain on his face. He's been walking around campus with Ingrid grabbing him at every turn. Why is he acting as if he wants me instead? Does he really think I'll forget that I found them together? Maybe he's upset that he didn't get everything. Yet… I never see Ryder reaching for Ingrid. He doesn't want to be with her.

Ryder straightens, smoothing his coat and picking off imaginary lint with fake nonchalance. It's a move he uses to hide himself. The muscles in his throat shift as he composes himself.

Ingrid's fury radiates from every pore, and her hate towards me is unmistakable as she approaches Ryder again. With one furious glare, Ryder stops her in her tracks. The two Royals face off silently for a minute before Ryder storms off.

"I'm going to the washroom to clean up," Liam says to me a bit too loudly.

Well, if Liam wanted to make a fuss, he certainly made it happen. And did he really use the word *washroom*? He leaves to do his sneaky government work, but no one notices because Ingrid's demanding Ryder to come back.

Celeste consoles me. "I can't believe Ryder did that," she says, shaking her head. "I mean, I've never seen him lose control, even when he was mad at what Ethan did to him."

Connor murmurs, "Ryder's always gotten what he wants, either by throwing his body around or with money. What he wants is Mira, and he doesn't have her."

My eyes slide to Connor. "Are you sure about that? Because when I walked in on him the day I left, he seemed pretty cozy with Ingrid in bed."

"What?!" Celeste practically screams, and several students eye us curiously. She claps her hands over her mouth.

Connor goes pale. I guess he didn't know about that. But then something Celeste said connects with what I read on that horrible Discord site. "What do you mean about him and Ethan? I thought their fight was about old versus new money."

Pushing her hair back as we walk towards a quieter spot, Celeste says softly, "I thought Ethan would have told you by now. As you know, Ryder has a reputation of being a womanizer – a modern-day Lothario or Casanova, if you will – and his father disapproves of that behavior."

"My uncle fears that some woman is going to claim that Ryder fathered a kid with her," Connor explains, his mouth twisting in a way that makes me think he's holding something back. "In our sophomore year, it was pretty clear that Ryder intended to sleep his way through half the wealthy girls at school. Ethan was trying to secure support to date Darcy. Unfortunately, he decided to use Ryder's reputation against him."

My heart squeezes as Celeste continues for Connor. "Ethan brought in a girl – a call girl. Ryder's father never made much of a fuss if the girls in question were rich. But prostitutes? Not something his father's cool with. The girl posed as a student from another school and got Ryder to a room. Ethan had a hidden camera and recorded the encounter."

No. Not Ethan. Ethan wouldn't blackmail someone, would he? I remember how protective he was of me last year, demanding that I check in with him repeatedly. Was he worried that someone would do the same thing to me?

"To secure Ryder's support, Ethan threatened to send the photos to my uncle," Connor says, and I know Connor regrets how his words cause me pain. "In Ethan's defense, I think he was willing to do anything for Darcy. And Ethan never sent the pictures. But Ryder – could never let it go." His blue-gray eyes canvas the Royals and Court members around us.

"So, Ryder used me for a variety of reasons," I say, but Connor shakes his head.

"That's what doesn't add up. When he told me how he felt about you, he sounded so sincere that I forgave him. He's never lied to me, Mira. He was crazy about you. Ryder's been different since you entered his life," Connor says, his hand reaching for Celeste. "After you disappeared, Ryder was a wreck. He and Ethan fought, you know. Ryder didn't lift a finger; he just let Ethan beat him. I think the only reason why Ethan stopped was because Ryder wouldn't fight back."

I absorb this, unsure how to interpret everything I'm hearing, but I can't stop the niggling in my mind that tells me I'm not seeing the whole picture. Liam returns, and his wink tells me he accomplished what he wanted. He chitchats with Connor and Celeste like we're all old friends, and I'm glad when Connor and Celeste are equally friendly.

"I need to find a reason to stand by Ingrid. You can see the outline of her phone in that godawful dress she's wearing," Liam murmurs in my ear. "Are you up to dancing with Ryder?" He adds that last bit when he sees Ryder return.

Ryder stands as far from Ingrid as possible. "You are going to owe me ice cream," I grumble as we follow Celeste and Connor out to dance. I think for a moment. "We're going to have a fight on the floor, then. I can't promise to make my acting skills on par with yours."

"How monstrous do you want me to be? Don't forget I'm into RPGs. I love this stuff."

"Jealous, less monstrous," I say with a sweet smile as we start dancing. "Celeste called Ryder a Lothario."

Liam fashions his mouth into a frown. "You know, I'm going to use that as my next in-game name."

I furrow my brow, pretending to get upset. "It's probably a banned name."

"Do you really think the companies from Asia know what that means?" Liam scoffs, but his expression is petulant. "You ready? I'll follow your lead."

I push Liam away fiercely. "Just drop it!" I shout because I can't think of anything else better to say.

"He's the one who punched me!" Liam rages back, just loud enough to make everyone notice. "Maybe you need to show more concern for me!"

"You're making mountains out of molehills!" Got to love generic statements, right? Except I'm running out of generic statements to say.

"I'm not the one dressed like a whore! You look like you want everyone to screw you!" Liam yells, pointing a finger at me.

My mouth drops open, and I clap a hand to my mouth. Excuse me? I see the immediate apology in his eyes, but my shock comes off as genuine when I get teary. I mean, that's such a horrible thing to say. And he gave me the dress! Slut-shaming is harsh!

Ryder's at my elbow, bristling. My plan to walk towards him is no longer necessary. "Walk away now, Jacobi, before I bash you senseless," Ryder growls so that only Liam and I hear. "You don't fucking talk to her that way."

"Screw this!" Liam storms off in Ingrid's direction and it takes all my willpower to not laugh at the absurdity.

Guilt hits me when Ryder faces me, his face shining with concern as he puts his hands on my arms. "He shouldn't have said what he did. I don't love the fact that every guy is ogling you and having fantasies, but that doesn't make it right. You look beautiful." My heart flutters at his words. I fiercely recall finding him with Ingrid in bed.

"Will you just dance with me for a bit? Or stay with me. I need to think." For a moment, I worry he'll say no because he hesitates.

His hands appear to shake when he settles them on my body. Within a few seconds, though, his confidence returns. Drawing me deliberately closer, he doesn't notice the students around us or Ingrid throwing a hissy fit on the side. His warm hands brush my exposed skin, and I hear his breath hitch as his pupils dilate. My pulse goes a little crazy. I'm going to hell.

After a minute, his head presses against the side of mine. "Mira, please let me explain about last year." He whispers close to my ear, and my tummy flip flops. "Let me tell you what really happened."

My teeth clench as I avert my head. To say that I'm not affected would be a lie. Ryder, whether he's being bossy, demanding, or romantic, has always gotten to me. I'm about to say something when Liam moves abruptly.

I watch out of the corner of my eyes as Liam stands beside Ingrid, his mouth moving as if he's muttering under his breath. Ingrid is so predictable. After seeing us on the floor, a calculating look crosses her face. She engages Liam immediately, her lips curving suggestively as they talk. She's so fixated on his face that she doesn't see him slip his hand in his pocket as he clones her phone through her eternally-on Bluetooth. (There's a reason why I disable mine on my devices. Bluetooth is a hacker's friend.) He needs to keep her engaged for about five minutes. I tense when Victoria pulls on Ingrid's arm, saying something. If Victoria pulls Ingrid away, Liam will either need to follow or restart the process.

Liam interrupts the talk, gesturing with his hands to Ingrid as if he's asking for more details. She's a sucker when it comes to trashing people's reputation, and there isn't any doubt who she's talking about as she flicks her glance our way a few times.

It doesn't take long for Ryder to realize I'm distracted. He hisses when he sees Liam and Ingrid talking to each other. Stiffly, he says, "Liam would be a fool to choose Ingrid over you."

Like you did? I restrain my inner voice.

"You must… really like him. You can't keep your eyes off him," Ryder continues, his voice flat. He's rebuilding his façade of indifference.

I can't say anything – at least not yet. The song ends, and Ryder politely moves to let me go. "Not yet," I blurt, confusing the heck out of him. Liam hasn't moved away from Ingrid. She's now running her fingers over Liam's jacket lapels, glancing at my fake boyfriend through lowered lashes.

I clear my throat. "Sorry. What were you saying?"

The astonished expression is priceless, but he recovers quickly. "When did you two get together?" Ryder finally asks, and I can't tell if he's making polite conversation or if he's truly curious. It doesn't escape my notice that his hands remain at my waist.

"Um, this summer." Duh. I realize that Liam and I never established when we started dating, and it would have obviously occurred during the summer.

"How did you meet?" There's a taut intensity to his question, his fingers twitching and digging into my waist.

Oh, crap. What do I say now? "Online," I squeak nervously. Ryder tenses because it sounds shady. I can see the headlines now. *Teenage girl meets strange man in online chatroom.*

Perhaps Ryder senses my anxiety because he tries to change the subject. "Where did you go this summer? I… I looked for you."

My eyes widen. He looked for me? "I stayed with a friend." I read somewhere that the best lies are ones that are close to the truth. I turn hot and cold at the same time.

Ryder takes a deep breath. "I don't want you to hate me. I never deserved you, but I… What happened between us wasn't a lie."

Liam meets my eyes. He's done. He must see the sheer panic on my face because he walks over, Ingrid tottering behind him.

"Mira, let's go." Liam is all business now that he's cloned Ingrid's phone.

I step back as Ingrid coos, "Mira, Liam told me all about your escapades this summer with him. How naughty! You've been living with this hot boy."

Ryder freezes. "You lived with Liam this summer?"

Liam glances at Ingrid briefly. "Of course. Our relationship exploded the moment we met." A cruel glint shines in Liam's eyes as he adds, "She's fiery in bed but sweet after."

The carpet's been ripped out from under me. What is Liam implying? Ryder swallows. "You slept with him?"

"I don't see how that's any of your business," I snap, but I'm flabbergasted. I am two seconds away from killing Liam. And why do I feel so awful? The look on Ryder's face…

Ingrid runs a hand over Ryder's chest. "Leave me alone!" he practically screams at her, violently shaking her off. The look he fixes on Liam is filled with murderous rage.

"Ryder, don't!" I blurt, grabbing his arm. What's wrong with him? We're not together. He's acting like he has a claim to me. "Whatever this is, just stop. You have Ingrid and your stupid title. I've moved on."

Connor, Celeste, Nate, and Xander surround us uneasily while Ingrid gloats as Ryder unravels.

Ryder reels back like I've sucker-punched him. His eyes are filled with anger, pain, and confusion.

Liam wraps an arm around me possessively. "Come on, making up is always sweeter when you're in this mood."

What the hell?! I don't get a chance to respond as Connor and Xander catch Ryder before he punches Liam again.

Liam ignores my death ray glare, dragging me to his car.

Celeste mouths *call me* when I glance back. I know Liam wants to check if the cloning worked, but he just told the school that I slept with him this summer. I never even saw him shirtless!

"For a guy who cheated on you, he sure acts like he wants you," Liam muses in the car.

"I am going to rip your balls off!" I seethe. "How about you warn me before you tell people we had sex?"

Liam winces. "Sorry. I had to tell Ingrid something to keep her interest. It just came out."

I can barely speak. "You owe me ice cream, chocolate, and a whole tower of Red Bull!" I bury my head in my hands. "I swear, this better be worth it. Because I'm not doing this again! Why don't you just tell people we're having a baby?!"

Liam wisely keeps his mouth shut the rest of the evening. Helping the government blows.

011001

Despite curious messages from Celeste, I lack the energy to respond. The worst part? I feel guilty. As I grip my head, I relive the devastation on Ryder's face. I can't focus.

Liam messages me that everything went well, and he'll update me on Monday when he picks me up for school. Meanwhile, our mysterious RatGh0st has gone strangely quiet. I wish I had the energy to dig more, but I'm so exhausted from the drama that I consider taking a long nap.

My phone rings and Connor's face flashes across the screen. Groaning inwardly, I debate not answering, but I find myself pushing the green button.

I don't get a word out before Connor blurts, "Mira, I need you to come over."

I hesitate because Connor sounds worried, almost panicked. "What?" I ask stupidly.

"Look, I know you hate Ryder, but I'm freaking out over here. I've never seen him like this." His words grow distant like he's holding the phone away to check on something. "I think... Mira, I think Ryder needs you. He won't calm down, and I don't know what to do. I didn't want to say anything last night in front of Celeste because she's borderline homicidal with respect to Ryder, but he's barely holding it together at school. And now, I think he's falling apart. I'm worried."

What does Connor expect me to do?

As if he can hear my thoughts, Connor says, "Mira, I don't understand what he was doing with Ingrid, but I do know one thing. He's crazy about you. He searched for you frantically all summer. When Celeste told me you were back, I mentioned it to Ryder. He left to find you before I could stop him. When he came back, he was broken, shattered. Do you know he trashed his entire room when you disappeared? He dragged his mattress out and burned it. His feelings for you were real last year, and he is not over you. As a favor to me, I think he needs to see you."

I close my eyes. "I'll be there in twenty."

I don't want Aunt Erika to drive me, but when I tell her I'm heading over to Ryder's, she gets worried. She knows the gist of why I ran months ago. "Connor is there, Aunt Erika. I'll be okay. It's something school-related." She gives me this look, shaking her head, but she doesn't stop me.

That's the thing about Aunt Erika. She tries to warn you and give advice, but she believes you have to fall to learn.

Ryder's home is a mile away, so walking isn't an issue. It gives me time to think. My emotions are all over the place. Images of his face when I caught him with Ingrid haunt me. His words sounded like every cheater's words since the beginning of time. And yet, if I had been nothing but a game, the pain on his face makes no sense. Dammit. I'm doubting myself and looking for excuses on his part. I need to hold on to my anger. There is no way I'm going to become one of those weak-kneed girls who give in the moment a guy pretends to be sorry.

Connor is outside when I arrive, pacing in the driveway. "You walked?" he asks as if he doesn't know that I don't have a car and don't have a driver's license. "Never mind." He runs his hand hastily through his hair, trying to calm himself. "Come on."

Once again, I can't help but think how lonely it must've been to grow up in this huge home with only a nanny. I may still be angry, but I have compassion for their lonely childhood.

Connor leads me down a long hall, and there's a lot of symbolism in the echoing sounds our shoes make on the floors. But our footsteps are soon joined by another sound. At first, I think it sounds like faint drums, but the tempo is uneven at times, faltering, then picking up. As it gets louder, I realize the sounds are not drums. Something hitting a mat, maybe?

I'm not prepared to see Ryder slamming his fists into a punching bag. This is not like a scene from *Rocky*. His hits are haphazard and frenzied, and he occasionally grabs the bag in exhaustion before he rages again. Shirtless, sweaty, hands wrapped but showing traces of blood, he's both savage and frantic. His breaths are punctuated by choked sounds and unintelligible words, and his body is on the verge of collapse. With a wordless sound, he collapses against the bag before falling to his knees. He groans, grabbing his head, and a strangled word escapes his lips. I think I hear my name.

"Ryder." When he freezes, I realize I've spoken. Ryder's hands, still twisted in his hair, fall to his side. When he looks at me with red-rimmed eyes, sweat dripping down his forehead, he's so unlike himself that I almost gasp. A flash of confusion, disbelief, a growing comprehension. He becomes aware of his state, of his hands, of where he is. His eyes dash from me to his cousin and then back to me.

"You're—" He breaks off, panting erratically.

I grab the first thought that enters my mind. "You said you wanted to talk to me, to tell me everything," I say evenly. "I'm here to listen." It's the truth. I am here to listen. Whatever he needs to tell me, I'm ready to know because my next steps are contingent on it. "But, before we speak, I think you should take a shower. Because you're a mess. And you stink." I say the last bit apologetically as Ryder gapes at me.

Connor helps his cousin up silently. Ryder sways, but he doesn't take his eyes off me. As they move past me, he asks, "You'll wait? You won't leave?" His hand lifts as if to touch me but hesitates. He lowers it.

I can smell the sweat, the lingering scent of alcohol, and blood. My heart cracks a little. "I'll wait, Ryder."

He searches my face, and his vulnerability floors me.

Connor directs me to a sitting room before helping Ryder up the stairs. While I wait, I ask one of the wandering people if

I could make some tea, but the woman assures me that the tea will be brought to me immediately. By the time a large pot of tea and several cups arrive, Ryder and Connor return.

"You didn't leave," Ryder murmurs in a low voice. He sounds uncertain, relieved, exhausted. If the shadows under his eyes are any indication, he could use some sleep.

At least he looks more like his usual self in his immaculate gray slacks with a fitted, long-sleeved shirt. His wet hair is combed, and he smells of toothpaste and soap. When I hand him a cup of tea, his hand trembles slightly, and he flinches when I examine his bruised and bloody knuckles.

"I can wrap those for you, Ryder," Connor says awkwardly, lifting the first aid kit he's carrying. "But I can also leave so you two can talk."

"You stay, Con," Ryder says, remaining focused on me. There's so much sadness in his gaze. "You should hear this, too, because it involves you."

That surprises Connor, but he nods while looking for gauze and tape.

Ryder steps towards me, and when I sit abruptly, he sits near me, putting his tea down so that Connor can deal with his hands. I take a sip of my drink, aware of Ryder's attention. Maybe I have something on my face.

Finally, when Connor is done, Ryder speaks again. "Will you... I don't even know where to begin." Taking a deep breath, he tries again. "Do you remember your favorite memory with your mom? The basketball game?" When I nod, he swallows. "I was there, too. I saw you before you came to RBA."

My jaw drops.

"I should start at the beginning. My father and I have a – contentious relationship. He believes in the whole adage 'spare the rod, spoil the child.' Ethan forced my hand regarding Darcy, and I – was angry. I was tired of being controlled. I was... in a bad place." His throat moves with emotion. "My father dragged me on some business trip, and one night, we were invited to a basketball game. We were in this suite above everyone, and my life felt empty and meaningless. And then, on the screen, a birthday message." Ryder closes his eyes as he relives the memory. "When the camera focused on you, I felt something. Most girls wouldn't want to be with their parents on their sixteenth birthday, but I could see your connection with your mom. I could see that light in your eyes. For a moment, I was happy."

My hand covers my mouth to prevent my sound of surprise from escaping.

Ryder's eyes open. "I felt something the moment I saw you. It sounds crazy, but I dreamed about you. I planned to find you after I graduated from RBA. And yes, I know how creepy that sounds."

Is it bad that I don't find it creepy? His reaction when I first met him now makes sense.

Ryder pauses to examine his wrapped hands. "Last summer, Erin reached out on Discord. She created the site long before she realized Ethan had no intention of dating her. Erin loves toying with and manipulating people. I was still bitter about Ethan's actions, so when I learned about a cousin, I was game. No one knew his cousin's name or anything except that she would be attending RBA. I said what Erin wanted to hear, what Ingrid wanted to hear. My whole existence would be meaningless until I graduated. Who cares what kind of monster I became at RBA? Redemption would come when I found *you*." His laugh is bitter. "And you end up being Ethan's cousin. You stood before me. Flesh and blood. Ethan would have told you stories. You weren't supposed to see me like this: cruel, petty, arrogant. You were supposed to meet me after I'd left my past behind. You were... fragile from your mother's death. And yet, I could still see your light." He shudders. "Erin and Ingrid were watching so I tried to act the way they expected. I worried that Erin would send Cage or Arthur after you. So, I lied; I told everyone that I would use you to get to Ethan. I planned to play the game and protect you. But Ingrid was suspicious. She tried to scare you in the pool. It was a warning to me that if I didn't deal with you, she and Erin would take over. I did my best to convince her that you weren't important, but then Connor took an interest. When Connor gave you his jersey... I lost it."

That's an understatement. I bite my lip to hold the words in.

"I didn't know," Connor says.

"I can't explain my rationale. Connor isn't like me. He's – kinder. The thought of losing you to him... I'd never experienced jealousy like that before. I lashed out. I – I wasn't thinking clearly. There was so much going on, and I—" Ryder closes his eyes. "When you turned Connor down, I took the opening to make my move. I hoped Erin would think I was playing her game, but when Ingrid saw us at the winter dance, she saw through my lies. Ingrid told me some bullshit about your mother, but when I laughed at her, she threatened to show you the site. She threatened to tell my father and have him come after you. With how much Ethan detested me, I knew the Discord site would ruin any feelings you had for me. So, I pulled away. But Erin still wanted vengeance. She sent Daniel after you. I knew my actions would get back to Erin and Ingrid, but I couldn't keep pushing you away if it meant losing you forever. I just had to keep you safe from the other Royals. But I got careless. I should've known Erin and Ingrid wouldn't give up without a fight. I know Ingrid was the one who orchestrated you being on the roof. Mira, I believed you, but I couldn't tell you why. When I confronted Ingrid, she confessed her involvement. I almost hit her." Ryder opens his eyes and looks directly at me. "That's when Ingrid showed me the photos of Celeste." Connor makes a sound. "Con, Celeste got involved in some sexting dare her freshman year. Daniel had the pics and Ingrid threatened to send them to your parents."

Connor's lips thin. Rubbing his neck, he explains, "My parents aren't much better than my dear uncle. They hate scandal. They wouldn't hesitate to yank me out of here and throw me in a boarding school in England."

"Right before the party – before everything fell apart – my father came back to confront me. He heard that I was involved with a girl with no fortune. He—" Ryder breaks off, anger flushing his face. "He was furious. But I was done hiding. You deserved the truth: Discord, Erin, Ingrid, my father. I wanted you to know what was going on so we could protect Connor and Celeste together. But you didn't show up at the party. Ethan said you were sick. I thought a day wouldn't matter, but in the morning, before I could leave, Ingrid showed up." Revulsion fills his face.

Ryder stands, pacing with nervous energy. "She has pictures of you, Mira, from the girls' locker room. On top of that, she has old pics of your mom on her phone. Your mom is young, so this was probably before you were born. She's in – compromising positions with Ingrid's father. Ingrid wanted to post them publicly and I panicked. I couldn't let her do that. Not after what had happened to you. Not after I failed to protect you. I never deserved you anyway. If it meant she wouldn't hurt you again... Everything that happened to you was my fault." Ryder licks his lips. "She promised to delete everything if I – if I... She wanted sex in return. I don't know what I was thinking... I just – I was so damn desperate. You could've died on that roof. And Connor... I didn't want Ingrid to have that power over Connor."

Disgust spurs me to speak. "Ryder, that isn't sex. That's rape," I state harshly.

Connor is pale. "So, you slept—"

"I didn't!" Ryder snaps, pushing his damp hair back. He immediately deflates, his voice growing weary. "I would do anything to protect you, Mira, but I couldn't do it. When she touched me and kissed me, it was too much. I was about to tell Ingrid when you came in and saw us. Saw me." His dark blue eyes are bright with unshed tears. "The disgust on your face. The way you looked at me." He exhales heavily, looking up at the ceiling like he can't continue. "That's it. That's everything. I can't ask you to forgive me for being stupid, but... your hate and indifference. I can't handle that."

Flabbergasted. No, that word isn't strong enough to describe how I feel. Shocked, stunned, really creeped out by Ingrid. I'm also glad that I waited on my whole revenge thing. But first things first. I walk to Ryder and wrap him in my arms. My actions aren't from pity – he would reject pity. I hold him because of the simple compassion humans should have for one another. I don't want him to clarify what he's implying with his words – at least, not until I have a plan in motion.

"Don't. Don't toy with me," he whispers, his body taut with pain and tension, but he doesn't fight my touch.

"Ryder. This isn't your fault." I make him look at me. "I believe you." How could I not? His pain is palpable, plus Connor is right there. It explains the push-pull relationship we had last year. I can't even begin to contemplate Ingrid's actions. To force someone like that... It's wrong. I don't know the details of Ryder's relationship with his father, but it doesn't take a genius to realize that Ryder grew up without parental love.

I remember the heated words I threw at Ryder when he tried to talk to me and cringe inwardly. Pictures of my mom. Pictures of Celeste. Pictures of me. The Discord site. The devastation on Ryder's face. It's a lot to process.

My relationship with Liam isn't real. It's a means to an end, but I can't disavow the relationship without talking to Liam first. "I don't hate you, Ryder. I never hated you."

Ryder shudders, leaning into me. "Mira," he murmurs, burying his face in my hair. The way he says my name...

"I'll just give you two a minute."

I twist in Ryder's arms. "Wait, Connor. Who do you trust at school, Ryder? If Ingrid's been blackmailing people..." I let my words dangle.

Ryder thinks. "None of the Royal girls. I trust Xander and Nate. They both know how I feel about you. I know Xander sounded like a sleazeball, but he wrote most of that because I asked him to. Nate sided with Ethan early on. Other than Celeste and Connor, I don't trust any of the Court members. Ingrid's slept with most of the guys. Daniel Jameson does most of her dirty work and she has sex with him regularly."

As I plotted my revenge, I did thorough checks on Xander

and Nate. I'm sure they're clean, even by Liam's standards. With the additional background checks I did earlier, I'm willing to trust them if Ryder and Connor trust them.

"I do not need to know Ingrid's sleeping habits. God, she's repulsive," I say, making a face. "Connor, can you get Xander, Nate, and Celeste here quickly?"

Connor nods. "Sure. I'll give you two some privacy here." Connor clearly wants to leave, so this time, I let him escape.

When Ryder tightens his hold, his eyes glowing with need, I stop him. "No. No, we can't do that," I say firmly. "I'm not angry with you and I believe you, but we need to stay focused."

I see him retreat, hiding his emotions behind the wall he constructs every day at school.

His nod is stiff. I want to tell him that I never stopped caring. But sometimes, we don't have the freedom to say what we want when we want.

011010

I text Liam to get here ASAP and to bring his laptop and one that I can use. He has a government-paid condo about ten miles away – yes, this is how our tax dollars are spent. I'm not sure if it's ritzy or not – his place in Washington was simple, clean, and neat – but very few things in this area are cheap.

Celeste arrives first, hugging me and asking me questions before I can speak. I pull her aside and talk to her quietly, stopping only when Xander and Nate appear. Xander's handsome face is puzzled when he sees me, but he and Nate surmise that something's up.

Liam, in his damn Range Rover, chooses that moment to arrive. He's a walking poster child for the FBI. Why couldn't they have picked a more "teen" car?

"What the hell is he doing here?" Xander snarls, looking over my shoulder as he spots Liam.

Ryder's façade shows signs of cracking. "No," he says to me. "No, I don't want him here, Mira."

Moment of truth. "I need you to trust me." Liam may dislike Ryder, but I need his help now that the scope of my revenge has changed. "I need you to trust me enough to tell him what you told me."

Pain. Anger. "No. Don't do this to me, Mira. Not him." The cracks grow bigger. He doesn't want to deal with Liam because he thinks Liam and I are in love.

Ryder walks back inside, Connor and Xander following quickly. Nate's lips tighten as he glares at me. "I hope you know what you're doing," he says in a disapproving tone.

Liam, wearing an annoyed pout while dragging his computer bag, walks up to me and says, "You know this is my day off, right?"

Seriously? He's on some mission to save the world and he is taking a day off? We're online all the time! We don't take days off!

He scans me, taking in the set of my mouth and anger in my eyes. He immediately collects himself. "What's going on? This is Cabot's place."

"I need your help," I whisper. "And you owe me."

Okay, I can see Liam's desire to record this moment. I never need Liam's help, so he wants to rub it in that I'm asking for a favor. I grab Liam's arm. "I want to tell Ryder the truth about us," I say, watching his green eyes widen.

"Mira," Liam says in disbelief, "please don't tell me you're one of those weak-kneed girls, melting every time the bad boy smiles at you."

I scowl before I swat him. That's a low blow calling me weak. "No. He's hurting, Liam. And I think what happened last year may not have been what it seemed."

"Was he or was he not in bed with Ingrid? And she isn't just a mean girl, Mira. She's scary. I have never met a girl so gleeful about causing people pain. She's like the nightmare mean girl."

"She's blackmailing people," I explain. "She has pictures of my mom. Not the nice kind either. And she has pics of me from the girls' locker room. She's been using that to control Ryder."

That gets Liam's attention. I see him gnaw his lip. "It'd be easier to say no if it didn't involve you," he grumbles. "But we can't trust this guy and his friends with the truth. I'm sorry."

"I trust them, Liam. The ones in there." I gesture vaguely to the mansion. "I trust Celeste and Connor. Ryder trusts Xander and Nate. We don't have to tell them you're with the government and all that."

"Ryder is now the good guy?" Liam rubs a hand across his face in frustration.

"He's being blackmailed."

"What a convenient excuse. He could just say no. This is dumb, Mira. He's messing with you. You want to tell him we're faking it? Tell him who I am? You could blow this whole thing just for a stupid crush!"

I underestimated Liam's obstinance. "I agree some of his decisions are stupid, but we are still teenagers, Liam. Just come in and listen first," I finally say, and he realizes how much restraint I'm showing.

His resistance wavers with a resigned sigh. "Fine."

When I talked to Celeste earlier, she agreed to tell her story openly. Once we're seated, she admits how Daniel got the pictures of her. She explains how she got carried away at a party and was flattered by the Court's attention. She did the pictures on a dare. She never expected Daniel to use them against her.

"How old were you?" Liam asks with a troubled expression, but he's paying attention.

"Fifteen," she says in a shaky voice. Connor rubs her shoulders.

Liam exchanges a look with me. "Mira, she was under the age of consent. There are other ways to get—"

I already know it falls under child pornography laws, but I'm trying to protect Celeste from exposure. "What if someone finds out?" I interrupt. "Her parents. Connor's parents may find out. And from what I hear, Connor's parents aren't the forgiving type. Do you want to put her through that?"

Liam exhales sharply. "Dammit, Mira, think this through. You're smarter than this."

Ryder snarls from his corner, but I raise a hand for quiet. "That's not fair and you know it. All I'm asking is for you to trust me."

Liam rests his hands on his hips. "What's his story, then?" he asks, jerking his chin at Ryder.

Ryder's blue eyes grow cold. "There are only a few people

I care about. Connor is one of them. I've been trying to keep Ingrid from going further with the pictures, but short of sleeping with her, it isn't enough."

Liam crosses to a window and stares outside blankly. "So, sleep with her. Ingrid's not bad looking. Some earplugs may be required because of her voice."

Wow. That's casual and crude. I scrunch my face in distaste and give Liam a *what the hell* gesture.

Ryder makes an angry sound, but Liam continues, "Or can't you do it? Because Ingrid wouldn't be doing this if you were satisfying her."

Xander and Connor grab Ryder before he can reach Liam. Ryder spews a slew of expletives while Xander holds him back. "Why are you being an ass?" I ask Liam, pushing on his shoulder roughly.

"If we're going to do this, I need to be sure, Angel." Liam's green eyes are serious and far older than his near twenty years. "You're going to get me in a lot of trouble." He sighs. "You screened them?" At my nod, he exhales again, looking at Ryder. "You said Connor is someone you care about. Where does Mira fit in all of this?"

Ryder stills, a hint of wildness as his eyes dart between me and Liam. For a moment, I think he's going to walk away or hide like usual. After a minute, his shoulders straighten defiantly. "I'm in love with your girlfriend," he says through gritted teeth, lifting his chin as if he expects Liam to attack him.

This is unexpected. Celeste gasps out loud, Nate and Xander elbow each other, and Connor smiles faintly.

Liam chuckles. "Is that the case?" After a second, he rests his hands on my shoulders. "Is that why you brought me here, Mira?" I shake my head. The way Liam tilts his head tells me he's come to a decision. "If you think you're a threat to me, Cabot, you're wrong. And you are definitely not in love with my girlfriend."

Ryder's lips thin. I wait for Liam to finish his thoughts. Liam opens his backpack and hands me a laptop. As he does this,

Liam continues calmly, "You're not in love with my girlfriend because Mira's not my girlfriend."

The room explodes into questions and shouts as I hold the laptop dumbly in my hands. Ryder's in shock.

"You win, Mira, like always." There's no bitterness to Liam's voice, just resignation. "I guess we're doing this, but we need to find a way to deflect it from me. From both of us. I want safeguards in place, Angel."

I huff, but Ryder shouts above the din. "What the hell does that mean? Mira's not your girlfriend?" Ryder shakes Xander's hand off, and he surges forward.

Liam sits down, not bothering to glance up. "Mira and I are friends. Friends *without* benefits, I should add." He turns his laptop on. "This is your play, Angel. What do you need first?"

"Wait, wait, wait!" Celeste practically screams, stomping her foot. "You guys have been acting like lovebirds since school began!" Her small frame rounds on me.

Nate shakes his head in confusion. "So, you two are faking it? Why?"

I perch myself at the end of a table, accessing my files remotely. "We'll need to install something that works on phones, Liam. Destroying the operating system or installing a variant of a ransomware is easiest."

Liam grumbles, oblivious to everyone else. "Easiest? Different operating systems for different phones, Angel. And we need to make sure they aren't backed up in the cloud." He sighs. "Where was I? Oh, right. We were pretending because I planned to help Mira complete her revenge by destroying your lives online. It allowed us to spend a lot of alone time without questions being asked."

"Wait, what?" Xander blurts.

"Be glad we waited," I add. "I mean, you won't believe the things I had planned for you, Xander. Disappearing homework, college applications sent awry, emails not received, nasty social media posts."

Ryder briefly fists his hair before grabbing the laptop

from my hands and handing it to Connor. "We need to talk now," he snaps, slinging me over his shoulder.

Really?

"What the –?" I never finish my expletive because Ryder hauls me to the kitchen, unceremoniously dumping me on the counter. He corners me with both hands and places his face inches from mine.

Ryder breathes heavily. "I am very close to losing my shit, Mira, so you have a minute to explain to me what the fuck is going on between you and Liam!"

I frown at his language. How confusing can it be? "Wow, very Neanderthal-like, Ryder." I pat his shoulder placatingly. "Liam's a hacker. Like me."

"Like you? What are you talking about?"

Shrugging, I say, "I tinker around with stuff online." When Ryder continues to look confused, I ask, "Can I trust you? Like really trust you?"

Ryder's pupils dilate. "I'd do anything for you, Mira. I hurt you before. I know that, and I know I screwed up. I won't do anything to hurt you deliberately again. You can trust me. Even if you need me to keep things from Connor."

Reality check. Why should I trust him? A more accurate question would be why do I trust him? Instinct. Because he's vulnerable. Because he's in love with me. That last bit will take some time to process. "Liam's not really a student. He works for the government, and he's here working on something."

Ryder swears softly. "Is this like *21 Jump Street* or something?"

I squeal because it's nice to know I'm not the only one who thinks that way. "It's almost exactly like that, but he isn't twenty-one," I say excitedly. "I've known Liam for a few years – you know, chat forums and all that. But you can't tell anyone that. It's complicated." Maybe I'm not the best at explaining things, but I hope Ryder gets the gist of it.

"What are you saying? That he's an agent for the government?"

I place my hand on Ryder's chest, and his eyes close at my touch. "Ryder, he's not an agent. He's part of their cybersecurity division. Something is going on in the area and someone's using the school's servers. It's complicated. He's here because it's easier to investigate if you have someone on site. It would take a while to explain everything. Let's just say he's following the money."

I make a move to leave the counter, but Ryder holds me fast. "Just to be clear," he says, a muscle twitching in his jaw, "you're not with that dipshit out there. You didn't sleep with him. You didn't live with him this summer."

"Correct. Correct. Wrong. I crashed at his place for the summer," I say, "but he was a perfect gentleman. The first time he kissed me was when you punched him." I make a face. "We've cuddled and gotten handsy but only in public."

Ryder grips the counter so hard that I'm surprised his hands don't start bleeding. "You didn't sleep with him," he repeats to me, relief in his face. After two steadying breaths, he cups my face. "Mira, I need you to be perfectly clear here. You aren't in love with that asshole out there?"

"I just told you we're friends. I mean, I love him as a friend," I say with a befuddled look. "Why are you–?"

Ryder kisses me, cutting off my words. I shouldn't want him – at least, not so suddenly – but I've never exerted common sense when it comes to Ryder. I kiss him back. When he groans against me, I break away. "Does this mean—?" Ryder stops and closes his eyes briefly. "I just announced to everyone in that room that I'm in love with you."

I bring his forehead to mine as his thumbs stroke my cheeks gently. "You can't take it back. I have witnesses."

He huffs at me. "I don't care who knows. Maybe that means I'm whipped. I don't care. I don't care if it means there's a chance for me. For us."

When he tries to kiss me again, I hold him back. "We have to be careful, Ryder. We don't know what else Ingrid has. We can't do anything until we're sure those pictures are destroyed."

His voice grows husky. "And after that… Once you fix my mess, do I get another chance? Because if you're not with Liam, then I'm not giving up. Please give me another chance."

"If it hadn't been me… If Ethan's cousin had been someone else, would you have gone through with the bet?"

Ryder's pained silence is answer enough. "I don't know, Mira. I'm not going to lie and say no with any level of certainty. I don't deserve you, but I want to. You make me want to be a better person. I-I don't want to lose you."

"Then don't put me on a pedestal. I'm not an angel. I'm not perfect." Our eyes meet, and I wonder if my feelings for him ever went away. "And I don't want to lose you either."

● ● ●

"Before you two disappear again, can we finish the plan first?" Liam is snarky, his eyes taking in the way Ryder lingers by my side. He cocks a brow at me. I flip him off.

Connor and Celeste snicker between themselves while Xander shakes his head in disbelief.

"Remember Echo? Modify the program." My flippant request doesn't sit well with Liam.

"Oh, gee, Angel, that won't take long," Liam says sarcastically. "You know I'll need a few weeks to do all that."

"Stop whining," I snark right back at him. "It's not like I haven't pulled all-nighters to help you."

Celeste and Connor look at me in a new light. Even Nate regards me differently. "I've never seen you like this before," Connor observes. "And why does he call you 'Angel' all the time?"

Liam chuckles. "She calls herself Arch4ngel101, but she's a terror when she works against you. I find it funny to call her Angel." He scrunches his face. "Mira is probably the best hacker I know. She can deconstruct code faster than anyone."

"So, what's the plan then?" Ryder asks, running his hand down my arm before entwining our fingers.

I start adding things in my head. "Halloween is two weeks away," I begin. Liam's eyes grow huge. "Oh, don't be a baby. You've pulled off more in less time before." I smile at Nate and Xander, enjoying the way they get nervous at my scrutiny. "Time to earn your keep. Start a rumor that all is not well between me and Liam. In the meantime, I will infiltrate their computers so that I can wipe their systems once we have their phones under control. At the Halloween party, we'll need to separate Ingrid, Judy, and Victoria from their phones. And Daniel, too."

"If you ask me to seduce Ingrid, I'm going to have issues," Liam drawls, typing on his laptop. Xander is befuddled like he can't understand how Liam doesn't care that Ryder walked off with me. "Mira, your rootkit, can it be modified quickly?"

"I was planning on sending it out to all the Royals to infiltrate their computers, but I guess we can spare the guys. Modifying it isn't difficult." I check to see that Liam has a copy of my program.

Ryder, Xander, and Nate exchange uneasy looks at my words. Liam smirks. "Don't worry, she won't destroy you guys now."

"That's how you knew the videos were fake," Celeste says slowly. "You got into the school's network."

I don't deny it. "Whoever Ingrid used is good." I pause. "Not as good as me, I know how it was done."

Liam rolls his eyes. "Angel, no one is as good as you. That's why everyone wants you. The Halloween party is on campus, right?" Liam asks. When Celeste tells him yes, he asks me, "Is there a chance there are cameras where the party will be?"

"There are, but no one monitors the feed," I tell him. "I can glitch them so it doesn't record anything in the building for an hour. I don't want it to be obvious, though, in case whoever Ingrid used takes a look."

Liam observes me with narrowed eyes. "Are you telling me there's a person who's better at this than you?"

My pride flares. Dammit. I hate being challenged like

that. "No, dumbass. Fine. I'll loop in a false feed. All I'm saying is we need to be careful." I scowl at Liam, who tilts his head back and howls.

"Are you really that good?" Ryder asks me.

I'm no longer shy about what I can do. "Yes. I am."

• • •

Ryder drags me away for some privacy. "I wish you could pull this off sooner," he murmurs, holding my hands. "You're mine, Mira." He gives me a cocksure smile.

He's so arrogant that I consider making him squirm. "Maybe."

"Maybe? How do I make that a certainty? Do you forgive me? Can you?" Some of his worry fades when I smile. "I burned everything she touched."

"Ryder, what Ingrid tried to do wasn't right. I might be angry with your decisions, but I could never hold them against you. You've been hurt enough." I pause. I want to talk about his father, but I decide to wait. "I do forgive you, Ryder."

Relief floods his body. "Whatever you're doing for Liam – it doesn't put you in danger, does it?"

I shake my head. "No, I'm just working on the periphery. They have real people to handle the dangerous stuff."

"I hope so." He hesitates. "Mira, promise me you'll be safe."

I nod absentmindedly. Honestly, what could happen? It's why I like working behind the scenes. Do all the work, miss all the drama.

"It's going to be a lousy month," he grumbles. "And tell Liam that I'll break his nose if he touches you again. I'm dead serious. The way he kissed you at the party… Once this is behind us, I'll do whatever it takes to make things right between us. My summer was hell." He pauses. "Liam made no moves on you all summer?" Ryder tilts my head so that he can see my eyes.

"He had an extra bedroom. He was incredibly polite. I

never even saw him with a shirt off. Besides, I spent a great deal of time crying in my room."

Sadness crosses his face. "I'm sorry I did that to you." Ryder drops a lingering kiss on my lips. "Just so you know, you can see me with my shirt off anytime you want. Or anything else off, for that matter."

I swat his arm. "Behave."

His mood lightens further. "Next summer, for my birthday, I'm taking you somewhere." His body is warm and relaxed against me.

"I missed your birthday? I didn't get you anything," I say with dismay.

He cups my cheek. "You've given me everything."

011011

Nate and Connor begin the rumor treadmill by telling the Court Liam and I had a massive fight after Ingrid's party. Celeste tells Victoria Little that she's sure I dumped Liam. Xander tells Judy Lee that he heard Liam broke up with me after he saw Ryder dancing with me. Celeste then tells Connor while Daniel Jameson is eavesdropping that I've been crying in my room, heartbroken. Ryder, per plan, pretends to not care. (Obviously, this is a twisted version of the game Telephone.)

Whether Ingrid believes Ryder is irrelevant. Since his actions during the party are telling, there's no point in trying to spin the narrative. Instead, Ryder continues to be sullen and resentful. Liam, on the other hand, relishes his new role. It takes a few tips from Xander and Nate to teach Liam how to come across as frustrated and upset. This is not easy since Liam learned his lines from role-playing games. Liam is nothing but determined. When Victoria flirts with him in the hallway, he fluctuates between vague interest and uncertainty. And during lunch, Liam and I sit together but ignore each other.

Amidst all this fake drama, I spoof Ingrid's school account to send emails to certain students. Guys will click on anything that looks like it might contain salacious pictures. I clear minor members of the Court first. Most of them are only guilty of following Ingrid blindly anyway. I spend some time going through Ingrid's files. After I saw the Discord site, I stopped snooping which was a mistake. This time, I find the files I should've looked for originally. I transfer copies and then set up a virus that will wipe her system completely when triggered. Of course, I remember her cloud storage. I stop the backup storage, delete everything on her cloud, and create a fake pathway to make her think she's backing up files to the cloud.

Ingrid has a few email accounts attached to her name. Her private account is primarily used to contact her father – most teens don't really use email anymore, but parents still do. Still, it's weird for a teen to email this much. And there's something odd about her emails with her father. At the bottom is what looks like random letters in the shape of a box. But the letters vary from message to message. It could be a cryptogram. I send a copy of the files to Liam. RReagan can use his guys to break the code. I'm still in high school and don't have time for that.

Judy and Victoria don't seem to have anything on their laptops – I still plan on wiping their phones – but since Liam's cloned Ingrid's phone, we know they're aware of the incriminating photos. I plan to be thorough about destroying any backups. We'll decouple the phone from the service provider before rewriting the operating system.

During my Zoom chat with Darcy and Brittany, I fill them in on what's happened. When Celeste joins us, our fifteen-minute chat goes to an hour. Brittany declares she always knew Ryder was in love with me, Darcy can't believe how evil Ingrid is, and Celeste tells us all that it was a lot more fun being in a quad than a single. Brittany plans on returning to Royal Bridge Academy in January now that we have a better sense of what happened among the Royals last year. I don't blame her for staying away, but I'll be glad to have another friendly face.

Because Darcy gives Ethan the gist of what transpired, I'm left with filling in the blanks. He's still hurt and angry I was targeted, but I know that deep down what Ethan feels is guilt. If he hadn't chosen Darcy over Erin, if he hadn't strong-armed Ryder, if he hadn't forced his will on everyone. It's easy to dwell on 'what ifs,' but doing so keeps you trapped in the past. (Yes, I learned that during therapy.)

Even though Ryder keeps his distance at school, he doesn't seem to think that applies to weekends. I barely have time to explain everything to my aunt and uncle – Uncle Robert is not as forgiving – before Ryder shows up on Saturday. He refuses to leave until my aunt and uncle allow him in. It's agreed that Ryder can visit me on the weekends if I keep my bedroom door open. When Uncle Robert *casually* walks by my room, neither Ryder nor I believe his "looking for a book" story.

"I wasn't going to tell you about the basketball part," Ryder admits to me the weekend before Halloween. He runs his hand along the back of my calf to my knee and then back again. Ryder has this thing for my legs. When I look at him curiously, he smiles wryly. "Honestly, I thought you would freak." He goes on his hands and knees to crawl towards me. "Ryder Cabot, student of RBA, stalker of young girls at basketball games." He brings his face close to mine.

I brush his hair back. I love the way it falls across his forehead, giving him a mischievous air. "I wasn't even dressed to impress when you saw me."

"I only saw you," he murmurs before kissing me.

"Oh, great, you two are being cute," Liam groans, entering my room since I'm required to keep my door open. "I need you to check my code, Mira. It doesn't work."

Ryder scowls, leaning back against my headboard. "You couldn't do this remotely?"

Liam plops onto my floor, handing me his laptop. "It gets boring working alone," he whines. "Besides, we can pretend I'm trying to win my dear love back." He makes a kissy face at me.

I throw a pillow at Liam, but Ryder's eyes narrow on the other guy. "You don't care that I'm with Mira." A statement, not a question.

"What is it you want to know, Cabot?"

"Your actions towards her looked real." There's a veiled threat in Ryder's words. I know he's trying to get a handle on his jealousy, but he doesn't have to interrogate every boy I know.

"Ryder, just because you're attracted to me doesn't mean

other guys are," I protest, rolling my eyes.

Liam's jaw tightens faintly. "I find her attractive, but she's still in high school. I was a complete gentleman when she showed up at my doorstep in tears. Acting on that would've been morally reprehensible." That's Liam for you. Noble dork at heart. "I value her friendship far more than her potential as girlfriend material."

Ryder averts his eyes for a moment. "I'm still trying to accept that," he says reluctantly.

"Oh, I found what's wrong!" I squeal, startling them. When they look at me, I smile sheepishly. "Sorry, I'll just fix it. It's easier than explaining."

Liam lies down on my floor, closing his eyes. "You know, Mira, when this is over, I'll be glad. Being a high school kid sucks."

I push the laptop away, and Ryder reaches over to pull me onto his lap. "Do you think the old guy will notice if we make out on your bed?" Ryder asks.

Liam groans. "Oh, for God's sake. I heard that."

• • •

As the Halloween party approaches, I run through the plan with everyone. I've adapted USB keys to connect to the phones. It'll take a few minutes to download the application, so we need to keep our targets distracted.

Our targets are the three Royal girls and Daniel Jameson. All three girls use Apple phones. The program will do a complete wipe. The process is no different from what happens when a phone is refurbished. Once that's done, I can proceed with unleashing the viruses. Daniel gets a special program since his phone is Android-based. Liam and I tinker with a ransomware program. These programs often work by using a simple popup so you can't see your apps. We're going to use that lovely popup to hide what is happening behind the scenes. We alter a few things so that his screen will be blocked, his files will be encrypted, and it will sync it as-is to the cloud. As for the Discord site? That's been shut down for a while.

Remember how I made copies of Ingrid's photos of my mom? I set the pictures aside for now. One problem at a time.

⦿11100

It's agreed the Royal boys will show up at the party together. Liam will go solo, while I'll show up with Connor and Celeste. Last year, my mask was white. This year, my mask is of black lace. My hands tremble a little as I slip the gown on. If all goes well, there will be one less thing to deal with.

I haven't forgotten that I came back to RBA to help Liam with his mission. Yes, even as I think it, the absurdity of the word strikes me. But I have no other way to describe it. And I'm still trying to find out if I can learn anything about my father. And what made Mom leave?

My floor-length gown is made of lace-embroidered tulle with a tulle overlay in soft gray. It has a bateau neckline with a plunging V illusion, so it's a bit sexy without being overly revealing.

Connor helps Celeste with her mask. "I feel like I'm in a *Mission Impossible* movie," he remarks, glancing at me with a smile. "You with your secretive computer talents and all that."

Celeste winks at me. "Maybe we should have undercover names like Boris and Doris."

Connor groans, shaking his head, but then he gives me a serious look. "I never thanked you for coming over that day. For giving Ryder that chance."

I bite my lip. I haven't talked to Ryder about his father yet. I plan to, but I want Ingrid neutralized before I cover that with him.

"Remember when Ryder and I fought over you last year?"

Connor glances warily at Celeste as he brings the topic up.

Cautiously, I nod as Celeste grows quiet.

"I knew then that he was crazy about you. Around Thanksgiving, I found his sketches of you, and I realized that anything I might have felt for you paled in comparison to what he was feeling for you. The strangest thing is that it didn't bother me. The only reason why I got upset at Halloween was because I felt like girls always preferred Ryder over me." He gives me a sheepish smile before looking at Celeste. "Except for one." He links their hands together. "I found the one girl who always put me first."

I let them have their lovey-dovey moment.

"Alright," I say, "let's get this party started."

• • •

Walking into the mansion, I reflect on how different I feel from a year ago. When I see Ingrid standing with Victoria and Judy, I'm no longer intimidated. Our eyes meet: hers filled with disdain, mine filled with confidence.

As if on cue, the three Royal boys enter. Ryder's careful not to glance my way. Ingrid saunters over to him, running her hand down his chest in that possessive way. She says something that causes him to frown right before he removes her hand and pushes her away. Before she can react properly, Xander is there to distract her, smiling. He flatters her, and she preens.

Victoria is first. Nate first borrows her phone to take a few pictures of the Royals together, then pulls her to a corner for an unsubtle make out session. (Nate told us earlier he was taking one for the team. Whatever.) Ryder walks by, snagging the phone and plugging in the key drive to run the program.

Liam arrives, glancing at me briefly before making a beeline for Ingrid. The gloating smile she flashes my way almost makes me laugh. Ryder returns to Nate, slipping the phone into his friend's hand. He makes a show of watching Ingrid with Liam before coming towards me and leading me to the floor.

The moment that happens, Ingrid snags Liam's hand as we predicted. Nate and Victoria join us with Xander and Judy. That's Celeste's and Connor's cue to act.

Judy's phone is an easy target – she takes a purse wherever she goes. While Connor blocks Celeste from being seen, she slips her hand into Judy's purse to grab the phone and attaches the drive while everyone is focused on the dancers.

Ingrid's displeasure is obvious, frowning every time Liam spins her. Ryder's done acting, though. He holds me close enough for students to whisper, his eyes on my face, his lips curved in pleasure as we brush against each other. I should remind him that we're supposed to wait until *after* I wipe the phones, but YOLO.

When the song is over, Celeste and Connor link their arms together, telling me Judy's phone is done. Two down, two to go.

Ryder brushes his lips against my temple as Ingrid approaches us, Liam trailing observantly. "Ryder, you forget yourself," she snaps.

Ryder's face hardens. "I haven't forgotten," he sneers. "You've forgotten that I'm the King."

"I'll end you," she hisses. "You know what I can do."

Now it's Liam's turn. Whatever he whispers in Ingrid's ear causes her to smile. She willingly lets him pull her away. Xander meets them halfway, and the three disappear together. I don't want to know exactly how they part Ingrid from her phone, but half an hour later, Xander reappears and winks at me.

Connor, Ryder, Nate, and Xander grab Daniel Jameson roughly and carry him into a hallway. There are no niceties – at this point, they just want to be done with this charade. Minutes later, Nate leaves, holding Daniel's phone in his hand. By the time Daniel reappears with a bruised eye and a bleeding lip, Nate's done and hands Daniel's phone back to him with a cold smile.

Celeste and I walk to the restroom so I can extricate my phone without anyone noticing. I execute the programs with

Celeste clutching my arm.

"Free," she whispers. "It worked, right?"

I smile at her. "Yes, I'm certain of it."

• • •

Returning to the dance, Ryder, Xander, Nate, and Connor look at me anxiously. Oh, ye of little faith. I know I have a confident little jaunt to my steps – it's the same walk I did when Liam and I were at the hackathon in March. It'd be too soon for anyone to notice their non-functional devices – on the outside, it would look like the phone was having technical difficulties, rebooting several times before shutting down – or their wiped computers.

Liam winks, doing his best to hide that arrogant smile he gets when he pawns another hacker, before leaving to work on his *other* project. I know everything has gone as planned.

Ryder isn't shy about kissing me possessively in front of the other students, even with Xander and Nate rolling their eyes, and Connor snickering. Ingrid is livid, but she can't throw her usual hissy fit because she, Judy, and Victoria realize their phones are malfunctioning. As midnight approaches, Ryder runs his hands through my hair. "Thank you," he murmurs.

My friends and I dance through the night.

☉011101

It's through the grapevine that we learn how successful the mission went. Daniel is completely shaken by his destroyed files. Ingrid tries to threaten Ryder, but when he dares her to show him proof, she backs off. Victoria and Judy walk around with paranoia plastered on their faces. (While my original plan had been to destroy them through social media, I settle for this gentler approach.)

The schism between the Royals widens. The Royal boys abandon the Royal girls, leaving most of the Court confused and clueless. While Ryder hasn't decided if he plans on retaking the Royals' table back, for now, they cluster at our table for lunch.

"I know what you said, but that doesn't mean I have to be happy about having that bully in our house for dinner," Uncle Robert grumps. Aunt Erika just told him Ryder and Connor are joining us for Thanksgiving again.

Aunt Erika shakes her coiffed head. "He and Mira are in a relationship. Be civil."

Who knew Uncle Robert would be this obstinate? But Ethan steps forward, telling his father and mother how the rivalry between him and Ryder began. It's brave to confess your mistakes. We don't tell Uncle Robert everything – not Ingrid trying to use the pictures to get Ryder to have sex, not the pictures of Mom. We keep the details high-level. The Discord site. The reason for the bet. The collection of pictures Ingrid kept on students. The only other thing to show Uncle Robert is the hackathon I won with Liam. He'd had a suspicion already – remember the videos and other evidence I found about my supposed suicide attempt? – but this cements everything. I swear Uncle Robert wants to adopt me.

Which reminds me, now that I have one thing out of the way, I need to work on my next problem. Liam's hardly around – the excuse given publicly is a family emergency – but he assures me that he'll be back in a week or so to fill me in. Apparently, there's been some "noise" in chatrooms that he's following, and I'm curious how it's linked to what we're working on.

Darcy isn't with us due to family commitments, although Ethan and I have invited her and Brittany over around Christmas, but Celeste is here because her mom is off in Rome. Instead of Aunt Erika greeting our guests, I take over the greeting duties. The way Aunt Erika and Ethan beam at me tells me how far I've come.

Ryder wraps his arms around me the moment he arrives. Once we put Ingrid behind us, Ryder hasn't held back. When I enter the classroom, he only has eyes for me. His love consumes me, and I don't mind it one bit.

I know he's been fighting with his father over the phone. Ryder doesn't like talking about his dad, but he's told me enough. A father who demands perfection. A father who keeps no mementos of Ryder's mother. A father who drags his son only to events when he needs to project an image.

Ryder doesn't want pity. He wants – and needs – the creature comfort I provide, the solace, the promise that love exists. "You okay?" I whisper.

Ryder's hand slides to grasp mine. "I am now. I'm perfect," he murmurs, some of the shadows clearing from his eyes.

Leaning against a wall, arms crossed, Ethan observes us. "All hail the king," he says, and Ryder tenses beside me. The two haven't talked since the incident by the pool. While Ethan doesn't know about Ryder's father, and it isn't my place to say anything, I believe he knows Ryder better than most. My cousin walks over cautiously and extends his hand. "Happy Thanksgiving," he says without rancor. A peace offering. A willingness to put aside differences. This is the cousin I know and love.

A brief hesitation before Ryder accepts the hand. "I – know why you did what you did for Darcy, Ethan. I'd do the same for Mira," Ryder says, his dark blue eyes on my face. He's talking about the brutality which Ethan used to ensure he could be with Darcy. Someday, I want to know how he convinced Darcy to be with him.

A moment of understanding passes between Ethan and Ryder. It's awkward and wonderful. "Good to see you brought your swim trunks, boys," Ethan says, leading us in. With ease which I still frown at, he hands out beer and gives me a mineral water with a grin. Ryder demurs and grabs a water, nuzzling me when I look surprised.

"Well, Mira did promise hot tub, popcorn, and a round of a game called Dominion," Connor says.

I roll my eyes at Connor. "It's like one of the most awesome board games ever." I put my hands on my hips.

"But it doesn't play on a PS4 or Xbox One or anything." Connor makes a face, and I feel like I'm talking to Gaston from *Beauty and the Beast.*

My phone buzzes and I check the message.

Get online now.

Liam is usually a lot more polite when he needs my help. My brow furrows.

"Mira?" Ryder's voice cuts into my thoughts as I check groups in Slack and Discord.

Both groups I'm in are exploding with messages about a new worm hitting hospitals. I run for my laptop, bumping into my uncle in the foyer. "You know," is all my uncle says as he heads to his office.

Snagging my laptop, I call Liam. "Tell me what you know."

"Someone stole a program from Homeland Security," Liam says, and I can hear his fingers moving rapidly in the background. "Whoever took it weaponized the program. The worm hit Europe first, but it made its way to the East Coast a few hours ago."

The timing makes me wonder if they meant to cripple the US's healthcare system on Thanksgiving deliberately. "I need to see the code. Can someone send me what they have?" I ask both Liam and Uncle Robert at the same time as I walk into Uncle Robert's office. Uncle Robert is on his computer, reading messages and texting his teams.

Ethan, Ryder, Celeste, and Connor stay out of my way. I have a simulated computer environment to run such worms. "I need to go into the office," my uncle says.

I'm still on the phone with Liam, but I stop my uncle from leaving immediately. "I can help," I blurt. I don't know if I'm saying it to Uncle Robert or Liam.

My uncle hesitates before nodding. "I have my teams on it, but if you're as good as I think you are, you'll be needed. Mira, I'll call you from the office?" I nod as he gives Ethan an apologetic glance before running for his car.

"They're calling the program KillRoy," Liam tells me. "It's targeting hospitals and emergency systems hard, Mira. People are going to die."

I'm reading as fast as I can. Teams in Europe have done a fantastic job analyzing the code, so we have a head start.

"I have you on speaker, Liam," I say, looking at the code online as Ryder comes over to watch. "No ransom?" Usually attacks like this come with ransom demands.

"None so far," Liam replies. He sounds grim. "Teams in Europe have been looking for a weakness."

"I need to see more," I mutter to myself.

"Angel, sending you what we've collected in the past hour." I hear Liam bark at someone in the background. Never pegged Liam as the bossy type.

Over the next hour, various groups pull apart the code, and I'm able to visualize how sections of code function in the worm. It's a blend of programs pieced together like a jigsaw puzzle. I move Liam over to Discord where we begin a call with several other programmers we know.

Aunt Erika checks in, aware that some emergency is going on. She has food brought to us while I hunker down to work. Ethan, Connor, and Celeste eventually leave, but Ryder stays by my side, quietly watching me work.

I call Uncle Robert and his team, and we dissect what we've learned. He's already working with the government, and he's able to share with me the notes from the original program. And suddenly, the answer comes to me. Homeland Security had a line built into the code to ping a website. It was likely designed so that the worm could be triggered at will. Whoever manipulated the code either overlooked this or didn't understand it. "Hold on, everyone," I interrupt the rapid discussion. "Look at this part of the code. It has no obvious function."

Liam curses and then apologizes. "Why didn't I see that?"

"I think it's given us a way to buy time," I say, and everyone goes quiet. I give Uncle Robert the gist of what I'm suggesting. "It isn't a kill switch. It's a sinkhole," I tell them. "The worm won't do anything if it receives a ping. So, let's give it a ping. It's a way to stop the worm from proliferating and completing its program."

Someone in the background says, "Who's this girl?" Uncle Robert snaps something back, but I'm too busy to listen.

Liam's the first to respond. "I'm registering the domain name, Mira. Give me a few."

I stand up to pace, thinking. "Tell me if it works."

"I'm tracking it, I'll let you know," Liam says. "It'll take a few hours to be sure. Mr. De Vries, we'll loop your company in on the fix and get the other companies on board. We'll need everyone to cooperate to ensure this person doesn't attack the servers."

"Don't wait for me, Mira," Uncle Robert says. "I'll be home as soon as I can. I'll continue to have the teams work on this and ensure we have it stopped."

"We need to know how he managed to weaponize it so fast," I say, realizing how bossy I sound.

I sit down after I disconnect, exhaling suddenly. Ryder

approaches me slowly in amazement. "You're incredible, Mira." When I blink at him in surprise, he gently kisses me. "You're brilliant."

Suddenly self-conscious, I flush. "Can we eat now? I have a bad feeling it's going to be a long night."

•••

By the end of dinner, we know the sinkhole is working – at least, for now. If my method goes offline for any reason, the worm will proliferate; infected systems will shut down. I leave it to Uncle Robert and Liam's cohorts to find a way to keep that from happening. I want to keep my name out of the spotlight for now.

Uncle Robert sips some brandy and talks with us right before we hit the hot tub many hours later. "You seem to have an interesting assortment of friends, Mira," he says, swirling his brandy. The fireplace causes the liquid to glow in his glass.

I shrug. "I met some of them on the dark web."

My uncle curses. "How old were you when you met this Liam guy?"

"Fourteen." I wince when my uncle and Ethan start yelling at me. "I knew how to protect myself online."

Once Uncle Robert calms down, he addresses me directly. "You have a gift, Mira. I don't think I need to tell you how extraordinary you are."

Embarrassed, I shuffle a bit, but Celeste grabs my arm and says, "I always knew you were special. And you're right. It's not about money. It's about who controls the net." She wrinkles her nose. "I hope I said that right."

Connor chuckles with affection, nudging her into his arms. Ryder holds me from behind, burying his face in my hair. With a suspicious look, Uncle Robert asks Ryder, "And what are your intentions towards my niece, young man?"

Ethan grins while glancing at Ryder expectantly. He's enjoying my discomfiture.

I expect Ryder to look uneasy or squirm, but he returns my uncle's gaze calmly. "I love your niece, Mr. De Vries. Before you tell me we're too young, I'm aware that I'm eighteen and Mira is a month away from turning eighteen. I made some terrible mistakes, and I understand why you dislike me. I promise you that I will never take Mira for granted. Her family is important to her, which means that you all are important to me. I won't leave her unless she wants me to." The arm around my waist tightens. "I want a future with her. A permanent one."

My uncle spews his brandy while I gape. Okay, we have not talked about getting married or anything like that! But Ryder's face remains calm and sure. "And what if I say no?" I ask pointedly.

Ethan grumbles, "You're such an arrogant prick, Ryder."

Ryder closes his eyes briefly. "If you say no..." When he opens them, there's a fierce determination staring down at me. "I'll persuade you."

Celeste leans over to Connor. "I can't tell if that's borderline stalkerish or super-hot," she says.

"It's both," I reply, and yet, I confess it doesn't bother me. Ryder's lips tilt down for a moment at my comment.

My uncle stands and yawns. "Well, I'm going to bed since I suspect I'll need to be on my toes this weekend. There's the possibility of a DDoS attack while we work on security patches. Ethan, don't let that boy kidnap your cousin and marry her overnight. When I'm more alert, I'll grill him further."

I jerk free from Ryder. "It was too easy," I suddenly say. My uncle looks at me in surprise. "The worm was too easy to stop."

"I wouldn't say that," Uncle Robert begins.

But now I'm sure of it. "I would." The way the worm was put together, the way it proliferated... It was both clumsy and elegant. It did several billion dollars in damage, but we were able to mitigate it within hours. The loophole wasn't overlooked. It was deliberately left behind.

My eyes are clear when I repeat, "It was too easy. I don't think this was the real attack. I think it was a trial run."

⊙11110

I'm flipping through Mom's last journal when Ryder stops by on a weekend. We're a week away from the Winter Ball, and I'm about to send my special packet of files out to knock Ingrid down. It might just topple the Queen altogether.

He curls up next to me. "Did I freak you out when I told your uncle about my imagined future with you?" His tone is deliberately casual when I put the journal down.

I consider the question carefully. "No. But I'm not ready to get married or anything. You know that, right?"

His deep blue eyes are serious. "I do." When I'm quiet, he says, "My life is connected to yours, Mira. You're worth the wait." He brushes his fingers over the leather edges of the journal. "Your mother's?"

"Yes. Been trying to get some insight into her personality before she became a mom." I start flipping the pages aimlessly. Then I stop. I thought she never finished her last journal. Only the first twenty pages or so are filled. But as I flip through, I note that she started writing again three-fourths in. She deliberately left a slew of blank pages in between the older dates.

Ryder senses that I've found something important as I start on the first page in the new section. The date makes it clear that it takes place a year before I was born.

I hesitate to write this, but I have no one else to share this information with. I can't tell Erika. She just had a baby. Father is upset because I "blew" my chances with E. I wish I never had to see

E again. But I can't separate myself from seeing E because it means I may never see SJ.

I stop, glancing at Ryder. "I think E is Ernest Whitman," I whisper, my face a tad pale.

Ryder swallows. "Obviously, like father like daughter," he says with distaste. "But who is this SJ?"

I continue reading.

Father would never approve of SJ, so our relationship remains a secret. SJ thinks that once the money starts rolling in, Father will approve of him, but I'm not so sure. My father is a racist – I am sure of it. I know Erika and R would protect me, but I don't want to involve them in my drama. For now, everything is secret. I have a secret.

I flip the page and note a tiny square wedged deep between the sheets. I wiggle it free. It's about the size of a passport photo. It's old and the quality isn't great. It's a picture of three men, one of whom is Asian. I would guess the man is Korean.

Ryder frowns. "That guy in the middle. It might be Ernest when he was young. I've seen pictures of him."

"What if that guy next to him is my father?" I query. "I mean, this is the first picture I've seen that has a possible candidate."

Gently caressing my cheek, Ryder urges me to look at him. "I'll help you. We'll do this together and find out who that man is. If it's important to you, then it's important to me."

"Someday you'll need to explain why you like me so much," I mumble, tucking my hair back.

"I'd be happy to show you," he says back to me with a wicked grin.

He laughs when I roll my eyes at his corny line, but he stops when I lean in to kiss him.

• • •

"How did you do it?" Daniel screams at our table the following Monday, his eyes frantically jumping from Nate to Xander to Connor to Ryder. Considering they jumped him at the Halloween party, he's aware they're responsible for the wipe. He's been harassing Nate since, but he seems to have hit a breaking point.

I deliberately keep my eyes down as Ryder stands up. "Get out of here, Jameson. You're filth. You come near any of my people again and what we did to you on Halloween will look like child's play," Ryder snarls.

Daniel's ready hyperventilate. "The wipe was good. The virus on the computers. Who did you fucking hire?! The virus was custom. And what you did to the phones!" He's shrieking now. "I need to know who you used!"

I pretend to munch on chips, but a side glance at Liam tells me that he's bothered by Daniel's words. We both suspect there's someone here with some skill – how else would a mock account been created – and Daniel's description indicates more than a cursory knowledge.

"And you," Daniel says to Liam. "You and Mira broke up, but now you're sitting here like friends. So, you played us! You played Ingrid. Was it you?"

That's too close to the truth. I clamp down on the flare of panic.

"You know that I can hire the best money can buy," Ryder croons, stepping towards Daniel. Xander and Nate join him and all three Royal boys circle Daniel. Before anyone moves, Ryder punches Daniel in the stomach. "That's for all the girls you terrorized with your perversions. That's for touching my girl. Get out of my sight or I will break you right here."

Ingrid, at the nearly empty Royal table, watches with narrowed eyes as Daniel stumbles, fleeing the cafeteria. Except for that one shouting match with Ryder, she hasn't spoken to him since. Judy and Victoria mutter angrily, but Ingrid's gaze is directly on me. She still hates me, but now there is a darkness as she gazes at everyone at our table.

• • •

I'm not done with Ingrid. Not by a long shot. With access to her social media accounts, I compile a list of all the mean things she's done. This includes carefully redacted screenshots of her blackmail attempts, her bullying of friends and enemies alike, the list of boys she's slept with – this one is a doozy – and copies of her emails.

On top of this, I locate the messages she sent to Daniel where they spliced images and hacked the video feed the night I was thrown onto the roof. I even find the original video. This isn't even the worst of it. Her computer, before my virus, was a treasure trove of horrors: sex tapes, audio recordings, etc. I won't allow the sex tapes to go public. I don't keep any copies.

After compiling it into a neat little package, minus sex tapes, I spoof Daniel's email account and send the file to the school. I do this on a lovely Friday afternoon to ensure students have all weekend to stew.

☉11111

Since the email goes out without me alerting anyone, most of the immediate reactions come via text messages.

Celeste: *OMG. I think Victoria just peed in her pants in the parking lot.*

Xander: *School accounts are flooding with demands that Ingrid be expelled.*

Darcy: *I wish I could see this in person.*

Ryder: *That was beautiful.*

Ryder's father is in town, but I've been told that he'll leave Saturday. I know Ryder wants to keep me as far from his father as possible, so I figure it's safe to stop by on Sunday.

Going to Ryder's home makes me sad. It's such a large place. When the butler lets me in, I consider texting Ryder to tell him I'm here but memories of the last time I arrived without warning flood me. I'm frozen until a voice breaks me out of my reverie.

"So, you're the one."

A man about Uncle Robert's age approaches me. His hair is black with fine threads of silver. You can tell a lot about a person by a smile. This man wears no smile. In fact, there is no joy about him. He walks around me like I'm a car he might buy.

"I can see why my son is fascinated by you. You're pretty," he says with a faint leer.

Creepy older men – not my thing. I don't balk or flinch as he circles me. Even without names, I'm guessing this is Ryder's father. There's a similarity in their noses and jaw, but Ryder must have inherited the wideness of his eyes from his mother.

"Mira Bell." The way he says my name I can tell he's making all sorts of internal jokes. "I'm Clark Cabot, but I'm guessing you already know that. Tell me, Mira, what exactly do you think will ever happen between you and Ryder, hmm? You think he'll inherit the Cabot fortune and give you a life of luxury?"

Ryder and Connor have told me enough about this man. "No," I say firmly. "I intend to make my own way in the world. I won't need to rely on anyone."

Ryder's father laughs mockingly. "If you think for a moment I believe you…"

"I don't expect you to," I retort. "I'm certainly not going to waste my breath trying to convince you."

"Mira!" Connor rushes into the room, his eyes filled with worry. "What are you doing here?"

"I thought Ryder would be free today." With a calm glance at Mr. Cabot, I add, "I presume I'm wrong."

"Oh no, I'm enjoying this conversation, Miss Bell," Mr. Cabot sneers. "Ryder will end his relationship with you, or I'll disown him. I won't let my family name go down the drain with trash like you! If you have any sense, you'll end things now. You think he knows anything about surviving in the world without the wealth he's become accustomed to?"

"Father!"

The tension in the room rises when Ryder enters, anger on his face. He comes to my side and I expect him to be angry with me, but he isn't.

"She's certainly easy on the eyes, son," Mr. Cabot says. "Sleep with her and be done with her or be prepared to learn how the lower classes live. I will leave you with nothing if you continue to prance around town with this harlot."

"Don't talk about her like that," Ryder says through gritted teeth. The way he avoids my eyes tells me that he's hiding something.

"Well, Miss Bell?" Mr. Cabot questions me. "He gets nothing if you stay with him!"

Here's the thing about my life. Sometimes I meet people like Ingrid, and I can't help myself. Hacking into the school and hacking her accounts – not ethical but I'm willing to do it. I wouldn't, however, go after her family's wealth or harm them in any way. Mr. Cabot makes me want to cross all the lines I won't cross. But here's the thing – there's no going back if you abuse the power you have.

"Whether or not Ryder and I are together has nothing to do with you," I reply calmly, Mr. Cabot scrunches his face in surprise. "My choice is him – not his money, not his name, and certainly not his father. The world is changing, Mr. Cabot." Ryder turns to me, lips parted. I guess he likes me claiming him.

Mr. Cabot raises his hand – whether to hit me or grab me, I never find out. Ryder's there, twisting his father's hand back with a snarl before flinging the older man to the floor. "Don't touch her! I'll kill you if you touch her!" Ryder looms over his father threateningly.

Connor comes to stand in front of me – cute, but unnecessary. I'm done hiding in the shadows. I swipe my phone and call RReagan – the fact that his name is Ron Reagan still makes me laugh.

He recognizes my number when he picks up. "Angel." According to Liam, he believes using Liam's nickname for me makes him young and hip.

"I need a favor," I say with my eyes pinned on Clark Cabot. "Remember all those jobs I did for you?"

Ron and I have an amicable friendship. "Just tell me what you need," he says.

"How much pain can you inflict upon Clark Cabot? The one who owns a home in Royalton," I clarify sweetly.

Mr. Cabot gets to his feet, his eyes narrowing on me.

I hear a hum in the background as he types a few things. "How much you want? Just need to press a send key and he gets added to several lists," he adds with a chuckle. "But this is your only big favor."

"I'm guessing you'll owe me another one soon enough,"

I reply. "Make sure it hurts and don't let up until I say so. Tie everything up."

"Oh, it will. Bureaucracy and red tape go hand in hand." I hear him laughing. The thing about the government is that they're a mess and abuses are easy to hide.

I pocket my phone. "Mr. Cabot, the real power lies in who can manipulate the net," I say with wide-eyed honesty. "When you're ready to talk, let Ryder know."

Clark Cabot sneers. "What are you talking about?"

Ryder's puzzlement is obvious. "Mira?"

"You're going to find that your funds are frozen," I say, ticking items off my fingers. "You'll have the IRS looking into you and be subject to an audit. And that's just the beginning."

Ryder's father laughs at me. "You can't do that! I have lawyers that will come after you!"

"Really? A girl with no name?" I give him a skeptical look. "The government is a pain to deal with. Good luck sorting this mess." I smile at Ryder and Connor. "Why don't you pack a few things and stay with me for a few days?"

By the time they return, packed and ready to go, Mr. Cabot's learning how quickly the government works when they want something and how slowly they work when they're asked to fix something. We walk away to the sound of him shrieking into his phone.

• • •

It doesn't take long to convince Aunt Erika to let Ryder and Connor stay. Uncle Robert scowls a bit, but even he is a softie.

"What'd you do?" Ryder asks as he puts his things away in the guest bedroom. It's on the other side of the house because Uncle Robert doesn't want Ryder being next door to me. Since the guest bedroom has two beds, he'll be sharing the room with Connor.

I bounce on one of the beds. "You're not mad?" I ask.

Connor chuckles. "I've never seen my uncle so horrified."

"I have a friend in the government," I say. "I've helped him with a few projects." I shrug. "And I haven't even started. There's a lot you can do to someone with the Internet." Ryder knows more about my connection to the government, of course.

Ryder brushes my hair back. "It won't get you into trouble?" When I shake my head, he kisses my forehead. "You're amazing, Mira. I don't care about the money. You're the only thing that matters."

"You stood up to him, Ryder," Connor remarks. "You've never done that before."

Ryder rubs his side slightly, wincing when I lift his shirt to stare at the bruise. I gasp. "It isn't as bad as it looks," Ryder murmurs, pulling his shirt down. He brings me closer. "If he'd touched you, I would've killed him."

"You defend me but not yourself?" I query sharply. "That's messed up."

"Never again." His eyes darken. "I won't let him incapacitate me if it prevents me from protecting you."

Conner chuckles. "You do realize, cousin, that she just gutted your dad with a phone call, right? It's fine to *think* you're protecting her, but it's clear she's the one protecting us."

100000

On Monday, we witness a screaming match between Victoria Little and Ingrid Whitman. Victoria, who'd been pursuing one Emmett Solomon, has learned that Ingrid's been doing the same with greater success. Daniel is nowhere to be found.

"Why couldn't you leave Emmett alone?" Victoria shrieks, tears streaming down her face. There's a nasty claw mark on her cheek.

"It's not my fault that he prefers me to you," Ingrid spits out in that childish voice of hers. She sees me and her face twists. "You bitch! Did you make Ryder do this to me? I'll kill you!"

When she lunges at me, Connor and Ryder intervene. "You don't touch Mira. You don't harass her or address her," Ryder says coldly. "You're nothing, Ingrid, and Mira is everything." He glances at the students watching. "Mira's mine. She's the queen I want by my side. Come after her again, and you'll learn how brutal I can me. Don't cross me."

Xander and Nate back Ryder. "Don't cross any of us. Mira's *the* Queen," Xander announces, nodding at Ryder.

I tilt my head. Part of me wants to point out how juvenile these titles are, but mad Ingrid is entertaining. She looks ready to pop a blood vessel. "Your mother's a whore, Mira! My father told me all about her! She threw herself at him!" Ingrid points a painted nail at me. "And you're just like her! Spreading your legs —!"

Celeste slaps Ingrid, breaking her tirade. Wow, go Celeste!

"You're a hypocrite, Ingrid! Just because you've slept with half the boys in this school doesn't mean that's what everyone else does!" A ripple of laughter comes from the student audience. "The worst part? You target guys your friends are interested in. That makes you all sorts of disgusting."

Ingrid goes white. Celeste – sweet, kind Celeste – pokes Ingrid in the chest. I've never seen Celeste so indignant. "Tell me! Is there anyone that wants to stick up for this *thing*?" Celeste asks out loud. "She's a terrible friend, a terrible role model, and a terrible person. Is it any wonder why Ryder's repulsed by you?"

The ripple of laughter gains momentum. As the other students join in on jeering Ingrid, Ryder raises his hand for silence. He's still King, after all. "You should leave," he suggests, wrapping an arm around me. "You're done, Ingrid."

Tears of outrage roll down Ingrid's face as Victoria and Judy distance themselves from their fallen queen. A hush falls over the crowd as two staff members approach Ingrid. "Miss Whitman, you need to report to the principal's office now," one of them tells her.

"You can't order me around!" Ingrid screams at them.

"Miss Whitman, we would prefer not to make this public, but we have evidence that you tampered with security cameras last year and caused the injury of a student here," the other person says. "Come with us now or we'll have the police remove you forcibly."

Ingrid looks ready to throw up. She's terrified. I deliberately look away, hiding my face in Ryder's chest. I'm not afraid of her – I'm hiding my smile as she's dragged away.

•••

Since I found that encrypted file containing the fuel air explosive mix ratios, there hasn't been any activity from that mysterious account. I discuss this privately with Liam.

"Have you looked into Ingrid's emails?" I ask. "Is there a hidden message?"

Liam grimaces. "There are hidden messages there, but we're not sure what they mean or whether it's tied to the fuel-air thing you found. We're sure he's doing some sort of money laundering thing – we just don't have enough evidence to make it stick."

There's a knock on my door and Ryder pokes his head in. He frowns because Liam is on my bed. "Chill," Liam says. "We're just talking. Go hug your girl instead of glaring at me." He stands up and gestures Ryder over. "You need to trust Mira."

"I trust Mira," Ryder growls. "I don't trust you."

"You're skipping the winter dance, then?" I ask Liam, changing the subject.

"I'm off to D.C. Besides, this guy," Liam says, pointing at Ryder, "stole my date."

Ryder positions himself so that he's tucked around me. He's unrepentant at Liam's words – in fact, he's downright smug.

"Can you set up alerts for me before I go?" Liam asks. "I want an alert if anyone accesses that lab or uses that account." I agree to do so. "You be good to her, Cabot. And try to stay out of trouble until I get back."

After Liam leaves, I poke Ryder in the chest. "Be nicer to Liam."

Ryder has the grace to nod. "I know. But when it comes to you, it's hard to remember. When you disappeared… The only thing that kept me going was hope. I can't lose you again." Running his fingers through my hair, he adds, "The dance. Then your birthday." He blinks a few times. "I almost forgot. My father left a message. It just said to ask you what you want. He sounded ready to cry." Ryder flashes me a smirk.

I giggle before I straddle him so I can give him a haughty look. "Your *queen* suggests you make a list of what you want. I think your father will agree to anything."

Ryder's eyes shadow. "I wanted to talk to you about that. I'm okay with him disinheriting me. The Cabot fortune. It's tainted. I don't want it. How do you feel about that?"

I squint. "You know that I'm worth a lot in bitcoins,

right?" I respond with my arms crossed, enjoying my ability to still surprise him. "I've made a lot in bounties alone. I don't care about your money, you idiot. I did this to teach your father a lesson. Do what you like." I lean over him. "I have enough to take care of us for the time being." I see the protest on his lips, but I shush him. "All that matters is that he leaves us alone."

"You are a very dangerous young woman," Ryder whispers, reaching up to caress my face. "I say you're mine, but the truth is I'm yours. I've always been yours."

1⊙0⊙01

It takes a bit of courage, but I finally show Aunt Erika the pictures I retrieved from Ingrid's laptop. I know the pictures will hurt her. After the initial slash of pain, my aunt takes a closer look.

"That's Ernest," she says with a heavy sigh. "He got married that year." Then she pauses. "Look at the body language. Gwen's hands." Erika begins to look distressed. "I don't think she wanted him to kiss her. She was revolted by him. I think he was forcing her to kiss him. She's trying to push him away."

On closer inspection, I notice the same things. My mom's hands are clenched, and the angle of her shoulders indicates resistance. It would be consistent with mom's journal, too. I show Aunt Erika the tiny photo Mom had hidden. "I found this in her old journal. She actually wrote a few pages right before she disappeared," I tell my aunt.

Aunt Erika's fingers tremble as she takes the photo. "I think that's Ernest. I don't recognize any of the other men. You think… You think that man there might be your father?"

"It's the first Asian I've seen. She calls him SJ in her journal."

Aunt Erika searches her memory banks. "Nothing comes to mind. Our father – there was always some sort of business deal at play. I wish I'd paid more attention, Mira. I'm so sorry."

I shake my head. "You have nothing to be sorry about." I gnaw on my lip. "You and Uncle Robert – I couldn't have asked for better people to take me in. You gave me the freedom to leave this summer. And I needed it. You didn't push."

My aunt smiles wryly. "I didn't push because you're like your mom. When Gwen left, I always thought she'd get back in touch. I only made half-hearted attempts at first because – because I knew she left for a good reason." Fingering the picture gently, she sighs. "Maybe it was wrong of me."

We embrace, both shedding tears for the woman that connects us and a history we now share. Aunt Erika pulls back. "You and Ryder Cabot," she begins. "Are you being... safe?"

I turn beet red. "Oh, God. We haven't. I'm not ready," I blurt, flustered. I bury my head. "I know about the birds and the bees."

My aunt bursts into laughter. "Well, that's good. But if you want to start the Pill or talk about anything..." She trails off expectantly. "You're seventeen, and Ryder seems rather serious about you. And I think you're serious about him." She hugs my shoulders. "I'll spare you further embarrassment, but please consider *things* before your hormones get the better of you."

• • •

My dress is a deconstructed ball gown in pale pink. The V-neck bodice looks a bit daring with spaghetti straps, but the deep cuts in the front and back are an illusion. The skirt has flowers outlined in sparkling glitter with sheer and textured layers so there's a dreaminess to the skirt's movements.

Darcy helps with my hair, pulling it into a sleek side ponytail that goes over my right shoulder. Silver pins with crystal cut flowers help hold the style in place.

"We should've taken Ingrid down last year," she muses aloud as she applies some translucent powder to my face. She steps back like a proud sister. "You look magnificent. He might not even wait until you're eighteen to propose."

"What?!" I squeak, ignoring her wicked laughter.

Darcy fluffs out my skirts. "I'm teasing. Maybe. Ryder's never been so serious. Even Ethan notices how Ryder looks at you. He's beyond smitten."

I grow pale. "I need to ask you something awkward. Please don't laugh."

Darcy cocks her head at me. "I won't."

"How will I know when I'm… ready?" Feeling faint, I sit down. "I know a bit about Ryder's past." I wrinkle my nose.

Darcy is careful with her questioning. "Is he pressuring you for sex?"

I flush. "No. Oh, God. No. I mean. We kiss and stuff. But he's very – restrained." This is harder than I expect. "He's never asked, but I'm going to be eighteen. At some point, it happens."

My friend nods. "The timing is different for everyone. I can't stress enough that you want to be ready. If you're freaked out, then you're not ready." She waits for that to sink in. "Ryder should respect that. If he pressures you, you need to tell someone you trust." She adjusts my hair. "The first time is often – awkward. It helps if you're with someone that you have a connection to."

I'm not clueless about sex, but this is a talk I expected to have with Mom. If Darcy weren't with Ethan, I'd be asking more questions, but I have no desire to dig into my cousin's personal affairs.

Ryder, formal in a tux, quietly converses with Ethan when I join them. They'll never be best friends, but the animosity between them is gone. Darcy slips under Ethan's arm, and they step back while my aunt takes about twenty pictures with her phone.

Ryder, conscious of Uncle Robert watching, takes my hands and presses his forehead to mine. "You're beautiful," he whispers, brushing my cheek with a kiss. He and Connor are back at the manor now that Clark Cabot has left the States again. His father has agreed to let Ryder live there until he finishes school, but Connor already has plans to purchase a place for them once he accesses his trust fund. (I know, tough life, right?)

With Connor's assistance, Ryder splurges for tonight. It's not enough to arrive in a limo. Nope, Ryder has us arriving in a

Rolls Royce Phantom that I'm sure Connor paid for. The driver puts up the privacy screen once we're inside.

Imagine two big seats with enough legroom to lie down. It's quite luxurious. "You look nervous," Ryder says with a chuckle.

"I don't even want to know how much this cost," I whisper, frowning when Ryder shrugs. "I won't ask."

"Only the best for you, Mira," he murmurs, reaching over to kiss me solidly. He runs a hand down the nape of my neck.

My pulse beats a little faster when his lips follow his hand's path. I feel very warm and confused.

"Too fast?" he whispers.

Great question. I don't know. I'm filled with too many emotions to think clearly. "I don't think so," I whisper back.

He observes me, kissing the corner of my lips lightly, before sitting back. "You have that look on your face – the one that says you're thinking about three things at once." He rubs his thumb over my wrist. "Is something wrong?"

I hesitate. "I can't go fast, Ryder. That's not me, and I'm worried that you aren't happy with that." I'm not sure if that came out alright. And how bad is my timing?

Ryder's thumb stills on my wrist. "Are we talking about sex?" When I turn beet red, he exhales slowly. "I guess we are." He removes his hand and straightens in his seat to look at me directly. "I suppose I only have myself to blame. The day we officially met? Everything changed. There hasn't been anyone since. We'll take the next step when you're ready, Mira. We have time. I'll wait because I want you to be sure." He reaches over to pull me against him.

I relax, leaning my head on his shoulder. "Thank you," I say, feeling shy.

When we kiss, he lets me take charge, and we spend a good deal of the drive kissing. I hardly register the moment we enter the dance. Dimly, I'm aware that Nate and Xander clear the floor so that Ryder can dance with me alone. What stays with me is the expression on Ryder's face, the soft smile on his

lips, and the warmth of his eyes.
Everything else pales in comparison.

100010

I turn eighteen with Ryder, my best friends, and my family around me. Darcy, Brittany, Celeste, and I stay up all night exchanging stories and experiences. (Brittany speaks French like a native!) A moment of painful honesty occurs when Ryder, Xander, and Nate apologize to Brittany. It feels right that Ethan is there to oversee the apology, and I'm happy when he claps Ryder's shoulder in support after Brittany tears into them for twenty minutes. It's been a year of growth for all of us.

With Ingrid under suspension, Royal Bridge Academy is quieter and pleasant. Victoria and Judy keep a low profile. Daniel, once part of the Court, disappears when Ingrid implicates him for altering the school's videos.

When I mention that to Liam, both our thoughts navigate to the encrypted file I intercepted. Liam's investigation into Daniel provided few clues, but that doesn't mean Daniel is not involved. If he's anything like me and Liam, he'll cover his tracks. But the bigger question is why?

In January, my tracking program in the computer lab room registers a surprise visitor: our mysterious person with the fake email account is back. Since I handed access fully to Liam, I only get told after Liam intercepts the email, which was not going to a "friendly." (When Liam talks like that, I know he thinks he sounds all cool and government-like. He also likes to call our mysterious emailer "the unsub.")

We work together to access the camera footage. I pull up the feed to the lab. "Look," I show Liam. "The camera in there is wirelessly connected – the signal was jammed for an hour." I check the feeds for the cameras in the hallway. They've been disrupted, too.

"What the hell," Liam breathes. "Do you know if this happened before?"

"I didn't have it set up before," I reply, "so either the person knows someone's watching or it's a precaution." I glance at him uneasily.

Liam's brow furrows. "Maybe. What about the wired cameras? They're not all wireless, right?"

I wrinkle my nose. "No, but I don't have time to watch videos. The wireless ones capture feeds in spurts so it's easier to filter. You'll need to do that or get a lackey."

Liam nods, leaning back on my bed. We're in my dorm room since it's midweek. "What are you doing after you graduate?"

This is a common discussion of late between me and adults. "Haven't decided. I've applied to a few schools, but I may take a gap year."

"Come work with me," Liam suggests. "We make an amazing team."

I scrunch my face. "For the government? I don't know. It sounds dreadfully dull."

Liam doesn't get a chance to protest. A quick knock announces Ryder's arrival, and my boyfriend is not happy that Liam is so close to me on the bed.

Liam sighs dramatically, giving Ryder a cursory glance before rolling off. "It's not like you found us in here naked, man. Chill."

After Liam leaves, Ryder is semi-apologetic. "I'm trying," he mutters. "What were you two talking about anyway?"

"Work stuff," I reply. He knows I can't go into detail about Liam's investigation.

Ryder quietly wraps his hand around mine. "Is it dangerous? Is there a chance you could be in danger? Because if so, Liam shouldn't be involving you."

"I'm not in any danger. I'm just making it easier for him to find information." I hesitate because there are really two things going on. One is the money transfers that got RReagan's attention. The second is the strange email that went out followed by the fact that Liam's traced activity from the school. Whoever is doing this is not being subtle. The noise is loud enough to get attention, but not so loud that we know who it is. "Ingrid's father is involved in something weird," I finally say. Ernest Whitman has been clever and quiet; the only reason why RReagan pinged him was by luck – an inside accountant providing information.

Ryder lowers his body next to mine, kissing me persuasively while running his hands down my body. When I kiss back enthusiastically, my response snaps something within him. Pinning me to the bed, his mouth fixes on mine until I'm a confused mess of emotions. With one hand, he tilts my head back as his lips continue down my neck. His other hand parts my uniform's blazer and runs along the waistband of my skirt. When I gasp, he stops.

His eyes rake over me with need, and I catch my breath – which is difficult when you're breathing hard. "Mira, do you know how much I want you?" he murmurs.

Considering he's on top of me… "I have an idea," I whisper. How far do I want this to go? When I avert my gaze, he gently kisses me on the cheek before settling beside me.

"You were… saying something about Ingrid's dad," he finally says.

"Even I don't know all the details of what's going on, Ryder. What I do know is what I've uncovered. But there's something weird happening. Ingrid's father's been moving chunks of money around."

Ryder stills. "Are you serious? This is what you work on so secretly? This isn't a game, Mira. Ernest Whitman is not someone to be trifled with. If he's laundering money…" He sits up and jerks me upright. I can see the worry in his eyes.

"You're worrying over nothing. No one knows I'm involved."

Ryder shifts until I'm straddling him, burying his head in my neck. "Promise me you'll be safe. I won't lose you, Mira. I can't. I love you too much."

"I know." Then shyly, "And I think… I love you."

Ryder lifts my head, a startled sound escaping his lips as his eyes stare at me in wonder. Then slowly, he smiles.

● ● ●

Later that week, Liam approaches me with a list of individuals seen in the area leading to the computer lab that also accessed the lab within that hour: Principal Philippe, Brittany Khan, Daniel Jameson, Emmett Solomon, and Judy Lee. When I watch the videos, though, I note that you can't see Judy's or the principal's face. I remember all too well the video of me that was faked.

"Well, we can remove Brittany as a suspect," I say confidently, but Liam's tight expression worries me. "What? What is it?"

"While Brittany was gone, we saw zero activity," Liam points out. "But now that she's back… Think about it, Mira. Also, there's her father."

Huffing, I point out, "No, that's way too obvious." I may be closer to Celeste, but I can't see Brittany being involved in this. She loves life way too much. "Daniel Jameson would be a better suspect. He hasn't been around since Ingrid was suspended. Why is he roaming around campus?"

"We have our eyes on him, too. Look, we believe Mr. Khan may be using his business to channel funds to several terrorist organizations." He waits for me to absorb that.

Chewing my thumb, I think about the way the message was encrypted, and the activity we've seen. "No," I say, thinking out loud. "Whoever is doing this would leave tracks to point us elsewhere. If it points to Brittany, then it is likely a false trail. We need direct evidence."

"She knows we're hackers, though," Liam mutters to me.

"We need to be careful, Mira. Don't share what we've learned. I mean, you already know too much." Running a hand through his blond hair, he adds, "I know too much. The plan was to filter the information you gleaned, but this is getting to be more than I expected."

Liam's worried. Which means I should be worried. I decide this is not something I need to share with Ryder.

1·0·0·0·1·1

Brittany and Celeste decide we need a girls' night at school. (Brittany and Enrique are an item again.) We send Ryder, Connor, and Enrique off, grab a pizza, and settle down for homework and chitchat.

After an hour, we give up the pretense and start talking. "Ryder's totally in love with you," Brittany declares, taking a long drink of her soda. "Are you attending the same college and all that?"

We've only talked about it marginally, to be honest. I haven't decided what I want to do. On top of that, Ryder's financial situation has changed. "I don't know. We're still talking about it," I say honestly. "What about you and Enrique?"

Brittany gives me a coy look. "Hard to say. But I'm keeping my options open." She winks at me. "And what about you, Celeste? You and Connor got serious pretty quickly, too."

Celeste blushes. "We're staying close, joining Ethan and Darcy at the U."

I bring out my mom's journal – the one with the picture of my potential dad. "I was going through my mom's old journals, and I found something. I think the guy in this pic is my father."

Wiping the grease off her fingers, Brittany takes the photo. She squints because the picture is tiny. "Who are the other guys?"

As Celeste leans to look at the picture, I say, "The middle guy is Ernest Whitman, Ingrid's dad. Not sure about the other two."

"I've seen that picture before but bigger," Celeste says slowly, tapping her lips. She snaps her fingers. "I had to go to Ingrid's house a few times with Erin and there was a picture in her father's study. It was for an award."

When Celeste begins searching online, I take the photo back with nervous fingers. I mentally slap myself. I should've shown this to them earlier!

"I found it!" Celeste triumphantly angles her phone towards me. "That must be a copy of the original photo or something."

I scan the article, but what I'm drawn to is the caption beneath the photo used in the story.

Businessman Ernest Whitman poses with Mayor Howard Ulmstead and Korean businessman Suk-jeon Park.

"Are you okay?" Brittany asks in alarm. When she reads the article, she gasps. "Oh, my God. Is this your father?"

I have a name. Is he alive? Korean. I'm half-Korean. What if he's in Korea? Do I ask for a DNA test to verify I'm his daughter? He could have a family! I could have half-siblings. Maybe they're programmers like me.

A sound of dismay escapes Celeste's lips. "Oh," she says, her forehead wrinkling. I can see the sadness on her face.

I hold my hand out even though I know what I'm about to read. *Korean businessman killed in hit-and-run.* The date of the accident is roughly seven months before my birth. Numbly, I read the details. *Middle of the night... declared dead on scene... police continue to investigate...*

Mom left Royalton and never looked back. Was she simply escaping a lifestyle, or was she running because of my father's death? As quickly as hope appears, it's ripped from me brutally. I may never know.

It's absurd to experience grief. I never knew the man. He might not even be my father. And yet... The possibilities disappear before I could explore them. I remain an orphan. I lose Mom again. Raw. My chest relives the pain of my mother's death.

I shut down and sob like my heart might break.

Warm hands encircle me. "I'm here," Ryder murmurs in my ear. I don't know who contacted him – probably Celeste – but I turn to him. I seek him out. I cry for my mother. I mourn for a possible father. I weep for losing the truth before I found it.

• • •

After carrying me to his room, Ryder holds me, the physical contact telling me I'm not alone. My words and thoughts come out in fragments, and I'm not sure if I make any sense. The times Ryder came to me for that basic creature comfort? I understand why he did that. I need that very thing right now. In his arms, the sadness abates. It's still there, but I'm solid, whole. My mind and body respond to his touch, his scent, his warmth.

"Do you want to talk about it?" he asks, his body loose and reassuring. I know he's vulnerable like this only with me. Although his voice is gentle, there isn't a hint of pity. I don't think I could tolerate pity.

"It's stupid," I say, sniffling. "I thought I'd found another connection to my mother. I want to know why he never knew about me. Mom gave me a good life, but we were alone. Why?" I shift in Ryder's arms. "I love hacking, programming, all of it. A well-written program is elegant. I make the rules, I find the answers. This whole thing with my mom… I don't know if I'll ever have answers."

His breath is warm against my head. "If you had these answers, what would it give you other than closure? Sometimes we're not meant to know, but whoever your father is or was – it doesn't change who you are."

I'm silent as I consider what Ryder's saying. "Who am I?"

"Everything."

I roll my eyes even though Ryder can't see my reaction. "Is that the best you can do, Mr. Cabot?" My mood lightens a little.

Ryder hums thoughtfully. "You are the cousin Ethan De

Vries doesn't deserve. A person who makes a friend's happiness a priority. A girl with frightening programming skills. Also, you think I'm the sexiest man alive."

"And what else do I think? Enlighten me."

"You think I have stunning good looks. You love my incredible wit. You're obsessed with my body."

"Ah, yes. I also appreciate your modesty and humble demeanor." My lips twitch.

Ryder's huff of laughter tickles my ear. "When I first saw you, I was drawn to that simple joy in you. I knew I loved you when Connor was crushing on you. You were attracted to him, but you weren't willing to hurt Celeste for something that wasn't deep. When people grieve, it isn't abnormal to want some physical comfort. You could have turned to him, but you thought of Celeste – your first friend here – before yourself. You change people, Mira. You changed Ethan by making him less of a pig."

My startled snort stops him. "Ethan's always been nice." I flip over to face him.

Ryder gives me a look. "Not always." Brushing my hair back, he cups my cheek. "What I feel for you isn't perfect. It's borderline possessive and obsessive. If we have sex, there's no way I'll let you go. I won't be able to. So, don't take that step with me if you aren't sure, Mira."

I trace his lips with my fingers, and he kisses my fingertips. He's trying to warn me because he thinks I don't understand him, but I do. I'll never forget his devastation when he thought I was with Liam. A relationship like this is not for everyone, but maybe it's right for me. "When I'm ready, I want it to be you," is all I say, and I mean every word. Some say young love doesn't last, but this feels real and right to me.

His eyes glint as he runs a thumb over my lower lip. His voice deepens. "Feel like being distracted?"

I giggle when he maneuvers me to straddle him. "I could be persuaded," I tease before I bend down to distract him instead.

100100

A few weeks later, Liam receives additional feedback on the weird letters in Ingrid's emails. His teammates (or are they coworkers?) uncover words like 'alone midnight' and 'bad weekend' but haven't a clue what they mean. Unfortunately – or is it fortunately? – Liam gives me no insight into what else has been uncovered. When I ask him about their investigation into Brittany's family, Liam simply zips his mouth shut with an indecipherable look.

Ingrid's suspension from school remains indefinite. Ryder believes RBA is reluctant to expel her because the Whitmans donate lavishly. Regardless, no one has seen her for a while, and rumor has it that she won't be returning at all. Daniel withdraws from RBA altogether. There is less drama without those two, and things settle down at school.

I begin focusing on Mom and my potential father. I now have names, but what do I do with this knowledge?

Celeste and I discuss this as I grab a few items from my room that I'll need for the weekend. Ryder and Connor are already off-campus. They've been secretive all week, and Celeste and I believe they plan to surprise us with details of our spring break getaway.

Since Ryder's Maclaren is under his name, he plans to sell the car and get something far more reasonable. It's been fun teaching Ryder money management skills. In return, he's teaching me to drive. I know Aunt Erika is dying to buy me a car for graduation, but I haven't decided yet if I plan to accept the gift.

My cell rings, and I stare at the unrecognizable number. I debate not answering, but curiosity gets the better of me. "Hello?"

"Miss Bell, this is Ernest Whitman."

Whoa, that is not a name I was expecting to hear. "How can I help you?" I ask. Celeste notices my tense voice.

"I'm not calling because I'm angry about Ingrid's situation. I'm calling because I knew your mother. And I have something of hers that I think you'll want."

There's something oily about Ernest Whitman's voice that sets me on edge. "What is it?"

"If you stop by in the next hour, I will give it to you. Otherwise, I will rescind my offer."

"Alright, I'll be there in less than an hour." I motion for Celeste to remain quiet. "I may have a question or two for you."

"I would expect nothing less from Gwen's daughter. Goodbye, Miss Bell."

"Could we stop by the Whitmans before we meet up with Ryder and Connor? That was Ernest Whitman, and he says he has something of Mom's." I stop at Celeste's Porsche.

Celeste nods. "Of course, absolutely. But aren't you worried about Ingrid being there? She's a borderline psychotic bitch."

I gnaw on my lip. "I know. But I can't pass up this opportunity. Will you come in with me?" I plan to ask him what he knows about my potential father, and it might give me a proper starting point if decide to investigate on my own.

"As if I'd let you walk into that place by yourself!" Celeste says.

•••

One of my favorite lines from the Star Wars franchise is "I have a bad feeling about this." When Celeste and I are taken to some sort of waiting room or living room – how do you keep track of the rooms in your home when you have more rooms than fingers? – I get an uneasy sense of the place. Maybe it's because Ingrid lives here even though I don't see her anywhere. I fully expect her to appear raging at any moment.

Ernest Whitman arrives alone, but he seems surprised to see Celeste with me. A petty part of me is so tired of people assuming I have a car! How else did he expect me to get here?

"Miss Bell," he rumbles.

I take a good look at him. He's not ugly by any means, but he has a long, narrow face, thin lips, and squinty eyes. He may just have bad vision. He's gray and pale.

"So, you said you had something from my mother?" I pointedly remind him why I'm here.

"You look a tiny bit like her. Your eyes are different. The hair."

Ernest has Rambling Man syndrome. "Getting back to why I'm here?"

Ernest shakes himself. "Yes, of course." He fishes in his pocket and pulls out a gold ring.

I take it from him and examine it closely. The gold band is etched in fine detail with two ducks. "Why would she give this to you?" I ask. I have an inkling behind the symbolism. Inside the ring, I see the words "Gwen Forever" inscribed.

"She didn't." Ernest steps towards a window. He pretends to stare out the window, but I have a suspicion his attention is on me. "She left a bag here and that was inside."

I slip the ring on and find that it is loose on my ring finger. What I know is that Mom and I wore the same size in rings. I don't think this is Mom's ring. In Korea, ducks symbolize faithfulness and eternal love because they supposedly mate for life. This is a wedding ring.

Celeste blurts, "I'm sorry, I need to use the bathroom."

Ernest nods. "You know where it is. You've been here before."

With an apologetic smile, Celeste leaves while I stare at the ring. "When did she leave the bag?"

"The day she ran away, of course." The expression on his

face is odd. It is almost full of anticipation.

He expects me to recognize the ring! I realize he's trying to see what I know about Mom's departure from Royalton. But why?

"You saw her that day?" When he nods, I press the issue. "Did anything odd happen?"

Ernest is about to answer when the man who let us in enters to whisper something. "You'll have to excuse me for a minute. Something urgent has come up. But don't leave just yet."

I pace until Celeste returns, her face anxious. Before I can tell her anything, she says, "I just saw Daniel Jameson."

"Here?" No one has seen Daniel since he left school.

"Yes. Going into the library I told you about." Celeste bites her lip. "He didn't see me. But why is he here?"

"Probably up to no good," I mutter, pulling out my phone. I use a remote access tool to tie myself into the Whitmans' network – how useful that Liam's access is there for me to piggyback on.

Celeste lowers her voice to a whisper. "What are you doing?"

"Checking if there's a camera I can access in the library," I say, going from device to device off the network. (Okay, this is not what a nice person should be doing, but I'm curious why Daniel might be here.) I get lucky. There is a computer in the library. I know it's the library because I see Daniel before me. I turn the audio on while Celeste peers over my shoulder.

"Why did you bring Mira here?" Daniel asks, moving out of view.

"I'm curious to see what she knows about her father. You do know her father was a talented programmer, don't you?" Ernest asks off-screen. "Does she show any ability?"

There's a pause. "Not that I know of..." His voice trails off. "But my phone and laptop got wiped. A lot of weird things have happened since Mira's arrival."

Celeste grips my arm as Ernest says, "How interesting.

Maybe Mira's inherited her father's gift? If so, then she probably had a hand in why Ingrid's been suspended. Is it possible she knows more?"

"You mean about the fuel-air combinations?" Daniel snorts loudly. "I don't think so. We left enough clues at the school, though. We can launch the worm anytime. That's what our contact said anyway."

I turn to Celeste. "Oh, my God. We need to get to Liam. We need to leave."

"Why? What's Daniel talking about?" Celeste picks up on my panic.

That's when I hear Daniel say, "Why is the light on your computer camera on?"

I don't wait. Grabbing Celeste's arm, I start heading towards the front door. But when we get there, our way is blocked by a person I don't recognize.

"Going somewhere, Miss Bell?" Ernest asks from behind us. Daniel peers at us from behind Ernest with surprise.

Celeste gasps at the gun in Ernest's hand. I don't hesitate; I fling my phone as hard as I can on the marbled floors. The screen shatters beautifully, but my joy is short-lived when Ernest points the gun at me. I guess we aren't going anywhere.

100101

Ernest takes Celeste's phone after we're escorted to the library. Oh joy, Ingrid has joined us. Daniel and Ingrid stand on the side as Ernest circles me.

"It was you, wasn't it? You hacked our phones," Daniel says, shaking his head. "All this time, you were right under our noses. Ryder didn't hire anyone. It was you."

What do they say to do when you're cornered? Deny everything.

"I don't know what you're talking about." There you go. That ought to convince them. All kidding aside, they did catch us fleeing after noting the camera on the computer was on.

"You shattered your phone. Tell me why," Daniel demands while Ingrid taps her fingers on her arm nervously.

Celeste looks ready to pee in her pants. Hopefully, she really did use the toilet earlier. "Why should I?" I ask.

"How about we remove fingers from Celeste until you do," Ingrid demands, setting her hands on her hips.

Celeste gives a little shriek. They wouldn't hurt us, would they? "Are you sure you want to deal with that type of DNA cleanup? You'd have to burn the house to the ground," I say with false bravado.

Ernest looks at Daniel, but Daniel isn't sure and looks at Ingrid. A part of me panics, but I can't help the snarky part that wonders why Daniel thinks *Ingrid* would know anything.

"Well, what do we do, then?" Ingrid asks out loud.

Ernest waves the gun around while he talks. "She heard

far too much. My partners won't be happy about that."

"Again, I don't know what you're talking about," I insist. "We were leaving because we're expected somewhere."

But Ingrid's father ignores my words. "If you have a smidgen of your father's talent, Miss Bell, then you know more about computers and networks than you let on. It's better not to make me angry." He shakes the gun in my face, and I can't stop my flinch. "You were eavesdropping on us, weren't you? The camera turned on here." He points to the now powerless computer. "Did you destroy your phone to hide the evidence?"

Daniel looks at the cracked screen. "I can't tell what she saw or if it was her. But it had to be someone close enough to be on the network."

"You may think you're clever, Mira, but Father holds all the cards," Ingrid says, but she sounds uncertain to my ears. Maybe she isn't completely sold on her father's lunacy.

Ernest thumps the gun on the table in the library. I wish he weren't so cavalier with it. "We need to change our plans." While he paces, I hear Celeste's phone buzz repeatedly. Both Ryder and Connor are probably worried now. "Alright, Miss Bell, you have one chance to save yourself and your friend. I need you to go to the school and go to the maintenance room underneath the chemistry lab. There's a backdoor exit. You will unlock that door for us."

"She doesn't know how to drive," Ingrid says. "It'll have to be Celeste."

"Why do you need access to the school?" I ask.

Ernest scowls and ignores my question. "Fine. Celeste, I will have Ingrid follow you. If you go the wrong way or do anything, your friend here dies. Go to the school and do as we ask."

Celeste has been silent the entire time, but her brown eyes are filled with fear. "It's okay," I say. "It'll be fine."

"But I can't leave you here," she whispers.

She can and she has to.

"Before you leave, let your friend use your phone, Celeste," Ernest orders. "I want you to call Ryder Cabot and tell him something so he doesn't raise the alarm about you two missing."

"What do you want me to say?" I ask. I need time for Ryder and Connor to panic enough to reach out to Liam. No one has turned off Celeste's phone yet, which means that Liam may be able to see that her phone's last ping occurred from the Whitmans. I listen to Ernest Whitman's request. When I make the call, I can only hope that Ryder truly does trust me.

• • •

"Is my father Suk-jeon Park?" I ask after Ingrid and Celeste leave.

Ernest and Daniel escort me to another car. Daniel's driving, Ernest sits in the back with me. At first, I think Ernest is going to ignore me, but he gives me a creepy smile before answering. "Most likely. I knew they were seeing each other."

I don't need to ask who *they* refer to. "You were already married." I clasp my hands in my lap to hide my feelings. "You weren't happy about Mom's relationship with him."

Ernest grows petulant. "Gwen turned me down. I was one of the richest, most eligible bachelors, and she turned me down. I got married. I offered to make her my mistress."

Wow. Underneath all that slime is... more slime. I can't imagine anyone being thrilled about such an offer.

"We were losing our edge," Ernest continues. "We still are. Foreigners coming here. Men like him, stealing our technology. Our women."

"But he was your business partner," I state. "You hated him?" My eyes dart around as Daniel begins to drive.

His loud snort startles me. "Business partner? Pfft. A means to an end. He developed the software I needed, but then he got greedy. Wanted more money. People only wanted to work with him because of me. Him and his soft hands." He stops to think for a moment. "It's fitting that his daughter brings about the justice we need so badly."

Ernest has gone from creepy to insane. "Justice?"

"Justice. For our country," the older man says. "You still don't have a clue, do you, what I'm doing?"

It occurs to me that maybe I don't want to know. But who am I kidding? I'm being held at gunpoint. The chances I'll be kindly released are next to none. I should die knowing everything, right? Okay, I guess it's time to bite the bullet. (Wow, bad choice of metaphor.) "I have a clue," I say.

Ernest and Daniel exchange a look using the rearview mirror. "Enlighten me," says Ernest.

"You're using the school's computers so that it looks like someone is studying fuel-air explosives," I begin. I note that we're heading to the school. "The crumbs make it look like Brittany Khan is involved, but I think that's a red herring."

Of all things, Ernest laughs. "You are a clever girl. Your father was smart, too, and he clever. But he was a terrible liar." For now, he pockets the gun. "And why is Brittany the red herring?"

"I don't know."

"Good. You're an honest girl. Just like your daddy." Ernest seems to enjoy commenting on my father. "You see, people like your father come to America to steal our ideas. Like leeches, they suck us dry and profit from us. The worst part? They force us to integrate them into our society. We're forced to change and accept their weirdness. And they take our women to create half-breeds like you." For the first time, I realize that he views me with distaste.

"You want people to think Brittany is doing something terrorist-related?" I ask.

"Consider it a purging, Miss Bell. Once your mother tainted herself, she was no longer suitable as a wife." Ernest shrugs. "I offered to save her."

Bile rises in my throat. "As your mistress?" Ernest has lost his marbles.

"We're here," Daniel says, taking the car past the main school buildings.

I've never been on the delivery and maintenance side before, but I recognize the building that holds all the labs. Ingrid, bundled in a coat, holds a door open and I see Celeste peering anxiously. Relief floods her face when she spots me in the car.

I avoid Daniel's offer to help me out of the car – creep! – but I don't attempt to run. Once we're all inside, I finally ask the question on my mind. "Why did you bring us here?"

The smile I receive chills me. "Because, my dear, we're going to blow up the school."

100110

My cousin and I have an entire weekend planned for the girls. Celeste and Mira hang out at school a lot, which makes the whole "double-dating" business easier. If you had told me two years ago I'd be contemplating double-dating seriously, I would've laughed my head off. Part of the weekend is to surprise the girls with our spring break ideas. More accurately, I'm taking the remains of my bank account that my father hasn't confiscated and taking Mira away for spring break. Connor's reserved a private home for us in Florida away from most of the crowds with a private beach and a pool.

The last text from Celeste to Connor didn't indicate anything amiss.

Mira and I are taking a small detour. I'll let her tell you both in person what's going on.

And then silence. Connor's worried, so now I'm worried too. My calls to Mira go straight to voicemail, which is odd because Mira rarely turns her phone off.

Then, my phone shows an incoming call from Celeste over an hour after our last message from the girls. With a concerned glance at Connor, I pick up. "Celeste?"

"It's me."

Relief floods my body when I hear Mira's voice, but it doesn't quite translate into my words. "Mira, where are you?" I sound like a demanding boyfriend. Dammit.

"Um, Celeste and I talked."

She sounds funny like she's trying to think but she's distracted at the same time. "Okay."

"We're not coming over. Change of plans. I think we should take a break." She says the sentences quickly.

It takes me a while to respond. A hit to my gut would hurt less. "Mira, what are you talking about? Where is this coming from?" I sound whipped and desperate. "Just come over so we can talk." I've done this to her before. Told her we need a break without justifiable reason. But she knows that was under duress.

"I still love Liam."

Jealousy hits me hard and fast. She said they were just friends! My insecurities rage as I grapple with what she's saying. "Don't say that. Mira, you told me—" I break off, struggling for logic and reason. She's not like this. Her emotions don't flip back and forth. *She's never given me a reason to doubt her.* "We can work through this. We love each other."

"I don't. I knew during Thanksgiving. I just didn't want to accept it."

Reason and logic win. Thanksgiving. The worm she stopped. She's mentioning it for a specific reason. I want to be a better person for her, so I want her to know the only thing that matters. "I will always love you."

Her voice sounds choppy when she speaks again. "Liam and I connected over the summer more than I expected. Whatever you do, leave Liam out of this. Celeste and I are disappearing for the weekend so I can think clearly. I'm sorry."

When she hangs up, I force myself not to fling my phone in rage. *Think!* She wouldn't do this. She wouldn't dump me over the phone. Thanksgiving. I remember I was worried about her safety. And then I remember. She thought the attack was a test to see how fast it could be stopped. Her awkward mention of her summer with Liam? She's talking about the work she does for the government. Leave Liam out of this? She wants me to do the exact opposite. My stomach turns. Mira's in danger. She couldn't speak to me honestly because someone was there. That's why she didn't use her phone. Somehow, she's not on the periphery anymore.

"Connor, do you have Liam's number?" Connor must see the fear on my face despite the calmness of my voice. My insecurities disappear in the wake of a worse emotion: terror for Mira. I can't – I refuse – to lose her.

Connor wordlessly makes the call to Liam and hands me his phone. "Liam, this is Ryder. I got an odd call from Mira," I begin without letting him speak. "She called me from Celeste's cell."

Liam is quiet. "What did she say?"

"She's in danger, isn't she?" When Liam doesn't say anything, I swear. "If anything happens to her, I will kill you, Liam! Help me find her!"

That causes Liam to rage right back at me. "Let me work, Ryder! Her phone is off, but we should be able to triangulate Celeste's last phone call. Tell me what she said."

I do my best to relate what Mira said over the phone.

"She mentioned Thanksgiving specifically?" Liam asks.

I bite back a snippy reply. "Yes. And the work you two did this summer. What does it all mean?"

"God, she's clever." Liam's admiration is obvious. "It means she knows what the attack was about. I can't tell you everything. I'll get back to you or Connor once we have more information." When I start swearing, he cuts in, "Listen to me! You may not realize this, but I do care about Mira. We're going to find her, okay? She'll be okay. But I can't have you barging in and making this worse. I know it sucks, but if you sit tight, I will notify you as soon as I learn anything."

It rankles me a little to know that Liam understands Mira so well, and yet, it's probably a good thing. I hand the phone back to Connor. With dread, he sits down to listen when I tell him that Mira and Celeste are in danger.

• • •

Hours later, I wonder if I should call Ethan. But what is there to say? *Hey, Ethan, Mira's in danger, but that's all I know.*

Sorry. No, even I'm not that cruel. Until I know something beyond vague ideas of trouble, the less panic, the better.

"You really love her, don't you?" Connor asks with a sad smile. "You held it together. The old you would've believed she was dumping you."

I wish I could muster a smile, but I can't. I wish I could feel equal concerns for Mira and Celeste, but I can't. The truth is that I only care about getting Mira back, and to do it, I would sacrifice anything and everything, even Celeste. Even Connor.

"I do." I struggle to offer some words of comfort to my cousin. "We'll get them back." We have to. Mira is clever and strong. She adapts.

My mind plays back the past twelve months. The first time I held her in my arms as we danced... I lost my heart completely then. Up to that point, it was infatuation, obsession. It still might be an obsession. Trying to juggle Erin's and Ingrid's games and my feelings for Mira muddled everything. Even now, I cringe remembering the hurt on Mira's face when she saw me with Ingrid. She shouldn't forgive me for being so stupid.

I think of all the things I want Mira to know about me. What if--? No. I'll tell her when I see her. I need to stay positive. I won't just tell her. I'll show her.

Out of habit, I walk to the liquor cabinet and grab some brandy, but then I stop. No, I need to stay lucid. If Liam calls, I can't be wasted. With deliberate focus, I put the brandy back in the cabinet. In a moment of candor, Mira told me how her mother died because of a drunk driver. I don't need alcohol.

"They'll be okay," Connor says in a half-broken voice. "No one has a reason to hurt them."

Helplessness. Connor experiences it, too. My mind flips from fear to anger and back to fear. I find myself praying, bargaining with whatever higher power will listen. Every minute feels like an hour. Time creeps into the early hours of dawn, but I can't sleep. My frantic energy is wearing and exhausting.

When my phone rings, I shake so bad that it takes me two tries to answer. "What?"

"We have them."

100111

It takes me a while to wake up. Jumbled images confuse me further. Ernest Whitman in the car with a gun. Celeste sobbing. Phone calls to Ryder and Liam. An explosion. Am I dead? No. I don't think I would hurt if I were dead. Then I remember Daniel slapping me.

That explains why my face hurts, but it doesn't explain this out of body experience I'm having. I hear people, but my body refuses to move.

"When will she wake up?"

I recognize that voice. Seriously? Am I in the hospital again? Twice in less than a year. I am going to owe Aunt Erika her full deductible.

"I'm awake," I grumble. Oh, wow. My voice sounds terrible.

Aunt Erika starts crying when I open my eyes. It takes forever to bring my aunt and uncle into focus because the world is bleary. They fuss over me while the nurse takes my vitals and asks how I feel. She tells me I have a mild concussion, and Aunt Erika insists I stay overnight for "observation." I let them fuss because I'm bruised, battered, and disoriented.

"Celeste," I say hoarsely.

"She's alright," Uncle Robert assures me. "Right down the hall. She's a little less banged up. I even hired private security to be right outside her door."

My lips tighten. There are questions that need to be answered. When the nurse leaves after upping my painkillers, I expect an interrogation, but my aunt simply holds my hand.

"There'll be time for questions later," she says. "First, rest a little. Liam filled us in a little. When you're better, we're going to have a chat about secrets."

That doesn't sound good. Before I can ask her what she means, there's a tiny commotion outside followed by Ryder bursting through the door. The moment our eyes meet, my emotions get the better of me. I burst into tears, and my aunt and uncle take that as their cue to give us some privacy.

"Please tell me you're okay." He's anxious to hold me, but he hesitates, analyzing my injuries. His eyes darken as he takes in the scrapes and bruises. "They wouldn't let me in at first. There's no way anyone could keep me from you." Ryder doesn't hide the tears as he bends over my hand.

When Ernest tied me and Celeste up in the basement of the school, I expected to die. I wasn't sure if Ryder or Liam understood what I tried to tell them. To still be alive... "I'm okay," I murmur. "A little discombobulated." I get a huff from Ryder.

"I was terrified I'd lost you," he whispers, and his kiss is excruciatingly soft against my lips. "I'll do my best not to be obsessive about every move you make, but I'm going to need to know that you're okay. I hope you're good with that."

I laugh through my tears. "I think so." I wipe his cheeks, and he kisses the palm of my hand.

"Tell me everything."

In halting words, I do my best. I start with Ernest finding me and Celeste about to bolt. After I broke my phone, Ernest and Daniel interrogated me, but I played dumb. It didn't work.

"He knew my father. My father is – was – Suk-jeon Park," I say sadly. "He was a programmer. A genius."

"Like you," Ryder murmurs.

I shake my head. When Ernest learned Mom was involved with my father, Ernest threatened him. But my father refused to back down. They fought. My father lost. Ernest staged his death to look like a hit-and-run.

"He's insane. That whole family is insane," Ryder states in disbelief.

That's just the tip of the iceberg. "He tied me and Celeste up in the maintenance room beneath the admin building," I say, trembling at the memory. "He was going to kill us." I touch my bruised cheek, and Ryder's fury intensifies. "Daniel hit me. When they made me call you… I wasn't sure if you understood. But you must have."

"I'm not as dumb as I look," Ryder says with a humorless smile. "But I also know you. That wasn't you. I trust you, Mira. You would never act so callously."

"I don't remember much of how we were saved. Only bits and pieces. There was smoke, and then something exploded. To be honest, I thought—I thought the explosives had gone off." Ryder bends his head to my shoulder when I take a shaky breath, explaining how Ernest planned to blow up the school and blame it on terrorists.

"I could kill Liam." Ryder's lips thin. "He put you in danger."

"He didn't. Ernest called me." When Ryder looks at me in surprise, I add, "I think with everything that happened to Ingrid and Daniel, Ernest suspected my involvement. Maybe he's been watching me for a while. He lured me with information about Mom. I should've told you we were going there, but I didn't want you to stop me or get worried."

"I'm not upset with you." Ryder presses my hand to his face. "There's no way you would've known Ernest was deranged. Liam is still to blame." It's clear that Ryder intends to blame Liam regardless.

I yawn. "I'm so tired," I whisper. "Is Celeste really okay?" Great friend I am. I've barely asked about Celeste.

"She's fine. Connor is with her. They're waiting for her parents." Ryder arranges the blanket over me. "Rest. I'll be here when you wake."

I mumble, "Promise me you'll stay and keep the nightmares away."

"Always."

...

When I wake hours later, Ryder is slouched in a chair nearby. He's asleep. A note from Aunt Erika tells me they'll be back with Ethan. I spend a few minutes admiring Ryder from afar. A lock of his black hair falls across his forehead charmingly. I must still be on pain medication to be waxing poetic.

My hospital door opens, and Liam peeks in, clearly not expecting me to be alert. His green eyes are dark in the dim lighting. He tiptoes across. "Hey," he says quietly. "You doing okay?"

I manage a shrug as I gesture for some water. Liam hands me a cup and I down it in one gulp. "As well as can be. I don't remember that much of my rescue."

Liam grimaces as he refills the cup. "That's probably for the best. Ron was there. I was behind the lines waiting." He waves an envelope. "It's a letter explaining stuff, but since you're awake, I guess I can tell you what I'm able to."

"That leads me to believe you're going to hold information back." I continue to sip water.

Liam doesn't deny it. "Ernest Whitman has been on Ron's radar for a bit. Whitman's part of a domestic terrorist group focused on white supremacy. He planned to blow the school up and frame Brittany Khan."

My initial shock gives way to understanding. "Because her father has ties in Pakistan."

"By targeting the children of some of the wealthiest families in the nation, he wanted a race war to erupt. He didn't act alone."

"Daniel? Ingrid?"

"Daniel was a tool," Liam says, "as far as we can tell. We think Daniel has ties to RatGh0st, but he was a medium for Ernest to control. Daniel understands technology enough to implement what they got from RatGh0st."

"What about Ingrid?"

I jump when Ryder speaks.

"Tell me that bitch is going to jail," Ryder hisses. "I woke up when you tried to tiptoe in." He glares at Liam pointedly.

Liam sighs. "Ingrid knows far less than Daniel. We're still questioning her. Considering what she did to you last school year, she's certainly capable of murder. But that's all I can tell you." He pauses. "Oh, school will be closed for a week while we remove some stuff."

"What stuff?" I eye Liam suspiciously.

"Best not to worry about it."

"You're still removing explosives, aren't you?" Ryder swears when he hears my question. "And you guys came in with guns blazing!"

Liam winces. "Yeah, I didn't say we were smart. The explosives weren't set up to go off when we got there, though." He ignores my eye roll. Then, with a nod at me, he adds, "You were right about the worm. The plan was to slow rescue crews from reaching the school. We did a ping trace on Celeste's phone and saw it pinged near Whitman's home. We then tracked his phone and realized he was at the school. Things started to come together. We assembled a crew as quickly as possible after body heat signatures confirmed there was only a handful of people there."

I blink. "Wait. Ernest isn't the mastermind?"

Liam draws back, shifting on his feet. "I can't answer that. I can tell you that you don't need to worry anymore. Unless you come to work with me, that is. We have the information we need." He turns to Ryder. "Take care of her, Ryder. She's special."

Ryder scowls at Liam. "I know."

Liam gives me one last look. "If you ever change your mind about working with me officially, let me know."

I roll my eyes. "Go save the world, Captain America."

101000

You don't go from being kidnapped, being strapped near bombs, and learning about your dad's murder, then recover like nothing happened. There are nightmares. Therapy. Long talks. Amid all of that, interviews with the FBI (or is it Homeland Security or the CIA?) where I get asked the same questions five different ways. Sometimes Ron Reagan is there. Sometimes Liam's nearby. Mostly, I become numb to the faces.

There are things I don't know still. Who is RatGh0st and did he know what Ernest Whitman planned to do with the worm? Or did he take the money and run? Is there a larger (shadowy) group at work? The media doesn't cover the details, only linking Ernest Whitman to domestic terrorists. Ingrid suffers a complete meltdown and is considered unfit to stand trial. Daniel is found dead in his cell. The media reports suicide, but conspiracy theories abound.

I'm allowed time to process. And I'm not the only one. Celeste decides early on that she can live with a boring life. We've had enough drama and excitement to last us a lifetime.

After I recover, there's a long heart-to-heart discussion with Aunt Erika and Uncle Robert. While she respects my rights as a near-adult, she is not okay with how I kept Liam's identity hidden from her. "We're family, Mira. Your safety *is* my concern," she points out during the long conversation, Ethan hovering nearby. "I get you don't want our money or our charity, but you are my niece and the only thing I have left of Gwen. You don't get to push me away in a bid to be independent."

Remember how I used to think Aunt Erika was lax and all that? I find out quickly that she can be just as fierce as Mom. I'm also less prickly about accepting things, which is why I'm now in Florida.

"We're in trouble, Mira," Ryder says, running up to me breathlessly. The thin white shirt hugs his torso. "They're coming to take the fort."

He hands me a Super Soaker filled with blue water. "Guard my back." He moves to a higher vantage point with a water gun looped around his neck.

Celeste, hiding behind a wall of plants, gestures to me that someone's approaching from around the beach house. We don't see Connor, who has been tasked with getting the opposing team's flag. We hear a shout, and Connor comes screaming around the corner, waving a red plastic flag. Behind him, Brittany and Enrique attack him with Super Soakers, but Connor is just out of reach. Only part of his shirt gets stained with orange-dyed water.

Celeste and I pump our soakers to maximum pressure and start hosing the attackers down when a sudden crash announces Ethan bursting through the foliage. Celeste jumps in the way and is taken down as Darcy backs up her boyfriend. I'm trying to reload the pressure, but I'm doomed as Darcy aims for me. Ryder appears from the upper deck, unloading his water gun, and drenches Ethan and Darcy.

"That's cheating!" Brittany cries. "You can't climb!" She sounds outraged, but she's laughing through her mock anger.

"Hey, you never said we couldn't," Ryder says, winking at me before climbing down. "I would say we won that round. Shall we put on clean shirts and go for Round 3?"

Darcy examines her skin. "I look like a Smurf. I thought you said this dye wouldn't stain."

"You need to wash it off, silly," Celeste says, shrieking when Connor picks her up.

"That sounds like pool time to me." Connor strolls off with Celeste over his shoulder.

"I'm hungry." Enrique pretends to complain, making puppy eyes at Brittany.

"Oh, come on, you big baby." Brittany grabs him by the ear and drags him off.

Darcy strips off her shirt, revealing her yellow polka-dot bikini. Ethan's been singing the song all weekend. "This was a great idea, Ryder. We've never really spent spring break together. To be honest, I never thought we'd do anything together."

Ethan's arm is relaxed around Darcy's shoulder. "I think we were too busy being mad to plan anything."

"Have you guys thought more about college?" Darcy leads us back into the main house.

"Gap year," Ryder and I say simultaneously. His grin warm and friendly, so unlike the tense boy I met over a year ago. I need a year to breathe, and Ryder's onboard with joining me.

"Every company, school, and government want you," Ethan reminds me. He's concerned, of course. Thanks to the brouhaha with Ernest Whitman (is it blasé to use that term considering what he tried to do?), my name is known in certain circles. Ethan's convinced North Korea will kidnap me someday. One thing hasn't changed: Ethan is still protective.

"I'll probably help out with the family business," I say. It's what I call Uncle Robert's company. Ethan isn't interested in internet security, so Uncle Robert has been giving me unsubtle hints about joining him. I remain undecided. Ryder and I want to take our time. It's been a trying few years. We're allowed to take some time to think, right?

And then there's Liam. We are one helluva team. But work for the government? I'm not sure I could handle the bureaucracy and red tape.

Ryder remains adamant about forgoing his family's inheritance. I think that suits Clark Cabot. He hasn't made any more threats since his run-in with me, but he hasn't bothered to reach out to his only child. Connor has already found a modestly sized home – luxurious by most standards – for him and Ryder.

Since Brittany and Celeste are heading to the U, he will too, but he wanted a place for all of us to gather. I haven't told Aunt Erika yet that I intend to move out during the summer.

Of course, Ryder and I are not poor by any means. Between the bounties I've collected, plus some side work – I'm not cheap to hire – I've amassed a nice buffer. Ryder sold off several useless "trinkets", and he's been working the stock market with success. I doubt we'll live conventional lives.

Once we're alone, Ryder brings me close for a lengthy kiss. When we part, I'm glad that there aren't shadows in his eyes anymore. "What is it?" he asks, noting my look.

"You're happy." Funny. I'm happy, too.

He runs his hand up and down my back. "So I am," he agrees. "I love you, Mira Bell."

"I love you, Ryder Cabot."

EPILOGUE

Ryder

The moment I set eyes on Mira, she became my future. She teaches me what it is to love. She teases me, she pushes me, she forces me to keep up with her.

I don't care what people say. What I feel may not completely healthy in the way it consumes me. My life begins and ends with her. I propose to her the moment we graduate from RBA because I need to see my ring on her finger. Her uncle throws a fuss until I agree to hold off on wedding plans for at least two years.

Her path is not an ordinary one. We eschew college so that Mira can help her uncle with his business. It's not enough for her. She becomes a consultant, helping companies, governments, and individuals. I find my organizational skills are a benefit to her. I learn the value of money – every penny of mine is untainted by my father. Mira and I make a strong team, and by working together, we're rarely apart. I help her uncle run his business, but like Mira, I remain a free agent.

Friends come and go, but Liam remains close. Those two are connected in a way that I am forced to respect. My jealousy and insecurity take a back seat; I trust Mira unconditionally and absolutely. It's more than that, though. Dimming that light within her would be a crime, and it would hurt her. I would rather die than hurt her. She needs the freedom to explore her ability in the fullest way possible, and that means taming my insecurities.

We don't live too far from her family. Now that she's found them, she wants them close, and I won't deny her that even if I want to be as far from my father as possible. Not that it matters. I never see my father again.

It's strange to consider that Ethan was once my enemy. Of course, that's changed. Our families are intimately meshed and connected, not just from our experiences at RBA but also through marriage and children. When I marry Mira, I gain everything. I gain all the things I once resented Ethan for: love, acceptance, family. Our children bear with our oddities, but they are loved and watched, never left to nannies. We sometimes abandon them to her aunt and uncle, who are more than willing to babysit any number of children.

Mira doesn't forget her humble roots – our home is warm, open, but not too large. The only extravagance is our master bedroom, which I specifically design so that, if we want to, we can gaze at the stars and I can be with her under the moonlight.

No one taught me to be gentle, but it's instinctive with Mira. I cherish every laugh and argument. I treasure her even when we disagree, or when she frustrates me with the rapidity of her mind. At times, I watch her, memorizing every breath, every sigh. When she's up all night tracking the latest cyber-attack, I'm content to be near her and watch the speed at which she seizes every challenge.

Connor tells me to count my blessings. And I do. Every single day.

ACKNOWLEDGEMENTS

Many people made this book possible.

First, to my online game friends:
In particular, AegentEight, Luckette, Brooke, Arranis, and Occisor. Thanks for answering the questions without laughing. Anchor and Kahlan, thank you for helping me with random questions.
A shout out to my guildmates and friends in the following games:
Hundred Souls, Heroes Charge, and Empires and Puzzles.
Klairebella – fingers crossed

Second, to my husband, Josh Byrne, and to our cousin Bill Alfveby for helping me with terms and the reality of Internet security. If I got anything wrong, it isn't your fault.

Third, to my friends: Darcy, Nicolle, Brittany, Tina. You know why I appreciate our friendship.

A whisper to my panda bear: remember not to leave lint on the windows! Never lose hope.

BOOKS BY THIS AUTHOR

Survivor

The Betrayal

Shattered

Turn The Tables